The
Rebuilding Year

Kaje Harper

Dedication

For my husband, with gratitude for his confident support, surprising patience, and unending supply of bad puns.

Many thanks to Eric Alan Westfall for proofreading this second edition.

Contents

Chapter One

He felt it happening, an instant too late. By now, he was sickeningly familiar with the sensation as the ligaments in his knee failed to hold, getting ready to spill him on his ass. Only this time his damned leg was giving out as he took the first step down a flight of stairs.

Shit!

He grabbed for a rail, realized there was none, and knew he was going to land hard. He slid, jolted at the painful crunch as his tailbone hit, and then the back of his head met the concrete.

Jesus! For a long moment there was nothing but flashes of light and a ringing in his ears. He would have begged it to stop, if he'd thought it would help. Eventually, his vision cleared a little and he realized he was looking up into a pair of concerned eyes. Really pretty eyes, the hazel that mixes gray and green and gold, framed by long auburn lashes.

Great. He'd managed to fall flat on his ass right in front of that gorgeous, tall redhead from his class. The one with the nice, um, assets. *Way to go, Ryan. Great first impression.* Except his vision was still clearing, and those pretty eyes were bracketed by laugh lines and the eyebrows were thick, and okay, *so not* the tall, gorgeous redhead. The man bending over him had to be in his late thirties, tanned and craggy-featured. His mouth was moving, and Ryan strained to make out the words through that damned ringing.

"...and I'll get some help, okay?" There was a hand on his shoulder, pinning him down. "Don't move."

When the face receded, Ryan made a grab and caught hold of fabric. *A sleeve.* "Wait. I'm okay. Just give me a second. I'm fine."

The man leaned closer. "You don't look fine."

"Rang my bell a little." More literally than he'd imagined, but the ringing was easing off. He tried to sit up and was pinned in place by that firm hand.

"You should hold still and let a doctor look at you."

1

"I'm fine." Bad enough that he'd left his cane at home, hoping not to start med school as the old guy with the cane. He would be damned if he'd start it as the guy who left halfway through the first day in an ambulance. He'd manage. It was just pain. God knew he could handle pain. "I'm going to sit up. I'll go slow."

"Um, okay." The hand left his shoulder, but slid behind his back to help him ease up.

The guy was strong. Ryan barely made an effort and he was sitting. And wow, the world was tilting. He held as still as possible and waited for it to pass. "See, I'm good. I don't need a doctor."

The man kneeling beside him offered a wry grin. "There's lots of them around. You should take advantage."

Meet your professors up close and personal. No thanks. "Yeah, I don't think so. I just need a minute. You don't have to wait."

"I don't mind." The man sat, clasping his arms around his knees, and watched closely.

"I'll get up in a minute," Ryan said. *He hoped.* When the knee gave out like that, it was sometimes really stubborn about going back to work. He looked around, and spotted his backpack beside him. At least it wasn't underneath him. He pulled it close and opened it to check his electronics for cracks, giving himself another moment to recover.

He was at the bottom of three steps leading from a back door out of Carlson Hall. The spot was pretty secluded, screened by bushes, so maybe his smooth move hadn't had much of an audience. This door evidently didn't get a lot of use. He'd figured it would cut a few yards out of his trek to Physiology class, and save his leg a bit, to come out this way. Talk about a plan that backfired.

Still, so far he hadn't drawn a crowd. He'd be all right if he could just get up. And then walk to class. *Here goes nothing.*

He closed the pack and slid the strap over his arm, rolled to his hands and knees and pushed up carefully, mainly using his right leg. A strong hand under his elbow steadied him.

"What did you do to your foot?" The man's hip was close to his own, bracing him as he swayed. "Is it sprained?"

"No. God, no." He tried a laugh. "I have a trick knee is all. It gives out on me sometimes. It just takes a minute to get better. I'll be fine now, thank you. You can get back to…" *Class? Work?* The guy looked too old to be a med student, but he wasn't dressed like support staff. He'd indicated he wasn't a doctor. A really laid-back professor? Ryan shifted his weight onto his left leg, and felt the knee give. *Nope, not walking yet.*

Those fingers still held his elbow in a secure grip. The man leaned closer, and Ryan felt a gentle touch across the back of his head. "You're bleeding." The guy showed him a smear of red on callused fingertips.

"Shit!" Ryan looked at his watch. Ten minutes to get to class. "I don't have time for this." He pulled his arm free and staggered a step. He didn't fall on his ass again. But that was about all that could be said for it.

"Did you have a cane or something? For your knee?"

"Left it at home." Ryan bit off the words. Yeah, that'd been stupid. But he'd been much better lately, and he got tired of the looks and the questions. This was what he got for underestimating the amount of walking between classes, and the dearth of elevators. *And the stupid pride that made you quit looking for one and climb the stairs twice, because your classmates were doing it.*

"Okay," the guy said. "Look, just stand there for a minute. Can you do that?"

As Ryan watched him, yeah, standing there because right now that was about all he could do, the man went over to a backpack on the ground. He reached in and pulled out, of all things, a short pruning saw. Ten feet away, a big maple tree spread its branches out over the grass. The guy walked over to it and, cool as you please, began cutting off a branch.

"Um," Ryan called, "I don't think…" The branch hit the ground, and the guy gave him a grin.

He brought the stick over, flipped it, and grounded the butt at Ryan's feet. "Up to wrist level okay?"

"Um…"

The saw flashed, short sharp strokes, and then the twiggy end fell away, leaving a thick cane with a serviceable bend as a handle. The lunatic with the saw held the improvised cane out. "Here."

"Thanks," Ryan said automatically. He took it, leaned his weight, and yeah, that was better.

The guy was still grinning at him. "Don't worry." His voice was an amused rumble. "You won't get arrested by the campus cops. Trimming that dead branch was on my to-do list anyway. This just means I got to it sooner." He held out a hand. "John Barrett. I'm the head groundskeeper."

And not a lunatic. Ryan was surprised at his relief. "Ryan Ward. Med school, first year."

The guy's grip was firm and dry, rough and callused. "Great first day, huh?"

"Peachy."

"Hang on one second. I've got something for your head." Barrett went over and rummaged in his pack. He came up with a disinfectant wipe in a foil pouch, and passed it over. Ryan must have looked bemused, because the older man smiled. "I have kids. You get used to carrying those around. Now they're useful to get the pine sap off my hands."

"Thanks." Ryan reached up, awkwardly swiping at the back of his head, hunting for the sore spot.

After a minute, Barrett said, "Here, let me." He took the wipe from Ryan's fingers and stepped behind him. The guy's touch was gentle. Ryan closed his eyes for a moment, as careful fingers parted his hair, dabbing at his tender scalp.

"Just a small cut. Doesn't look like it's going to bleed much more, but you're going to have one hell of a bruise. Are you sure you don't want to see a doctor? You might have a concussion."

"Nope." Ryan propped his eyelids back open and reached for a casual smile. "I've taken a whack or two in my day, and I know what a concussion feels like. This is just a pain in the…head. Thanks again. I imagine patching up students isn't in your job description."

"That's something I like about this job. I make my own job description." Barrett folded the red-smeared wipe into the foil, and stuck it in his pocket. "So if you're really going to walk to class, I'm going to tag along, just to make sure you don't fall over on the way. Okay?"

Not like Ryan could stop him. He took a careful step, then another. With the help of the cane, he could manage it. It wasn't fun, his head and leg and ass all screamed at him, and tonight would be bad, but for now he could still walk. Physiology class was in Smythe Hall. He could gimp that far. He pulled in a steady a breath. *Make it so.*

Bonaventure College was set on a pretty campus. The paths between the buildings wound through flowerbeds, bright with fall annuals. Mature trees showed just a hint of the color to come. This path was crushed rock, and the edges were bordered with embedded bricks, in color contrast to the stones. Ryan would've admired the effect, if he hadn't had to grit his teeth and concentrate on just putting one foot safely in front of the other.

Barrett walked beside him. He was three inches taller than Ryan, and had to be holding back his stride, but he made the easy pace seem natural. Ryan fumbled for something to say. "Don't worry about the blood," he offered. "I mean mine, on your hands. I've been tested recently and I'm negative for anything infectious." Which sounded like he'd done a gay date panel... "I mean, I tested after I had some transfusions and..." *Oops, not going there either.* "I mean, you should wash up, but you don't need to be worried."

Barrett had a great smile, slow and wide. "I wasn't."

"So, um, been working here long? I mean... the campus looks great." What was wrong with him? Maybe getting whacked on the head knocked out all of his small-talk skills.

"Two years. And thank you."

And here was Smythe Hall, thank goodness. With his classmates still streaming up the steps. Ryan braced his good leg and pivoted enough to hold out his hand. "Thanks again."

"You're welcome."

He shifted his backpack on his shoulder, and gripped the cane harder. Ten feet of path, seven wide stairs with, thank you, Jesus, a railing. Then the last class of this long, long day. At the base of those stairs stood one of his classmates, the little, perky blonde, smiling at him. He headed her way, walking as evenly as he could manage, trying to get his aching brain to come up with her name.

****

John watched as Ryan limped over to a short, blond girl, his steps almost steady. The guy was tough, no doubt about it. He'd really taken a bad fall. John remembered his own flash of fear as he'd seen Ryan go over, and the loud crack of head on unyielding concrete. For a panicked moment, John had thought the guy was dead. Ryan must have a skull like iron to get right back up from that and walk away.

He was older than most of the students around the college, probably pushing thirty from one side or the other. Of course, with the medical school on campus, it wasn't all undergraduates, and Bonaventure College was small, and not prestigious. The students were perhaps a more mixed group than at your standard Ivy. John liked that about it.

Today, as classes got underway, there was a new crowd among the old familiar faces. A new school year, the seniors gone, freshmen coming in. Although John had nothing to do with the students officially, he'd begun to recognize many of them. He'd put in work over the past two years to encourage them to spend more time outdoors on his campus, in the fresh air. New paths, new benches, arbors that invited romantic cuddling.

He had a lot more plans, but he already liked the way the campus was shaping up. His predecessor had been a dour traditionalist, known mainly for yelling at the students the moment they got off the paved paths. John wanted those kids to enjoy the space.

His pocket crackled as he turned, and he made a detour to unload the wipe wrapper into a trashcan. Good thing he'd had that. Wipes were handy for getting the gravel out of skinned knees and skinned hard heads. Although his smile dimmed as he remembered saying *I have kids.* Closer to say I *had* kids.

Cynthia had called that morning to postpone the kids' visit again. New year of school, hard to adjust, too much stress to travel right now— she had all kinds of excuses. Truth was, she just didn't want the kids around him, and he didn't have the money or the energy to fight her for his visitation rights every single time. He'd call them tonight. Or tomorrow, when he wasn't so angry and disappointed that it would show through.

He hadn't seen the kids in two months. And they were changing so fast. When they visited in July, his Torey had been wearing makeup! Not very expertly, but still, Jesus, last he remembered she was a tomboy climbing trees. That maple tree he'd lopped the branch off had been a favorite of hers earlier in the summer. He was missing so much.

He shook his head hard, to banish his foul mood. Kids grew up, that was life. He was still their father, whatever Cynthia's new husband, Brandon Pretentious Carlisle, might think. So what if he was now a groundskeeper and not some fancy high-priced lawyer. The kids had fun here. Anyway, he'd better finish trimming up that maple, before someone else tried climbing it and found the other dead branches with their feet. He headed off with long strides to take a sharp saw to some nice hard wood.

****

It took several hours of cutting, raking, and uprooting invasive buckthorn before he felt calm enough to head home. When he was tired enough, the shower beckoned more than the barstool. He'd gone back and hung around the entrance to Smythe Hall when classes let out. Just in case. The Ryan guy had made it down the stairs safely, still using the makeshift cane, and headed for the bus stop. He'd been moving pretty crap, but he got a lot better when the blonde ran up and walked with him. The wonders of testosterone.

John put his tools away, and locked up his office. His grounds crew had called it quits an hour ago. He had five guys, all immigrants. Legal, he assumed, but it was the college's problem to verify that. He just handed out the assignments and kept them on track. Truth be told, these guys worked a damned sight harder than many of the native-born Americans he'd dealt with over the years.

All was currently peaceful in his mini United Nations, at least since Manuel had left. Take out the one complaining hothead, and the others turned out to be a nice bunch. He'd put in a request for a replacement, but he still had enough good hands to think about a serious run at the buckthorn bushes. He wandered toward his truck, plotting his assault.

A light in the gloom of the aspen grove caught his eye. It looked like a flame, maybe a lighter. Given smoke-free buildings, he'd made a point of placing outdoor ashtrays around campus, but there were none over there. He hadn't spotted that location as a favorite for lighting up. New students, new choices. He headed over to have a word.

He wasn't a fanatic. The smell of cigarettes annoyed him, but everyone was entitled to their vices. Heaven knew he had his own. A little pot didn't bother him either. He figured it was pretty harmless stuff. But an open flame down there worried him. The aspen leaves were falling early this year, and the ground was dry and deeply carpeted. The last thing they needed was a fire.

As he neared the grove, the flame still wavered. Not a lighter, then. A soft voice was singing in a breathy whisper, something about the moon's orb. He spotted the singer and paused, surprised.

He didn't know the girl's name, but he'd seen her around. She'd been a drab, mousy thing when she'd arrived on campus two years ago. Mid-brown hair, mid-brown eyes, bad skin and a slightly hunched posture that screamed, *kick me.* She was one of those who'd bloomed in college. Her skin was now clear, her hair long and braided.

But she'd always seemed, if anything, too serious. She worked in the lab of one of the medical faculty, helping with some kind of research. Sometimes he saw her leaving work in the evenings. She always strode quickly down the well-lit paths to the dorms. She had never wandered the grounds with, of all things, a lighted candle.

"Excuse me, miss," he said softly from a distance. He didn't want to startle her into dropping the candle. The girl turned slowly to face him, her eyes shining in the flickering glow.

"The trees live, you know," she said, with a smile.

"Um, yes, they do." *What the hell?*

"It breathes, all around us. It speaks, if we could only understand it."

Okaaay. He edged closer. "What's your name?"

"Alice. I'm Alice. All of this is Alice too, in a way." She smiled again, and made a wide gesture with the candle that set the flame flickering and spilled wax. A drop of hot wax landed on her hand, but she ignored it. "Isn't it great?"

"Listen, Alice." He kept his voice gentle. "I think we should blow out the candle now. This place is too dry to have a flame burning."

"Is it?" She bent and puffed a breath onto the flame. It went out, leaving a small red glow at the tip of the wick. "Oh, that's lovely too." Her face was joyful and serene.

He wondered what she was on. He wondered where he could get some. "Come on, Alice," he said, holding out a hand. "You should head back to your room. I bet it's lovely there too."

8

"It doesn't sing like the woods." But she stepped toward him obediently and put her hand in his. He slipped a finger across her wrist. Her pulse was strong, slow, and even. Her skin was cool, not feverish. He didn't smell booze, or pot.

"Come on." He led her carefully up the slope. No way was he going to leave her to wander around the campus in her state. Their campus was probably safer than many, but if some man walked up to her and invited her home tonight, he'd bet she would find that lovely too. At least until morning.

"Which dorm are you in, Alice?"

"Where the moon shines down. Where the chestnuts grow."

As far as he knew there were no chestnut trees on campus. Horse chestnuts, yes. Maybe it was poetic license. He headed in the right direction for undergraduate housing. Maybe when they got close she'd give him a clue.

They walked past the first tower, the freshman dorms. Then past the second block of midyear rooms. He was rethinking his strategy when she turned abruptly in on the path to Clarence Hall.

"This is my stop," she said gaily. "Good night, sweet prince. Night's candles are burnt out." She pulled her hand out of his and gravely handed him the half-melted candle.

"Um?" said a voice from behind John.

He turned quickly, and found himself face-to-face with a sardonic young woman with dyed red hair.

"Oh good," he said quickly. He didn't want to give her time to start speculating. "Do you live here? Because this girl seems to think she does too. I found her wandering around the grounds with a candle. Whatever she's on, I think she'd be better off safe in her rooms. Could you see that she gets there?"

The girl made a face, but then shrugged. "I suppose. I've seen her around. She's on the third floor." She went to the door and swiped her card through the reader. The door clicked and she pulled it open. "Come on, then."

"Go on to bed," John urged Alice gently.

Alice looked at him. "If the moon lasts, there's always a tomorrow."

"Whatever you took tonight, I think it's a little strong for you," John said. "I would stay away from it tomorrow. Go on in now."

She gave him another radiant smile, but turned obediently and followed the redhead inside. John breathed a sigh of relief as the door closed. Of course she could just leave again, but the other girl didn't seem the type to take any nonsense. He could hope Alice would end up safe in her own bed.

It was a lovely night. The air was soft and cool. The moon had risen, and where the electric lights dimmed, it was still bright enough to see the beds of flowers, and the waving stalks of plume grass. The shapes of his bushes and trees took on a bulk and a softness they lacked in the sunlight. Maybe Alice had things right. There was always a tomorrow. John headed for home.

Chapter Two

A couple of weeks later, Ryan dragged himself down the hallway to his apartment and jiggled his key in the lock. Anatomy lab had gone way past the normal hour. His dissection partner was going to drive him crazy. He could already tell. Better too slow than too sloppy, maybe. But if he heard Kaitlyn complain one more time that the real thing didn't look like the book, he was going to pop her one. Real life never looked like the book. Real life was messy, and variable, and interesting.

And noisy. He stepped inside the apartment and sighed. It'd seemed like a good idea to share an apartment with a second-year med student, someone who was already established and could serve as a native guide for a guy whose undergraduate days were a decade back. And he was really too old for student housing. He'd met Jason for coffee, compared expectations, and signed the shared lease. It should have worked.

What he hadn't realized was that Jason was a pussy-hound of the first order. And good-looking enough to be all too successful. In the two weeks since classes had started, he'd had no less than six different girls parading through the apartment. At least there were separate bedrooms, but it did bad things for Ryan's nerves to walk into an unfamiliar, half-naked woman in his bathroom in the morning, when he needed to get to class. Especially when it wasn't his own half-naked woman.

And Jason liked his sex loud. Ryan wasn't a prude, but he had a hard time studying to the tune of *yes, yes, harder, do it to me*, that seemed to last for hours. Today's girl was already moaning and squealing behind Jason's closed door. No verbal directions yet, but Jason sounded like he was working up to it. Ryan cursed under his breath. His bed beckoned. He could stretch out, and review the names of the blood vessels of the foot. Except for *oh, Jason, oh, Jason, yes, Jason.*

He shoved his keys back into his pocket, grabbed the damned cane back out of the corner, and headed out. He could study anatomy somewhere else. Maybe with a snack and a beer. Maybe two beers.

The town sprawled out away from the college on its edge. He'd done some exploring the last couple of weekends and found that there were several bars within his walking distance. The two closest to campus were clearly student hangouts. The music was loud and bad, the patrons young and intoxicated, and the food mainly fried. The one called Sly's had looked promising at first, but proved to be stodgy. He was too young for that one by at least a couple of decades. He'd made a note to move on to The Copper Stein for his next round.

The interior of The Copper Stein was a bit dark for ideal studying, but the music was reassuring. It actually had a beat, and lyrics, but wasn't sixties rock. One end of the room had a short wooden bar with a brass rail, but most of the floor was filled with small tables. He went to the bar, requested a Harp's, and then carried the bottle with him in search of study space. Unfortunately he wasn't the only one who'd chosen this Thursday night to get out on the town. There were no empty tables.

He'd resigned himself to sitting at the bar when a vaguely familiar voice said, "Hey, Ryan, you can park it here if you like."

He glanced around. The guy's face was immediately familiar, with its strong chin, hollow cheekbones, prominent nose. He recognized his rescuer from day one, but damned if he could remember the guy's name. Oh well. He held out his hand. "Hey, thanks again. That makes twice you've rescued me."

"My pleasure this time. I hate drinking alone."

Ryan eased himself into the empty chair and set his cane on the floor. "Me too." He took a long pull on his beer. *When was the last time you didn't drink alone?* He couldn't remember. Back before, anyway. He sipped again, slowly.

"So how's class? They working you hard?"

"Not yet." The workload was heavy but not unmanageable. He just had to adjust from doing-things mode to studying-things mode. He hadn't been a student in a long time.

"And how's your head?"

He shrugged. "It's fine. My dad always says I have a thick skull. Sometimes that's a good thing."

"Yeah, my dad said that too." The other man raised his glass. Ryan realized he was drinking whiskey. "Must be a dad thing. Although I've never said it to my boy."

"You have a son?" Lately, he'd realized that the only thing he regretted about his no-strings dating history was that no serious relationships meant no kids. His brother Drew had two small boys, out in California, and Ryan was starting to envy him.

"Yeah, one boy. He's fourteen. And a girl, Torey, she's twelve."

"That's nice."

The man took a swallow of his drink, and then chased it with a sip of beer from a mug. "Would be nicer if they weren't a thousand miles away. Nicer if they were actually going to visit within the next decade."

Ryan realized that the guy was a little drunk. "Divorced, huh?"

"Yeah." The groundskeeper slumped down in his chair and stretched out his legs, long and lean in battered black jeans and old cowboy boots. "Let's talk about something more pleasant. Like the Bubonic Plague."

Ryan laughed. "*Yersinia pestis.* Still present, by the way, in the gopher population of the southwestern United States. There are cases in cats, periodically, and in humans now and then. Hooray for modern antibiotics."

"You're kidding." The other man sat up and looked startled.

"No, really. I studied up on that kind of stuff before my med-school interviews. It's out there. It's just that with modern antibiotics, the bacterial diseases are less of a threat. It's the viruses that get us now. Influenza, HIV, stuff like that."

"Okay," the guy said. "That's about all the optimism I can take for one night."

"Sorry." Ryan was enjoying talking to someone who wouldn't think of the nineties as ancient history. Hell, he was just enjoying talking to someone. "Tell me about your job. What does a groundskeeper actually do?"

"Well my official title is Landscape Maintenance Architect," the man drawled. "But that just means the same thing for more glory and less pay. Basically, I keep the outdoor parts of the campus tidy, healthy and esthetically pleasing. Fortunately, my predecessor held the job badly for thirty years, and

13

changed nothing. Which means I have lots of scope for improvements, and won't run out of work. I bamboozled the hiring committee with my credentials, and they gave me a budget and a pretty free rein. It's not half bad."

Ryan wanted to ask about those credentials. Not many gardeners he knew used terms like *esthetically pleasing.* Then again, how many gardeners did he know? "They had a committee to hire a groundskeeper?" he asked.

"Oh please. They're a college. They have a committee to decide what day to celebrate Christmas."

Ryan snorted. "I've met people like that."

"Plus this bunch has a bit of an inferiority complex, since they would like to be an Ivy League university, except that they don't have the staff, the space, or the reputation. The med school is their only professional program. They overcompensate everywhere they can. They've decided that since they have three hundred acres of campus, they will make it a showpiece. I'm not arguing."

"You have to keep three hundred acres groomed?" Ryan asked.

"No, thank God. At least not yet." The man flicked a finger toward his whiskey glass as the waitress passed. "Another of each, lovely lady."

"Coming right up, John," she said easily.

John. John. Ryan committed the name to memory. "You really want another shot?"

"That I do." John rolled his empty glass between his hands, staring at it. "I got a call from my lovely wife, Cynthia. Have you met Cynthia?"

"I haven't had the pleasure."

"Of course not. Because she's a thousand miles away, too. And not as lovely as she once was." John tucked a bill into the waitress's pocket and took a gulp of his fresh drink. "She never comes here anymore. But the kids do. At least they did. But according to Cynthia, they're busy again. Not only are they not coming this weekend, they're not coming this month. Or next month. She'll pencil me in for November. Maybe." He chugged his beer.

"Damn, that's rough." Even worse than not having kids would be to have them, and not get to be around them. His nephews were little hellions, and he missed them.

"She has custody. She calls the shots. The tickets I sent were full price. She can change the dates. Again."

"Mm."

John put out a big hand and wrapped his fingers around Ryan's wrist. "Sorry, man. I didn't mean to be dumping on you. You have a nice face, but you don't need to listen to me complain." He let go, and drained his glasses one after the other. "I'm lousy company tonight. I'll head out and let you have the table."

Ryan watched him stand. John was steadier than Ryan would have expected, after knocking back those drinks, but he was far from sober. He turned and managed to make his way through the tables toward the door well enough. Then Ryan groaned. John had reached into his pocket and come out with a bunch of keys. Dammit, no way was he okay to drive home, no matter how straight he was walking.

Ryan scrabbled for his cane under the table, hauled himself upright, and chased after him, grumbling about tall men and long legs under his breath. He caught up to John on the far side of the parking lot. The guy was fumbling around, trying to fit a key in the door of a battered pickup.

Ryan reached around and took the keys. "No way, dude."

"Huh?" John blinked at him. "The lock's just tricky. I got it."

"I don't think so. You just had four drinks in fifteen minutes. Let me call you a cab."

"Can't leave the truck here. I need it in the morning. I'll drive careful."

"You won't drive at all."

"I don't like cabs. I can just sit here for a bit. It'll be fine."

Ryan thought about it and sighed. He owed the man. "Get in and I'll drive you home."

"You don't have to do that."

"Yeah, I do." He unlocked the door, shoved his cane and textbook under the seat, and swung himself in. It was an automatic transmission, thank God. His left leg wasn't up to a clutch. He still missed his beloved Mustang.

15

He reached down and slid the seat forward. Way forward. Either John was even taller than Ryan realized, or he liked to drive like he was sitting in a recliner. For all its dents, the truck started up smoothly. John was still standing in the open door, staring at him.

"Get in already, and give me directions," Ryan said.

After another moment, John's whiskey-soaked neurons apparently started firing. He closed Ryan's door, walked around, and climbed into the cab. "Left on Calder."

The truck ran surprisingly quietly. Two more turns, following John's muttered directions, and they were on Central, heading out of town. John sat slouched in his seat, rubbing a hand on his knee.

"I'm sorry," John said eventually. "You're right. Trying to drive was stupid. I usually keep it to two drinks, no more, so I don't have to worry. I just slipped tonight."

"It sounds like you had a reason."

"I guess. All these years, she knows exactly how to get to me." He blew out a whiskey-laden breath. "I love my kids, you know? And Cynthia makes it as hard as possible for me to see them."

"Where do they live?"

"Los Angeles. Now." John leaned back and sighed. "We lived in Chicago. When we got divorced, Cynthia moved to Springfield. So I moved too, to be close to the kids. I commuted to my job. Then after a year, she announced she was getting married and moving out here to Wisconsin."

"That sucks."

"Mm. Well, I found this job, moved out, got an apartment here in York. Then Cynthia started telling me my place was too small for the kids to stay overnight. They were too old to share a room. Which was maybe true, so I bought a house. Plenty of space. Then she told me they were moving to LA."

"How long ago?"

"It's been a year. I thought maybe I'd go… but she went out of her way to tell me that her new husband's position in LA is temporary. They'll move again in another year or two. So I just stayed here."

"When was the last time you saw them?"

"July. They were here a week, between camp and a trip to Europe with the new hubby. He has money. She said they'd come this weekend— they have Friday off. Some school thing. I should be picking them up at the airport right now, with two and a half days before I'd have to drop them off again. But something came up. So then it was going to be in October, the school-conference week. But she just called again. They were invited to someone's mountain cabin to go horse trekking. Exciting stuff. And she knows I wouldn't want to deprive them of the chance to make new friends. So maybe around Thanksgiving."

"Can you take her to court? Is she breaking the divorce terms?"

John took a long minute before answering. "Yeah, but I really don't want this to turn into a war. She has too many ways to win."

"What do the kids say?"

"I don't know." John rubbed his forehead tiredly. "They're teenagers. Talking to them on the phone is like pulling teeth. I call a lot, but they don't say much."

"You should get a webcam. Skype them or something."

"Um, yeah, what you said. Except that I'm technologically incompetent, and barely manage to text on my cell phone. Which is the best way to talk to my kids, incidentally."

Ryan had to smile. "That was last year. Listen, maybe I could come over sometime, help you get set up. With a webcam you can see them and talk in real time. Better than nothing."

"Maybe." John seemed distant. "Here. Turn in the drive with the yellow mailbox."

Ryan took the sharp right and pulled in. The driveway wound between two tall old trees, and then ended in a circle in front of a big, two-story house. The place looked like a farmhouse, with a gabled roof and a long, wrap-around front porch. It was painted cream with butter-yellow accents. The trim had fancy gingerbread curlicues and it was well-maintained. Ryan pulled up in front and parked.

"Hey, nice place."

17

"It's too big. But the kids love it. And their rooms are here for them, when they do come. Right now it's pretty empty." John sat in the truck, staring at the house without opening his door.

After several silent minutes, Ryan figured he'd better make the first move. He slid out of the cab, taking the jolt of hitting the ground on his good leg, and walked around to open John's door. "Come on. I'll walk you in."

John seemed to come back to himself with a sharp breath. "Oh! You don't need to do that. I'll get out here. Except this is my truck, so you can't get home. Shit. Here, I'll call you a taxi. On my credit card." He fumbled for his cell phone and wallet. The phone went onto the gravel. The wallet ended up on the cab floor.

Ryan laughed. "Maybe I'd better do that. Later. Come on, I want to see what this place looks like on the inside."

"It still needs work." But at least John was moving toward the door. Ryan stopped to retrieve his textbook and cane and lock up, and then followed with the keys.

The entry hall was floored in old wide-board maple that glowed softly as John snapped on a light. Off to either side, dark rooms waited, while ahead a kitchen sat bathed in a bright gleam of moonlight.

"Come on in." John headed for the kitchen. "Can I get you something? I don't keep alcohol in the house but I have coffee, tea, apple juice, Mountain Dew."

"Coffee would be good." For both of them.

"Coming up."

As John slowly and carefully filled the kettle and set it on the stove, Ryan looked around. The kitchen was a mix of old and new. The cabinets were lovely wood, stained and varnished, with small glass panes in the doors. The countertop was old, stained Formica. The floor was laid with the same satin boards as the hallway, but topped with a rag rug that had seen better days. The stove was old, the refrigerator ancient. The small kitchen table was a piece of art. It looked like a slab of huge tree trunk cut in a three-foot-long oval, deep-grained and lovely, supported by curving legs that seemed too slender to hold its weight and yet balanced it perfectly. The chairs were metal, old and clearly the type that were made to fold. Although judging by the warp of the legs, they might not manage that anymore.

John turned on the stove, and then reached to fumble with the switch of a small lamp. Cupped inside the swirled branches of a fanciful tree, carved from dark polished wood, the bulb sent out soft rays of light. "I like the moonlight." John gestured at the huge picture window. "But it's not quite enough to see by."

"That lamp is cool," Ryan said. "I've never seen one like it."

"Yeah?" John shrugged. He pulled coffee out of the freezer and set a drip cone on top of an old, plaid-patterned thermos. "I'm going to make extra. It'll only take a few minutes."

Either the man was really into retro, or he was short of cash. Ryan pulled out a chair and sat down. "I'm in no rush."

"So what about you?" John had his back to Ryan, peering into the refrigerator. "You have family?"

"Two brothers." *Now.* "Sister-in-law, two nephews. All on the west coast. My dad lives out in Oregon. My mom passed away ten years ago."

"I'm sorry to hear that."

Ryan shrugged. She'd died two months before 9-11. Three months before David did. Maybe it was for the best. She'd always been a happy woman. He pulled his thoughts away from the past. "No wife, no kids. I'm starting to regret the kids."

"You have time. Although if you don't regret the wife, that may be a problem. Do you have a girlfriend?"

"Nope. Not right now."

John straightened. "No milk, sorry."

"That's okay."

John meticulously poured hot water into the cone, and then leaned up against the counter and peered at Ryan. *Still a little drunk*, Ryan thought.

"What about that little blonde?" John said. "The one with the cute nose and curly hair. She looks like she's interested in you."

Ryan blinked. *How does he know?* It was a bit creepy.

19

"I saw her chase after you out on campus," John said, apparently sober enough to catch the recoil. "A couple of times."

"Oh. Yeah, she might be interested. But she's so freaking young, you know? Not just years, although I'm betting she's barely over twenty-one. But in experience. She comes off pretty shallow."

"Don't need deep to have fun."

"Mm. I've done that but... I think I'm done with shallow." Because the next girl he went to bed with would have to look at his leg, and his scars, and be cool about it. Which he had trouble imagining. Which was why he hadn't gotten laid in a year. Hell, the closest he'd had to a tender touch in months was John cleaning up his head injury. Maybe he could stage another fall, in front of that tall, curvy redhead. She looked like she could handle it.

"That's okay," John was saying. "That's good actually. Shallow can get deep all of a sudden, and then you end up married to someone you thought was just a fun time."

Ryan softened his voice. "Is that what happened to you?"

John turned away, pouring coffee from the thermos into mugs. His voice was muffled. "Not exactly. No. Here. Best coffee in all of York."

Ryan took a sip and blinked. That was amazing. "Wow. I might stop by here sometime, just to hit you up for more of this."

"I get it mail order. Grind it fresh every morning. It's my biggest indulgence."

"Worth it." Ryan drank again.

"So." John seated himself at the table. "You know my whole sorry history. What brought you out drinking by yourself on a school night?"

Ryan laughed. "My roommate is definitely not done with shallow. In fact, he's a master at it. I'm waiting until the heat of passion cools a bit, so it's safe to go home."

"You don't like his girlfriend?"

"That's girlfriends, plural. No, even that's giving him too much credit. It's one-night stands. And he likes them young, loud, and air-headed. And did I mention loud?"

John smiled. "So you escaped to a pub."

"I like a beer or two. The Copper Stein seemed like a decent place."

"My favorite. The music's good and played at a reasonable volume, the bartender knows his stuff, and the bouncer doesn't tolerate much nonsense. They even have some live music on Saturday nights that can be worth hearing."

Ryan let a sip of liquid darkness flow down his throat. *Mm, good.* "I'll have to check that out."

"Not this week. Girl with a harp, and way too much affection for Irish ballads. Next weekend though, there's a decent trio with a fiddler who can burn up the strings."

"I'll remember that."

John pulled out his cell phone. "You must be tired of hearing me blather on. I'll call you a cab."

"No rush." It was relaxing, in this dim kitchen with the moonlight streaming in. No noise, no music, just someone to talk to, and the heavenly smell and taste of that coffee.

John stared at his phone. "Good, because the damned thing is dead. Let me put it in the charger for a bit." He pulled over what Ryan had thought was an abstract sculpture, and set the phone into it, plugging in a jack. Ryan leaned forward to take a closer look. The piece was made of wood, in long swooping curves that looked abstract. Until you put the phone in it, and then the shape resolved into a pair of hands, cradling the phone as if it were precious.

Ryan ran a finger over the luster of the wood. "Wow, that's cool too. Same artist that did the lamp, right?"

When John didn't answer, he looked up to see the man was…blushing?

"You made this?"

"It's just a hobby. I pick up the stray bits of wood I find and fiddle with them in my spare time. It's just for fun."

"Well, I've seen worse in fancy galleries with major price tags. If you're ever short of cash, let me know. My sister-in-law would love this." Grace had a thing for melding form and function. When it was done right, like these gorgeous pieces.

"It's just a hobby," John said firmly, almost angrily.

"Okay." Ryan took his hands off the sculpture and sat back.

John held out his hand. "Let me have your phone. I've got a number for the taxi company somewhere. I'll call you that cab and they can charge it to me. It's the least I can do."

Somehow the easy comfort between them had disappeared. Ryan pulled out his cell, passed it over, and silently drained his cup.

Chapter Three

The early-October air was still warm and pleasant on campus in the middle of the day. Ryan had a sandwich, a soda and a lovely biochemistry chart of the Krebs Cycle to study. He headed across the grass, looking for a shady spot to enjoy them.

At the bottom of the nearest hill, there was a stand of old pines. He vaguely remembered seeing a bench set under them. It was always easier to stand up from a raised seat than get himself back up off the ground. He headed downhill.

As he approached the trees, he heard women's voices raised anxiously. Two students stood under the tallest pine, looking up. One blonde, one brunette, both young enough to definitely be undergraduates, and both very anxious.

"Come on now. This is silly," the blonde was saying as he reached her.

"What's up?" He looked into the tree, following her gaze. About fifteen feet above them, another girl with long brown hair was climbing slowly.

"Come on, Alice," the brunette beside him called. "That's high enough!"

Ryan checked out the tree. Like many old pines, it had a veritable ladder of sturdy side branches running up its trunk. The girl had another twenty or thirty feet to go before the branches got too thin to be safe. Although she wasn't wearing good shoes for safe climbing. "What's she up to?" he asked the blonde.

"We don't know. She's been odd all morning, not really there. Then after poetry class she got spacey, talked about the squirrels of the air. Nancy and I figured we'd better keep an eye on her. She just marched down here and started climbing."

"Her name's Alice?"

"Yeah."

"Hey, Alice," he called up. "What are your plans? How high are you going to go?"

"Squirrels climb," the girl's voice floated down. "The trees are their highways, to reach the realms of sky." She pulled herself up another rung.

Not a good answer. "Alice. Your friends are worried about you. We'd like you to stop there for a bit."

"But the sky is above me." He could see what they meant by spacey. The girl's voice seemed to float on a breath with no emotion behind it. "Up, up and up. To real lightness of being." Another branch higher.

"What should we do?" the brunette asked.

"Does she do drugs?"

"I wouldn't have thought so," the blonde said slowly. "But lately she's been… different. And that shit about squirrels, that's not Alice. I had to convince her to take the poetry class, because she said it was too abstract for her."

"Okay." The girl was thirty feet up now, and the branches were smaller. Still safe enough, but she showed no sign of stopping. "You'd better call 911. Tell them you think she may be high on some kind of medication, and she's reaching a risky level in the tree." He glanced around. A couple more people were headed their way, but not close enough. He dropped his cane and kicked off his boat shoes. Knew he should have worn sneakers today.

"What are you going to do?" the brunette asked, as the blonde pulled out her phone.

"I'm going up after her. Maybe I can talk to her, convince her to come down. Or even grab her if she falls."

"Do you think you're able…?" Her eyes dropped to the cane.

Ryan hated that, freaking *hated* it. "Sure. Climbing is all about arm strength." He reached up and hauled himself skyward.

The old pine was like a ladder, an easy climb. Except for the needles in his hair, and the rough, sappy texture, it was easier than a ladder. He reached, chinned, braced his right foot on the next rung, and repeated. Fast and smooth. If it weren't for that fool girl, it would almost be fun. It was a long time since he'd done something like this.

"Alice," he called. She was eight feet above him now, four sets of branches. He didn't want to make her slip. "Alice. I'm just going to come up there and join you, okay? I bet the view is great from there. I'm just going to climb up slowly on the other side okay?"

"The squirrels are jealous of the birds," Alice said. "Flight is beyond them. But they can come close." She stood up on a branch where there was a gap in the tree. Holding with one hand above her head, she reached out with the other and leaned into space.

"Easy there." Ryan used his best talk-jumpers-off-a-ledge voice. "You don't want to slip. Why don't you hold on with both hands, honey." He slid farther around the trunk, and chinned the next rung. Two more levels.

She looked down at him and smiled. It was a scary smile, serene and empty. "But that's why they keep trying. Because next time, they *will* fly." And she leaned forward into the space, and let go.

He lunged for her, his feet slipping, grabbing at air. His fingers weren't even close as she plummeted past. He used all his core strength in an emergency twist, body arching, one fierce grip away from following her to the ground. Luckily, since his injury he'd put a lot of time into upper-body strength. He hauled upward, got his other hand on a branch, and pulled himself safely against the trunk.

He didn't want to look down. But he had to.

Alice had landed on the grass, taking a couple of branches with her. He remembered the crunches as they broke, as she hit. He didn't remember the girl making a sound. A group of people gathered around her crumpled body. One girl began trying chest compressions and mouth to mouth, but Ryan had no illusions. You don't survive a fall like that.

One person's face was turned up at him, rather than staring at the dead girl. The groundskeeper, John, was looking fixedly his way, his eyes wide. Ryan sighed, and began the descent. Easier than the climb up, he could just do this hand over hand. As he hit the ground, a newly familiar grasp on his elbow steadied him. "Here." His cane was placed in his hand.

"Thanks." He gripped it and took the two steps to lower himself to his knees beside the fallen girl. *Alice.* It was always better if you didn't know their names. The brunette who'd tried rescue breathing was sitting back on her heels, white-faced. Ryan reached for Alice's carotid pulse, unsurprised to feel nothing but clammy, lifeless skin. The no-resistance, loose roll of her head even at his gentle touch put an end to any idea of resuscitation. *Neck gone. No hope.*

Bracing the damned cane, he struggled back to his feet, then winced, and inspected his palm. Abrasions and pine sap. John was somehow still right beside him. Ryan asked, "I don't suppose you have another one of those wipes?"

"Not on me."

In the distance, a siren swelled, growing quickly louder.

"I wasn't fast enough," he said down to his sock-clad feet, rubbing his sappy hand on his jeans. Bad mistake. They were his favorite jeans. But he couldn't seem to stop. He worked his shoes back on, balancing carefully with the cane.

John touched his elbow and then withdrew. "I saw the end of it. She didn't hesitate. Just let go and boom. She didn't give you time."

Ryan looked up. Those hazel eyes were as wonderfully compassionate as the last time.

John added, "Did you hurt yourself? I almost had a heart attack thinking you were going down with her."

"No, I'm fine. A few scrapes."

"Good."

The emergency vehicles were bumping toward them over the grass, police and fire rescue. Too damned late. Although John was right. She hadn't hesitated.

The paramedics came running over and knelt beside the girl for a moment. The older one shook her head. "Skull, neck, chest. Not a chance. How far did she fall?"

"About forty feet," Ryan said.

The campus police were joined by a city police car, and more than one doctor drawn from the classrooms by the sirens. Ryan sighed and waited. So much for a lunch hour of studying. *So much for some stupid mixed-up kid's life.* At his back, John waited too, a solid presence, as the paramedics and police did their thing. *At least, there's no shortage of doctors to pronounce the death.* Ryan looked away from the too-familiar scene. After about five minutes, a cop came over to them.

"Excuse me, sir," he said to Ryan. "I'm told you were the guy who went up the tree after her?"

"Yes."

"And you are?"

"Ryan Ward. I'm a med student."

The cop flipped to a new page in his notebook and made a note. "Officer Danielson. I'd like to ask you a few questions, if you don't mind." He glanced at Ryan's cane, and back up. "We could sit on the bench over there, if you like."

Fuck. But his back was sore. He'd wrenched something in that wild grab. Sitting down was smart, not weakness. "Okay." He led the way over and eased onto the bench. John didn't follow them, but he leaned against the tree, listening. After a glance his way, the officer turned to Ryan.

"Do you have identification on you, sir?"

"It's California." He passed over his driver's license.

The cop noted the details, then said, "Please give me your local address and phone, and then run through what happened."

Ryan went through the story.

"What made you go up after her?"

"The way she was talking. She clearly wasn't thinking normally. You're going to want to do a complete drug screen on her."

The officer nodded. "Could you tell what drug she'd taken?"

"No clue. She was calm but not coherent, dissociated, but almost happy."

"She was like that the other night too," John said from where he stood.

"The other night, sir?"

"Yeah. The first day of term. I was working late on the grounds, and I came across that same girl wandering in the alder grove. She was talking nonsense, like disconnected poetry. I figured she was high. I guided her back to her dorm and asked one of the other girls to get her to her room. I assume that's what she did. I didn't actually go inside."

"You're sure it was this same girl?"

"Yes. I got a look at her just now before she… fell. And that night, she said her name was Alice."

"And you didn't report her possible intoxication to anyone at the time? Her dorm monitor or health services?"

"No, I didn't." John spoke more slowly. "She seemed happy, her pulse was normal, she just seemed high. It's not my job to police these kids, as long as they seem safe."

"But she wasn't safe, was she?"

"Not this time." John didn't look down. "She was then."

"Who are you anyway?" the cop asked. "What *is* your job?"

"John Barrett. Groundskeeper."

Barrett. Ryan figured he might actually remember that now. Although after an hour of sharing drunken rambling, he was probably entitled to think of the man as John.

"I'll want to talk to you afterward." The cop turned back to Ryan. "Even if the girl was high, what made you think it was a good idea to climb up after her?"

"I didn't like the way she was talking about flying," Ryan said carefully.

"And you didn't worry that you might scare her into falling?"

"Sure I did." He kept his voice even. "But she had that out-of-control feel, like she wasn't coherent enough to even realize the danger. I hoped I could grab her first."

"That's a difficult call to make."

"I was a firefighter for eight years. I've seen jumpers. And fallers. I made the call. But she was fast. I didn't get close enough."

"He's telling the truth." John sounded angry. "She went straight up, leaned out, and let go. He came closer than the rest of us to saving her."

"Firefighter where?"

28

"San Diego."

"And now you're a med student?"

"And now I am." The cop's eyes dropped to his cane again, and then rose. Ryan met them, trying to seem indifferent. *Don't ask.*

The cop gave him a more friendly look. "More excitement in the big city than we get here, I guess. You didn't know the victim before today?"

"Never saw her."

"Okay." He flipped a page in his notebook, and held out his hand. "I guess someone should say thank you for trying. If we have more questions, we'll be in touch."

Ryan held up his sticky palm. "You don't really want to shake my hand right now."

The cop nodded. "Right." He turned to John. "And now you, sir, if you don't mind."

Ryan closed his eyes and leaned back on the bench. He listened with half an ear as John described seeing the girl in early September. The cop was fishing for some kind of drug connection. John wasn't giving him much. He'd seen the girl around campus the last two years, had a few bits of information about where she worked.

"So, how come you know so much about a random student? You said you're the groundskeeper."

John's drawl got deeper. "Yeah. Which means I'm out on the grounds, every day, all year. If it happens outside the buildings, I probably know about it."

"But you were pretty familiar with this particular girl?"

"I'd noticed her. Mostly because she changed a lot from her freshman year. I like when college does that for a kid, makes them grow. I'm really sorry it ended like this."

"Taking drugs isn't growing."

"No, it's not."

"So how many of the undergraduates do you know, sir? Five, ten, twenty?"

29

Ryan could hear the suspicion in the cop's voice, but somehow John answered calmly. "I can probably tell you which year or program a couple hundred are in. The ones who stand out in any way. I know the names of about fifty." He nodded at the huddle of Alice's friends, still speaking to the paramedics. "That dark-haired girl is a senior, with an interest in literature. She likes to read Proust on the rocks by the daffodil bed in spring. The guy with the bright red hair over there is a med student. Second year, I think. The short kid next to him is Brian. He skateboards. Also a med student."

Ryan twisted to look at John, surprised. He got that warm smile in return.

"I like the kids," John said. "I have two of my own, not quite in college yet. And I have a very good memory for names and faces."

"Apparently," the cop said sourly. "All right, sir. That's all for now. We'll be back in touch."

As the cop headed back toward the body, John came over and dropped onto the bench beside Ryan. "Whew."

"He seemed like he was interrogating you."

"Yeah. I guess I can see it. Thirty-seven-year-old guy knows the name of a pretty undergraduate who may have committed suicide. They'd like it to be about sexual abuse, or for me to be her pusher. Tie the case up neatly."

"Too bad for them." Ryan frowned. "I don't think it was suicide. Not really. Maybe something like PCP or ketamine. She wasn't thinking right. But she was too calm for either of those drugs. Maybe acid, on a really mellow trip."

"Yes. Serene. That first time I saw her I thought it looked like a nice high. Maybe not so much now."

"Not so much."

Ryan was in no hurry to get up, and walk past that spot. John sat next to him, patient, his bulk warm and steady in the shade of the giant pines.

Chapter Four

Two weeks later, John was raking out the bushes in front of the library, when he heard a familiar voice curse inventively. He glanced up. Ryan stood at the top of the steps, pulling on the locked doors.

"They're closed," John called up to him. "Ceiling maintenance. It was posted yesterday."

"I forgot," Ryan called down to him. "Damn."

He came back down the stairs and walked over to where John was working. "What are you doing here so late? A gardener's work is never done?"

John smiled. "I was bored and restless. Figured it was this or the bar, and I'm trying to cut back."

"I haven't seen you drink too much. Well, not since that first night."

I don't when you're around. It was when he was alone in a darkened, anonymous room that the first glass became a second and a fifth. They'd met several times now at The Copper Stein, happening on each other by chance, and glad of the company. Ryan was bright and fun. They'd kept off the subject of Ryan's firefighting days and his own bad marriage, since that first time. But the conversation ranged far and wide. Ryan was interested in travel, and science, and politics, and comic books, and sports. John had enjoyed those evenings.

His two moves and the divorce had isolated him from his old friends. Here at the college he was in an odd position. The faculty were not about to socialize with him, and yet he didn't fit in well with his workmen either. Spending his time outdoors, he rarely talked to the other staff who kept the place running. Until Ryan, he hadn't found anyone whose company was more comfortable than an evening spent alone.

He'd recently realized how often those evenings alone included too much alcohol. "Yeah, well, I don't need to spend the money on overpriced drinks, either," he hedged. "What did you need from the library? Research?"

"Nah, just study space."

"Jason again?"

"Yep." Ryan leaned companionably against the stone pillar at the bottom of the steps. "He's got a new girl. Mona. And God, if anyone was ever more appropriately named it's hard to imagine. On top of which she likes rap. Now, when I leased the apartment, I specifically asked Jason if he listened to rap, and he was all like, *no, man, I don't like shit that doesn't have some melody.* But it turns out what Mona wants, Mona gets. Which is rap. On my own stereo system. I can't study."

John knew that Ryan's roommate considered requests for quiet to be suggestions with about a twenty-minute expiry date. Ryan got sick of asking. Several times he'd brought a textbook to the pub to study, until they got sidetracked into conversation. "I'm about done here. I could give you a ride to The Copper."

"No, thanks. I'm trying to stay away too," Ryan said. "I like it too much, especially when you're there. We start talking, I have a beer, and next thing you know it's midnight, and I haven't done any work. Besides this is biochemistry, and I suck at it. I need someplace quiet."

"How about my place?" John surprised himself, but now that he thought about it he liked the idea. Better than going home to an empty house and leftovers. "I was going to call out for pizza, work on a little project. You'd be welcome to a piece of the kitchen table. It's quiet."

"God, that's tempting. But I have to work, not socialize."

"Me too," John said quickly. "I mean, I have this present for Mark's birthday that I'm working on, and I need to finish it. And I could make coffee. Fresh delivery this morning."

"You're an evil man," Ryan said. "Lead me to it. Although I warn you, if it's as good as last time, you may never get rid of me."

Fine with me. John blinked. Man, he was lonely. Maybe he needed to get a dog. "Okay, let me put the tools away. Truck's in the green lot."

On the drive home, John had a moment's panic about whether he'd left the kitchen in a mess. That coffee had come as he was finishing breakfast. Had he washed the dishes? He made a point of preceding Ryan into the kitchen, and yes, he had. Which was stupid to worry about, because why would Ryan care?

He stuck his phone in the charger, and began getting out mugs. "There's a flyer for Domino's on the refrigerator. I think there's a coupon for a large deep-dish. I eat anything except olives and pineapple."

"Mushrooms and pepperoni?"

"Perfect."

Ryan pulled out his cell to make the call, as John lifted down plates. The kitchen felt warm and welcoming this evening. John found the real fabric napkins in a drawer.

"Hey," Ryan called with his hand over the phone. "I don't know your street address."

John fumbled a piece of mail out of the pile on the hutch, checked it for accuracy and passed it over. Behind him, Ryan's clear voice recited his address. The hot water rose over the ground coffee, filling the air with the amazing scent.

"They say twenty minutes." Ryan came over and leaned in beside him to breathe in the aroma coming off the grounds. "Oh, wow, nice." His hair brushed John's cheek, a light scent of man and lemon herb shampoo. John was struck with a sudden sense of déjà vu. Like he had done this before. Like he had smelled exactly this combination of rich coffee and clean skin and light citrus herbs. Then Ryan stepped back and the moment was broken. *Weird.*

"So, what's the gift?" Ryan asked.

"Huh?"

"The one you're making for Mark."

"Oh." He shrugged. "It's not much."

"Show me?"

He went to the workshop and brought it back. The bent roots had suggested the final form, an abstract of a baseball player, his bat in motion, shoulders swinging round. There was a lot of polishing to do, but the shape was there.

Ryan handled it gently, turning the piece in his clever hands. "Now that's something. How old is Mark again?"

"Turning fifteen."

"Yeah. That might be old enough to appreciate this. It's not realism, but God, you've got the heart of the motion there. You can almost hear the crack of the bat on the ball. You just know he's going to connect." He set it carefully on the table. "There's a reason you're not making a living charging a gazillion dollars for these, right?"

"Don't want to." Damned if he could explain it to himself, let alone someone else. Cynthia had wanted him to put a price on everything. Maybe that was one more reason he didn't sell the work of his hands. He shrugged abruptly. *Drop it.*

Ryan obviously understood when a topic was hands-off, because he just gave a sweet smile. "You're a unique man. Who makes amazing coffee. And was just about to offer me a big cup when I distracted you."

"Right." John poured, and passed over his favorite extra-sized mug. "Here."

Ryan sipped appreciatively. "The woman who left you was a fool." Before the words were out of his mouth he was making a face. "Sorry. So, is it okay if I crack the books until the pizza comes?"

"Sure." John felt off-balance. A retreat to the workshop would be good.

He was deep in the initial sanding when the doorbell rang. Before he could get his hands clean, Ryan appeared at the door of the workshop. "Pizza's here." His bright green eyes scanned around the room. "This is nice. You'll have to give me a tour some time. Now wash up and come eat."

"Yes, dear," John muttered as Ryan disappeared down the hall. His stomach felt oddly bubbly, like champagne. He obviously needed to put some food in it.

Ryan had cleared his books off the table and set it with the dishes John had gotten out. The pizza box sat open on a towel in the center, steaming lightly. Ryan eased down into a chair, and reached into the box, pulling out a big oozing slice. "This is one of the perks of small-town living."

"Domino's?" John sat down and took his own piece. "I hate to break it to you, Ry, but they have Domino's in big cities."

"Yeah, but the pizza's never hot." Ryan bit in, and licked a strand of cheese off his fingers. "You're always fifth or tenth on the delivery list and the pizza's lukewarm. It just isn't the same."

"Glad you like it," John managed. The pizza was good. Everything was good. He refilled their coffee out of the thermos, and found the remains of a pack of Oreos in the cupboard. Ryan ate six, dark hair falling into his eyes, his teeth dusted with black cookie crumbs when he laughed.

John turned down help with cleanup and set him back to studying his books. The only sounds were the scratch of Ryan's pencil, and the running water as John washed the dishes in companionable silence. He found it surprisingly hard to head back to his beloved workshop, and leave that simple warmth.

By ten o'clock he was done with the rough sanding on Mark's present. He stood to stretch the kinks out of his back, and looked over at Ryan's knock on the doorframe.

"Hey." Ryan's smile was bright. "I think I've got amino acid synthesis down cold. I should probably head out."

"Already?" John glanced at the clock. "It's not that late. There's more coffee."

"Get thee behind me, Satan. If I drink any more I won't sleep. Anyway, there's only more coffee if you make more, because I just might maybe have finished off what was in the thermos." Ryan gave him a little-boy mischief smile.

"You're welcome to it." John sighed and dusted off his hands. He was reluctant to have the evening end, even though they hadn't spent most of it in the same room. The house was a different place with Ryan in it. "Okay. Come on. I'll drive you home."

"You don't need to do that. I can catch a cab."

"Don't be silly." He passed through the kitchen and grabbed his jacket off the hook. "You're no millionaire either." They hadn't talked money. John didn't know what firefighters made, or whether there was disability pay. But he had the impression Ryan wasn't rolling in funds.

"I can pay for gas, then."

John aimed a swipe at Ryan's head, then converted it to a quick steadying touch on his back as Ryan's dodge brought his weight onto his bad leg. John pressed his fingers into solid muscle just for a moment, steadying Ry, then pulled his hand away without comment. Because it didn't take a genius to see that the most sensitive topic in Ryan's life was that leg. "Wow, big spender," he said lightly instead. "Gas both ways, in my truck, you probably owe me a buck fifty. Which is less than I owe you for the pizza."

"Which balances out what I owe you for the coffee."

"So we'll call it a wash, after I give you a ride home."

"Okay."

They drove in easy silence. Once, John slowed to point out a doe with her half-grown fawn under the trees along the verge. They eased past with his foot riding the brake. Luckily, Bambi didn't seem to be in a suicidal mood tonight.

Ryan directed him to a concrete apartment block near campus. It was… basic. Not bad but just a place. Reasonable-sized balconies. Smallish windows. Ryan looked up and then sighed. John followed his gaze.

On the third floor, one of the units was lit up like a Christmas tree. The balcony doors were open, and a young couple stood necking in the doorway.

"Jason and Mona?"

"Nope," Ryan said flatly. "But that's my place. I guess he decided to have a party."

"Great."

"Well." He opened the door and turned to slide out. "At least I have the right to be a party-pooper. We have a written agreement about no noise after ten on weeknights. It's in the lease."

"Good luck with that." John reached out impulsively and grabbed Ryan's sleeve. "Wait a second."

Ryan half turned. "Yeah?"

How to say this right? "You said your lease is monthly. Have you ever thought about moving out?"

"Only a hundred times. But then I'd have to apartment-hunt again. I don't have the time. And the next roommate might be worse than Jason."

John glanced up. "Hard to imagine. But no, what I meant was, I've been thinking about renting out one of the rooms in my house."

Ryan raised an eyebrow, but swung his legs back in and shut the door. "First you've said about it."

36

"Well, I hadn't decided. You see, I could use the cash, but…what if I ended up with someone like Jason? I mean, my kids come and stay with me sometimes. I'd have to find someone I trusted around them. And someone I wouldn't mind having in my space."

"And?"

"And you need a place to live that won't make you flunk out of med school. I need the money. We get along okay. You don't laugh at my hobby."

"John, believe me, no one would laugh at your artwork."

"You see?" This sounded better the more he thought about it. "You're older than most students. You find a twenty-two-year-old immature. You don't go cruising for sex. I don't have to worry about you looking at my twelve-year-old and seeing jail bait."

"Oh, now that's flattering."

"It came out wrong," he said, before he realized Ryan was laughing at him. "What do you think?"

"Seriously?"

"Yeah. What are you paying for your share of that dump?"

"Five hundred."

"So, there's a quarter of my child support, right there."

"A *quarter?*" Ryan stared at him. "You pay two thousand a month?"

"Yeah." He couldn't stifle a sigh. "At least there's no more alimony since she remarried."

"That's ridiculous."

"No, it's not. When we got divorced, Cynthia was a housewife, and I was a landscape architect with a big firm. She didn't want me buying the kids fancy presents, like that daddy-as-Santa-Claus thing, but I wanted them to have nice stuff."

"So you gave her the money and she bought fancy presents for them herself?"

"It was a mutual decision. It was…" He choked on the word *fair.* It had never been really fair, but… "It was good for the kids."

"And now? You can't be making that much. That's twenty-four thousand a year!"

I know that. "It's a stretch. But teenagers are expensive. I can do it. Rent money would help."

Ryan was staring at him. "It sounds too good," he said slowly. "I like your company. I don't have many friends right now. But sometimes living with someone is a good way to ruin a friendship."

"I'm easy." John coughed. "I mean, I'm pretty easy to live with."

Ryan glanced up at the light show in his windows. "I can't say no," he admitted. "In fact, when can I move in?"

"Whenever you like." John felt like he'd won a lottery, warm and happy. It would be great to have someone else around the house, someone who would fill those empty spaces where he should have had family. "How about this weekend? You pack your stuff, and I can help haul it in the truck. Except… what about giving notice? You don't want to end up paying rent on two places at once."

Behind Ryan, a fluttering motion caught their eyes. Something pink floated earthward from the open balcony and landed on the grass. It was a bra. The woman who owned it was undoubtedly a… healthy young woman. Ryan sighed. "Oh yes, I do. Saturday. 8 a.m. Be here." He slid out and shut the door.

"Right." John knew he was grinning. "Good luck with the biochemistry exam."

Ryan tapped his forehead. "No sweat. It's in here. Even that circus upstairs won't shake it loose. Saturday."

"See you then."

****

Ryan hated moving, but it was definitely easier with help, and getting away from Jason's never-ending party was a major relief. Worth any amount of effort. He'd kind of enjoyed getting up at six a.m. despite it being Saturday, thumping around and ostentatiously packing up the last of his stuff. He left Jason bleary-eyed, grumbling about losing the stereo. *Tough shit.* The girl who'd been with Jason this time— who was not Mona— pointed out that there was now room for her to move in. Ryan had savored the look of panic on Jason's face.

Ryan reached the top of the stairs in John's house, hiding the need to take a few fast breaths. This was the last box of his stuff. He should've let John help with more of it, except he'd caught the guy trying to be secretive, lifting all the boxes to see which was the heaviest. So of course, Ryan's pride made him want to lug those ones himself. Which was stupid. He was fucking lucky he hadn't taken another header down a flight of steps. He turned in at his room and sat down hard on the bed, letting the box slide to the floor.

John turned around from where he had been casually looking out the window. "That the last?"

"Yep. Ready to give me the tour?"

"In a minute." John slid down to sit on the floor, his long legs stuck out in front of him. "You don't have much stuff for a thirty-year-old guy."

"I've got a bunch in storage at my brother Drew's place," Ryan told him. "I didn't want to pay to haul it all out here. This was kind of a new start. I figured I'd go slow."

"I'm just as glad," John said. "I'm old and decrepit, and I can't take this much work."

"Bullshit." Ryan dropped back on the bed. *Nice, soft bed.* "You're not even forty and in better shape than I am, and that's saying something, because I've worked at it."

"Well, maybe. Outdoor work is good for keeping fit. When I was a suit in an office, I was pretty flabby."

"Hard to imagine."

"Me as a suit, or me flabby?"

"Either. Both." Ryan closed his eyes. John was built like a tree, tall and limber and not an ounce of extra fat. He had long lean muscles, nothing flashy except for his arms, which were nicely rounded from all the digging. Well, and his chest had some width to it. "Maybe you'll take me on as extra crew, save me lifting weights."

"When you can tell a maple tree from an oak, maybe."

"One little slip." Ryan smiled in the dark behind his closed lids. The room was quiet, with only a distant swish of traffic going by on the road out front. No rap. No duets of passionate moaning. "Man, this is nice."

"You sure you don't mind having the smallest bedroom?"

Ryan cracked one eye open and rolled his head to look at John. "What, you think I'm going to kick one of your kids out of their room, to have more space for my nonexistent things? Who do you think I am?"

John's smile was slow and warm. "I know who you are. You're welcome to use the rest of the house, you know. That parlor thingy downstairs has a desk in it that never gets used. I have the study and the workshop."

Ryan bit his lip. "The workshop might make a great place to study in, if it was cleaned up a bit."

John swallowed. "Um..."

Ryan laughed. "Just kidding. Come on. You're already giving me this great room and plenty of space, for the same rent as my half of Jason's Fantasy Playhouse. I'm good."

"Okay. Good. I'm glad." John got up and gave him a slap on the leg. His good leg. The man paid attention. "Come on, let me give you the ten-cent tour."

It was a great house. Lots of nooks and crannies, gabled windows, odd-shaped closets. It was a little dusty, but relatively empty of clutter. It was clear that kids visited, but they didn't live there. There was a small space on the end gable, accessible only by bending over, with a round window out onto the back lawn. It begged for a heap of cushions and a grownups-keep-out sign, but held only dust bunnies. The kids' rooms were personalized, filled with books and toys, but a little too tidy. And a little young, Ryan thought, handling an airplane lamp on Mark's dresser. Most fifteen-year-olds would have passed that along years ago.

Eventually, they ended up in the kitchen, sitting at the little table. "You made this, right?" Ryan ran a hand over the glossy surface.

"Yes," John said. "It's too small for when the kids are here. I have a regular one that seats four. But this one is okay for just me."

"Or for the two of us. Two plates and a large pizza—what more could we need?"

"I guess."

Ryan tilted his head and took a better look. John had seemed low-key all day. Ryan wondered if the reality of sharing the house was sinking in. Maybe John was regretting his invitation. "You know," he said tentatively. "I still have a month on my lease on the apartment, if this isn't working for you."

"Huh?" John straightened. "No! What would give you that idea?"

"You just seem a little down."

"I just...I think I'm finally realizing that I'm never going to have it all. You know, a normal life with a wife and kids in this house. I know it's been four years since the divorce, but I think all along I was hoping something would change, that I could get my life back. Not hoping in my head, but in my gut. And now I know I won't. Which is... liberating, in a way, but a little sad."

"It's hard to let go."

"Yeah."

Ryan knew he shouldn't ask, but he wanted to know. It wasn't the impression he got from all their conversations. "Do you still love her?"

"Cynthia?" John shook his head. "No. Not for a long time. I did once though, and I loved the life, loved the kids. I liked being the breadwinner and the dad, having it all. Cynthia was the most beautiful girl in school. I couldn't believe it when she agreed to go out with me. She was way out of my league, but she made it happen. We got married at eighteen, and I thought I had the world in my hand. Even when it wasn't still true love, it was good."

"What happened?"

John sighed. "Life? I'm not sure. I wasn't enough for her somehow. She was always needing more, looking for more."

"More?"

"She was ambitious and I wasn't. Like my job. She picked out which offer I took out of school. She wanted to play the upwardly mobile wife, give parties, help my career. I wanted to grub in the dirt. When the firm got bought out, I had a chance at a bigger salary in a management position. I turned it down. I guess that was the last straw."

"What work does she do?"

41

"Work? Well, the kids, she's always been busy with the kids. She's a great mom. Her new husband's a lawyer and she talks about all the stuff she does to help his career."

And how old are the kids now? Sounds more like a great parasite. His own mother had held down a job, even with mothering four kids. She hadn't needed to define herself by his dad's career. But it wasn't his place to comment.

"So," he said. "Do you want to make up a formal roster of household chores, and divide things up? Or play it by ear?"

John gave him that warm wide smile. "If you do dishes, you can live here forever."

Ryan was surprised at how good that sounded.

Chapter Five

They'd fallen into a routine easily, Ryan reflected three weeks later, as he dried the spaghetti pot from dinner. Okay, sometimes he wasn't as neat as John might've liked. He had become very familiar with the long-suffering sigh the man came out with, as he returned some straying utensil to its proper place. And John took the longest showers known to man, so there was never hot water in the evenings. Ryan had had to put his foot down, to make sure he got first dibs on Fridays after Anatomy lab. He needed to get the lab smell off his skin before letting John have his turn.

But in general, it was working even better than he'd expected. They liked the same music in the background in the evenings. They both got up early, but neither one was irritatingly chipper before the sun rose. They bought groceries for themselves, but didn't make a big deal out of whose carton of milk was open now. And as a side benefit, he got a ride in to campus in John's truck most mornings, instead of standing waiting for a bus. After just three weeks, Ryan decided he could handle living like this for the next three years.

Upstairs the water shut off at last. John appeared as Ryan was putting away the last of the silverware. John's T-shirt clung to his damp skin, and his hair was flat and wet, its auburn muted to brown. He moved easily past Ryan, and grabbed a clean mug out of the cupboard. "You want some too?" he asked, automatically getting down a second cup.

"Nope." Ryan grabbed a Sprite out of the fridge and opened his textbook on the cleared table. "I don't have much studying to do. I'm planning an early night and some real sleep. Without caffeine."

John filled his mug from the ever-ready thermos and waved it under Ryan's nose. "But it's sooo good."

Ryan laughed and flapped a hand at him. "Get away from me with that."

"Your loss." John took a big swallow. "I'm going on the computer for a while, planning the plant orders for spring. So don't shut off the network."

"You've got it." John had been pretty half-assed with his computer setup. No security, old software. Ryan had got him better stuff, and taught him to put his computer on a power strip and shut it off when not in use. Lower bills, and no one was hijacking your machine in the middle of the night. He hadn't sold the man on using a webcam yet, but eventually.

Ryan was deep in the intricacies of electrolyte controls in the kidney when he heard John curse from the other room. The tone had Ryan on his feet immediately. He stuck his head into the study.

"Computer problems? Something I can help with?"

"No." John cursed again and shoved himself away from the desk.

"What then?"

"Cynthia. She sent me a damned e-mail. Not even a phone call."

"About?" This was like pulling teeth, but the look on John's face was more pain than irritation.

"You remember I told you the kids have the whole Thanksgiving week off?"

"Yeah. Next month. They're coming here for the Saturday through Tuesday before the holiday. We've gone over that."

"Except now they aren't."

"What? Why not?"

John ran a hand over his head, standing his damp hair on end. "How the hell would I know? She gave a list of reasons, all this stuff they don't want to miss. She'll send them at Christmas."

The bitch. John made an obvious effort not to speak badly of his ex-wife. Ryan was under no such restriction, especially in his own head. After suppressing his first three reactions, he suggested, "Why don't you go out there?"

"What?"

"To LA. If she won't send them here, go out to LA yourself. Visit them there."

"Cynthia would have a fit if I asked for time with them on her turf."

"So don't ask," Ryan said. "God, you give in to her every time. Just go out there, show up at the door, and tell her you're taking the kids to a hotel for the weekend, to make up for all the time you've missed. How can she say no?"

"She could stop them from coming here the next time."

"She's doing that already. Look, I don't mean to butt into your business, but those kids must be wondering if you really want to see them."

"What?" John sounded pissed. "They know she has their tickets for a flight back here, any time she's willing to let them come."

"Do they? How do you know what she's telling them?"

John stared at him. "But... going out there... we're busy at work right now. And I don't know if I can afford... especially around the holiday. There won't be any seats."

"Now who's making excuses?" Ryan nudged John aside and got onto the Net. Ten seconds to log onto Expedia, and he was scanning flights. "There. Leave Friday at ten p.m., get into LA at eleven thirty. Love that time change. You can have all day Saturday and Sunday, and most of Monday. The rest of the week is booked full, if you don't want to spend thousands. But if you take the red-eye back Monday night, it'll only run you about five hundred dollars for the ticket. *And* you only miss one day of work."

"There'll be a hotel bill."

"So figure three nights, another four hundred, a couple of meals. You can do the whole thing for a thousand. You already have my first month's rent. How about if I commission a piece from you?"

"A what?"

"A work of art disguised as something useful. Stay with me here. A cane, I think." He smiled at John's open-mouthed stare. "You're catching flies. Yeah, I hate the thing. But you could design me something better. Something that would keep me from falling over and still have people going *that's so cool* when they look at it. A John Barrett original. Cover the other five hundred."

45

John blinked. "I could do that. I've actually had some ideas, but five hundred dollars…"

Ryan leaned forward and stuck out his hand. "A private room for a month and a John Barrett original artwork cane, one thousand dollars. A weekend with the kids, priceless."

For a moment he thought John would still balk, but then the man began to smile, and reached out a hand to seal the deal.

****

John stared out the window at his backyard. He usually loved late October. The color on campus was still close to its peak, the mornings were crisp, but the middle of the day still allowed for short sleeves. His crew had been busy raking, bedding down the perennials, trimming back bushes that might bend under the coming snow. But the annual beds still blazed with the fall colors he had planted. He didn't even mind the additional raking that piled up in his own yard after a full day on campus. So he wasn't sure why he felt discontented today.

He'd spent yesterday on his garden. It was winter-ready, except for the leaves still waiting to fall. He'd taken a walk around the property, and reviewed his plans for spring. He hadn't done a quarter of what he'd envisioned here this year. Maybe that was where this lingering sadness came from, this feeling of time slipping away from him. The reason a quiet Sunday felt sad, instead of peaceful.

He headed back to the kitchen, and Ryan glanced over at him. "Just the man I was looking for. Can you pick that pumpkin up off the floor for me? I put it down there, and now I can't lift it properly. I'm afraid I'll drop it."

"Sure." John grabbed the large pumpkin by its gnarled stem, and then, with a grunt, bent to put his other hand under it. He heaved the thing up onto the counter. "God, how much does this monstrosity weigh? No wonder you couldn't lift it."

"Isn't it great?" Ryan's eyes sparkled. "Biggest one they had. I about killed myself getting it home."

"I'll bet. So why the giant squash?"

46

"It's Halloween," Ryan said, as if that should make it obvious. "I'm going to carve it."

"I don't usually make a big deal out of Halloween." *Not when the kids aren't here.*

John remembered past Halloweens. Torey always wanted the most random costumes, like a cell phone or a milkshake. Somehow he'd become the costume designer. The milkshake had been his masterpiece, topped with inflated white-balloon bubbles flowing over the side, and a giant flex-pipe straw. He'd let the kids trick-or-treat longer that year, for the ego boost of having people admire the costume. Marcus generally wanted something dark and spooky. Purchased costumes were fine for Mark. He didn't have that obsession with being unique.

The kids had still been trick-or-treating the last year they'd all lived together. Now they were probably too old. For sure Mark would be. And it would be different in LA anyway. No crisp leaves, no chill air forcing parents to argue about wearing a jacket over that skimpy costume, no scent of burning leaves. Probably the kids were going to some fancy party, with Hollywood special effects. He'd bet they looked back on their younger days as corny and boring.

"Well, I like Halloween," Ryan said firmly. "And I'm going to carve this pumpkin, and the other one too if you don't want it."

"Other one?"

"Yeah. I bought one yesterday. But then I saw this, and it was just so awesome, I had to have it. So I figured you might do the other one. But if you don't want to, I'll do them both. As long as you promise not to laugh at my efforts, mister artist man."

"I won't laugh." John eyed the kitchen knife Ryan was brandishing. "Although I also don't want to drive you to the emergency room. Is that what you're going to use as a carving tool?"

"It's sharp enough." Ryan punched the blade into the thick orange flesh and began to saw around the top.

John winced. "Hang on. I think I have a better knife, and a small saw blade. Let me get them."

He hurried out to the studio and dug through his tools for something appropriate. A couple of short, strong knives and a saw-edged blade looked good. When he got back to the kitchen, Ryan had mangled a semi-oval top off the big pumpkin and was slicing the seed-goop from the bottom of the stem into a bowl.

"Here. Try these." John put the better tools on the counter and took the big knife out of Ryan's fingers. "Jesus. To think you might be a surgeon one day."

"Probably not," Ryan said cheerfully. "Too much standing involved. Can you get a metal spoon out of the drawer?"

John passed one over and stood, hovering, as Ryan began scooping handfuls of slimy pumpkin guts out of the shell.

He really should go do some work. There were things that needed his attention. Or he could put some time in on carving Ry's cane. It was going to be good. Not five-hundred-dollars good. For that money, he figured he'd be making Ryan a series of canes. But this one was coming out fun. Although, if he was going to carve something… "Where's the other pumpkin? At least I can fetch it for you."

"By the back door."

John trailed through the house and stepped out onto the porch. The warm sun of the late-October Sunday turned the yard to gold and green. No jackets needed for trick-or-treating this year. The day was edging toward dusk, but it would be a couple of hours before the little beggars came out.

The pumpkin was on the ground, leaning against the siding beside the door. It was no runt either. John grunted as he hefted it up in his arms, and lugged it back to the kitchen. "You had this one, and you needed bigger?" He slid it onto the counter a couple of feet down from Ryan's.

Ryan stepped back and compared the two for a moment. "Well, that one's not shabby. But this one's fucking fantastic." He dug back into the slime.

"So what are you making?"

"Making?"

"Yeah. On the pumpkin. What are you carving?"

48

"A face." Ryan gave him an exaggerated grimace. "That's why they're jack-o-lanterns, because they have a face."

"I liked to do other stuff," John told him. "One year, I made a pumpkin with cats all over it, in front of a full moon."

"You would. I'm making a face. If I'm lucky, the teeth won't fall out from being cut through too far, and it will have the right number of eyebrows."

"And what about this one?" John laid a proprietary hand on the big pumpkin he'd set down.

"Another face. My best pumpkins have cool faces. My worst pumpkins have kind of screwed-up faces."

"You don't want two the same, though. Maybe I could...I guess I could do something with this one, so we wouldn't have two the same."

"If you like," Ryan grunted, hauling slimy strings from the bowels of his squash.

John looked at the tall rounded shape of the squash, considering. Bats, perhaps. He'd had a design he didn't use once, for bats hanging in front of the opening of a cavern, and then flying off, silhouetted against a moon. Like the cats, but even better. Pondering, he hauled out another mixing bowl. He'd need to scoop it out first. That would give him some planning time.

He lost track, working with the firm orange shell. It was much easier to carve than wood, but you had to be careful about strength. He made the last bat's wing wider. It overlapped the rim of the moon, providing the free-flying shape with its anchor point. Too narrow, and the bat would break off. He should've scraped the wall of the pumpkin down thinner, for fine detail work, but he'd been impatient.

Then he shuddered and yelped as something cold and slimy went down the neck of his shirt. He jumped back, digging the pumpkin guts out of the back of his hair. Ryan eyed him from a safe distance, a hint of a smile on his face.

"What the hell was that for?" He wiped his fingers on the edge of the sink.

"Fairness. Take a look. Your pumpkin. My pumpkin. I figured a little slime down the shirt was required to balance the equation."

John glanced at the two pumpkins. Okay, so his had a cluster of slit-eyed bats with taloned wings hanging from stalactites, while two more soared off across the moon. Ryan's had… a nose, two eyes, fangs, and was that one eyebrow, all the way across?

John snorted involuntarily. "Um, it's very nice."

"Right."

"Halloweeny."

"Do tell."

"I think it will take more than pumpkin guts to even the score."

Ryan laughed. "You think?"

John's bowl was still on the counter. He was between Ryan and the door. His fingers slid toward the bowl as he spoke. "Really, we should save the pumpkin seeds and roast them or something."

"Except the ones in your hair."

"And the ones in yours." It was only one long step, and the handful of slime made a satisfying squish on Ryan's head.

Ryan blinked, and brushed a seed off his nose. "You know this means war."

"Just don't hurt the pumpkins. They're non-combatants."

It turned out that there was enough goo in two pumpkins to liberally coat two men, a counter, a table, and half a kitchen floor. John had Ryan pinned down, a final handful of guts held suspended over his face, before Ryan cried uncle. John was laughing almost too hard to get off him.

"God, that's disgusting," he said, trying to dig a seed out of his ear.

"But fun." Ryan lay back on the floor, grinning. "My brothers and I used to do that all the time, once the pumpkins were carved. That's one of the reasons to have the biggest pumpkin, you know. More ammunition."

"Your mother was a saint."

"She made us wash the kitchen after."

50

"And your clothes?"

"My mother was a saint." Ryan laughed and sat up. "Your pumpkin is freaking fantastic. It will be embarrassed to be seen with mine."

"I like yours. The spirit of Halloween at its purest." John stood and pulled his beslimed shirt away from his chest. "I need to shower and change before the kids start ringing the doorbell."

"Wait!" Ryan held up a hand for a lift off the floor. "I get to go first. I'll be fast. Promise."

John clasped Ryan's warm, gooey hand and hauled him upright. They stood chest to chest, smelling of pumpkin and sweat. Ryan wavered, and John shifted his hand to Ry's arm. *I hope I wasn't too rough on his leg.* He looked at Ryan's black hair, falling forward over those sea-green eyes. There were slimy seeds stuck to the strands. John found himself reaching out to pick the bits away from Ryan's face. "I could promise to be quick," he said. His voice was hoarse, for some reason.

"I wouldn't believe you. You're not one for a quickie." Ryan choked. "All right, not the way I meant that to come out. You take longer in the shower than anyone I know. I have no knowledge of...other things."

John let go of Ryan's arm as if it burned him. Because the words, the closeness, were reminding him how long it had been since he'd had sex of any kind. Too long, if wrestling on the floor with a *guy* could make him hard. Damn, he needed that shower.

"Okay, you first," he said. "I'll start cleanup here. But you *will* do your share."

"Yes, Mother." Ryan left the kitchen, limping a little more than usual, and headed up the stairs. From the sound of his footsteps, he went into the bathroom without pausing in his own room. In ten minutes, he'd be coming out of the bathroom draped in just a towel, skin damp from the shower. As he'd sometimes done before. John knew how Ryan's chest and arms would look, sparse dark curls over hard muscle, rounded biceps and strong forearms, flat lean stomach. John shook his head quickly to get rid of the image of a half-naked man upstairs.

Jesus, he needed to get out of the house.

Although not tonight. There was a bowl of candy waiting by the door, for the visiting munchkins. And he should find candles for inside the pumpkins. He thought there were a couple of tea lights above the stove.

He located the candles and dug out a lighter. The pumpkins weren't as heavy, now that they were scooped out. He set his by the door and Ryan's by the top of the steps where it would be seen first. It wasn't really that bad. It had a kind of rakish charm.

John centered a candle inside each one, and lit them. The sky was losing its color. The youngest trick-or-treaters would be out soon. The candles flickered, casting a homey glow on the yellow paint of the porch. John went down to the walkway and turned to consider the placement, his head tipped to one side.

The house looked like Halloween. More than just the pumpkins? He peered closer. Yes, that was a rubber bat hanging from the porch light, and a pipe-cleaner spider above the doorbell. He couldn't help smiling. When he was a kid, a house with cool decorations was a good bet for plentiful candy. He hoped he'd bought enough.

The front door opened and Ryan limped out. He wore a fresh T-shirt and jeans with bare feet, and his hair was wet and clean. He came carefully down the steps to join John, and turned to gaze at the pumpkins. "Okay, now I'm really embarrassed."

"No way." John stepped closer. Ryan smelled of soap, and lemon shampoo. At least as far as John could tell over his own pervasive raw-pumpkin cologne. "It looks great. It looks like home."

"I like Halloween. I guess I'm just a kid at heart."

John touched a muscled forearm with one finger. "Pretty big kid."

"You're bigger. It's been a while since I lost a pumpkin-guts battle." Ryan's eyes were colorless in the deepening gloom.

For a moment John just stood and breathed, his lungs filled with candle smoke and dried leaves and lemon shampoo. Something was moving, changing inside him, but he didn't know what. Then Ryan laughed and headed back up the steps. "You go shower. I'll listen for the doorbell, and work on cleaning the kitchen. Although you haven't done much, as far as I can see. You *will* do your share."

The return quip wouldn't come. John trailed after Ryan into the house and headed up the stairs two at a time. He needed a shower. He needed to get the drying goo out of his hair, needed the warm water cascading down. And maybe he needed his own hand, in the wet rushing darkness. Because there was no inviting woman in this home that he and Ryan were making, and his body was feeling that lack acutely right now.

****

The Copper Stein was crowded on a November Saturday night. Ryan took a quick look around the barroom. His beer glass was half empty again. He would've sworn it was full just a moment ago. Across from him, John sipped from his own glass and licked the foam from his lips. Ryan blinked and then looked away. *Not watching a guy lick his mouth.*

Ryan felt restless, itchy. Med school was smoothing out after midterms, from overwhelming to doable. The house was becoming a familiar haven. Stepping in the door was coming home. He didn't know why he felt so discontented. Maybe he was missing the excitement of fighting fires. There was no denying that sitting in class looking at slides didn't compare to climbing into his gear and walking into the smoke.

And yet, he no longer missed his buddies from the firehouse quite as much. John was good company. Sure, there were a couple of the guys he'd started e-mailing again. It was nice to keep in touch. But none of them had been as easy to be with as this man across the table. The firefighters' lives were different from his now, and their e-mail exchanges were superficial. With John, he could joke about deer stopping traffic on the parkway, or discuss the ethics of using embryos for research, and get a matching response. Or he could sit in silence, like tonight, and feel at ease.

Except tonight, he didn't. Lately, there were just times when his skin felt too small for his body. Or he would wake up from the weirdest dreams, so hard he was aching, and not remember which girl he'd been dreaming about. He'd decided he needed to get laid. It'd been over a year, after all.

Which was frickin' unbelievable, for Ryan Ward, playboy of the SDFD. There'd never been a shortage of willing women around the firehouse. Ryan hadn't been the biggest sleaze in the place, but he'd definitely taken what was offered when he was in the mood. Not as often as his thank-God now-ex-roommate Jason, but enough.

He'd even had a few girls who came back for more, for a week or a month. Until he started to detect clinging. At which point he'd always shrugged them off, and gone after the next new thing. The old Ryan did sex. He didn't do relationships.

That meant he hadn't had the right to complain, when Marla, his current flavor of the month when he was injured, took one look at his hospitalized corpse and said no thank you. He hadn't wanted her around anyway. At first, he didn't want anyone to see the pain. Then the work of healing and rebuilding had taken all his strength. He hadn't had energy for anybody, not even family. And then there'd been the scars.

Ryan flushed, remembering, and drank deeply to cover it. The waitress was passing by, and he grabbed her arm to order a refill. She smiled perfunctorily, but the new glass arrived promptly. He tipped her well.

Turning the glass in his hands, he drank again, slowly. Once, when he'd nearly healed, he'd thought he might try dating. He'd wanted to be sure everything… worked. But the girl he'd hooked up with had been too lightweight for him to go through with it. Even Ryan had his limits, and… he closed his eyes. *Not remembering. Not thinking about that.* He'd been the one to get up out of the bed and leave, after all. He clung to that.

"Are you okay?" John asked.

"I'm fine." Ryan opened his eyes and looked around again. He was looking for someone a little older. Older but hot, of course. Someone who'd be up for a little recreational activity without making too much out of it. A woman intelligent enough not to be fixated on appearance, even in a hook-up. *You could add wealthy to that list, owns a Ferrari, wants to put you through med school. Not asking too much, right?*

He shook his head. *Shut up. I just want to get laid.* "So," he said to John, "who do you think is the hottest woman in here?"

John looked startled. Ryan realized that, for all the stuff they talked about, he and John seldom discussed sex. He wasn't sure why, they just didn't. But

John looked around willingly enough and then pointed discreetly. "Over there in the red dress."

"Her?" Ryan took a closer look. "Jesus, she's a kid half your age. They should card her twice."

"You said hottest, not the one I would go for," John pointed out mildly. "I still have eyes and she still has…um."

"Tits."

"Oh yeah."

"So who would you go for, if you were looking for a date?"

John took a longer look. "Maybe the blonde with the blue blouse. She looks cute but smart. Or did you mean just a pickup?"

Ryan winced, which annoyed him. This was obviously why he didn't talk about sex with John. Because it somehow came out too… significant. "Yeah, a hookup for the night."

"Hm. Hard to judge if a woman is the type." John frowned. "Over there, the three woman at the corner table. All fairly cute, the right age, a little drunk and egging each other on. One of them might go for it."

Ryan looked over. He hadn't had to chase a woman in forever. When you wore the uniform, unless you were a slug, they would come to you. Those girls were okay, he guessed. Two brunettes and an obvious bottle blonde. They were drinking mixed drinks and laughing a little too loudly. And eyeing the men at the bar.

"Good eye," he said. "You going to go for it?"

John colored. "Not my thing. I don't date much, and I like to get to know someone pretty well before I take them to bed."

Ryan tossed back the last of his beer and stood, leaving the cane under the table. "Then wish me luck."

John looked startled, but didn't comment.   •

Ryan walked toward the women, keeping his stride as even as he possibly could. The beer wasn't helping, but he disguised a lurch as an effort to dodge the waitress. The women were still smiling as he reached their table.

"I couldn't help but notice you ladies laughing," he said with his best charming smile. "Are we men really that amusing to you, or are you all just in a really good mood?"

They looked him up and down with frank appraisal, and then the blonde slid around and tapped one long lacquered nail on the single free chair. "Why don't you have a seat and find out?" she said. "I'm Rhonda."

"Ryan." He slid the chair out and sat carefully. He hadn't screwed this up yet. The women turned to him, and he started the delicate game of flirt and response.

Half an hour later, he had all three phone numbers, although one of the brunettes was dancing with a salesman from Duluth. The other two women were giving a good impression of being fascinated with the exploits of Ryan the fireman and soon to be MD. He had no illusions. Two A-list professions for dating were the thing keeping their attention. Ryan had bought them another round of drinks, although he'd stuck to beer. If the women were leaving soon, he hoped the bartender was planning to take their keys.

Rhonda, the blonde, was actually the smartest of the three. She was clearly the leader of the group. The little brunette periodically glanced at her for approval. Ryan and Rhonda had verbally danced around the idea of going "somewhere else" for a while now. They both knew what was potentially on offer.

Ryan glanced over at John's table. He'd been sitting alone, sipping his beer and listening to the acoustic guitarist play. But now, that blonde with the blue shirt had wandered his way. She stood chatting, one hand on what had been Ryan's chair. She was prettier than Ryan had realized from a distance. She wore silver-framed glasses, which she pushed up her small, straight nose with one finger. She said something to John, who laughed.

John had a great laugh. It was deep and resonant, and you just knew there was nothing fake about it. Not like the social laughter these women at Ryan's table seemed to let loose with, at the slightest hint of amusement. They were trying too freaking hard. Suddenly Ryan was tired of the whole game of maneuvering and pretending.

He stood abruptly. "Listen, ladies. It's been great meeting you. But I think I've had one more beer than is really good for me. I'd better catch up with my ride before he leaves without me. You all have a great evening, and maybe I'll see you around."

"You have my number," Rhonda reminded him, running a fingernail over the back of his hand. "You can always call me." She slid the tip of her tongue over her pouty lower lip.

Ryan watched that slick motion. She was pretty, and seemed sharp enough. A woman who knew what she liked. She was also built. He wasn't sure what he was doing walking away from all that. But somehow, an early night in his own bed with a bottle of lotion sounded more appealing than facing a real live woman across the sheets.

He heard John chuckle again. The sound seemed to pull him across the room. "Maybe I'll call when I'm sober."

His walk back to the other table wasn't as smooth as before. Twice he put a hand on a chair-back for support. When he glanced behind him, the two women were eyeing him speculatively. Wondering if he was a gimp, or just really drunk? But John looked up at him with clear, unchanging eyes. "Going? Staying? What?"

"I could use a ride home," Ryan told him. "Unless." He suddenly realized he might be the one interrupting. "If you were staying for a while, I can catch a cab."

"No, that's fine. I was just chatting with Mary here, while she waits for her husband to arrive."

Ryan blinked. *Married.* It was a relief. Neither of them was getting lucky tonight. It made things more fair, he thought. "Your husband is a lucky man," he said gallantly to the blonde.

She seemed startled, but said, "Thank you."

John fished under the table, and passed Ryan his cane, as he stood up. "Here. You might want this. Beer not being helpful for walking in a straight line."

Ryan took it, feeling a sudden wash of sentimentality. "You're a good friend, John. And I think I'm a little drunk."

John gave him an odd smile. "Just a little. Come on. We'll go home."

The cool air outside sobered Ryan. He took his cane more firmly in hand and trailed John toward the truck. "I could've picked up one of those women," he said truculently. "I just didn't want to."

"Right."

John opened the door of the truck and gave Ryan a boost up and in. Ryan's head spun dizzily. John's hand was warm and secure on his elbow. John tucked Ryan's feet safely inside the door frame, slammed the door, and walked around. Ryan waited for his friend's face to reappear. When John sat down beside him, Ryan sighed. "I'm so fucked up. I don't know what the hell I want."

"Don't worry about it." John's voice was deep velvet in the darkness of the cab. "You'll be asleep before you figure it out. And then in the morning, all you'll want will be some aspirin."

Ryan tipped his head back and shut his eyes. "Y'know, John, you're a pretty smart guy."

"Right." John's voice rumbled into the distance. "I'm damned brilliant."

Chapter Six

John decided that coming into LA in November was like turning back the clock. Everything was warm and sunny and green. Where it wasn't dry and burned brown. Last night in the hotel, he hadn't slept much, wondering what kind of reception he'd get from the kids and Cynthia. Time to find out.

The Carlisles lived in a very nice house, just like all their neighbors. In this part of town, having a swimming pool was apparently required, and a half-circle driveway was standard. John parked on the drive and climbed the white steps to the front door. He resisted the impulse to check his hair again before ringing the bell. The first notes of the Pachelbel canon echoed behind the closed door. *Typical.*

Then the door was pulled open and he was looking at Torey. She hesitated for a second, long enough to make his heart sink. Then she shouted, "Daddy!" and her arms locked around his waist.

"Hey there, squirt," he said, hugging her back. "Missed you. Are Mom and Mark in?"

"Mark's up in his room," she said. "I think Mom's out back with the pool guy."

Okay, do not picture that, rein in the overactive imagination. "Do you think I can come in?"

"Sure!" She swung the door wide. "Why are you here? How long can you stay?"

"A few days, and I'm here to see you. How about we go find Mom, and clear it with her, and then you can pack a bag for the weekend and we'll have some fun?" Okay, telling Torey before asking Cynthia for permission was dirty pool, but he was tired of Cynthia's games and he was going to see his kids.

"Mark too?" Torey asked.

"Of course Marcus too." He chucked her under the chin. "Don't make that face. He's your brother."

"Exactly." She grinned, and pointed. "Mom's in the back. You can go through there. I'm gonna go tell Mark." She sprinted for the stairs yelling, "Hey! Butt-face!"

John sighed. God, he'd missed them.

He followed the directed route, and ended up at open patio doors. Outside, Cynthia stood on the tiled deck beside the pool, next to a slim, tanned boy in a white T-shirt and black pants. Quite innocently, of course. She was saying something about leaves in the filter. John leaned in the doorway and waited for Cynthia to notice him.

She looked younger than the last time he'd seen her, over a year ago. More tanned, more fit, a little heavier, her blond hair cut in a shining cap. She moved with confidence, gesturing about something. California obviously suited her. *Or maybe it was marriage to someone else that suited her.* She eventually finished with the pool boy, dismissed him, turned back to the house, and froze.

"John."

"Hello, Cynthia."

"What are you doing here? Who let you in?" She looked around as if expecting an armed assault team.

John bit his lip. "I rang the bell. Torey let me in. She's grown another inch."

Cynthia sighed. "What do you want, John?"

"I want to see the kids. My kids."

"This isn't a good time. They have plans for later."

"Break them." John let a hint of his anger show through. "Cyn, I scraped together the funds for those two plane tickets, which you've been sitting on for months now. If you won't let the kids come to me, I figured I'd come to them."

A voice came from behind John. "Won't let us?" Mark's voice squeaked, his new baritone cracking into a light treble. "Mom?"

John turned quickly. *Shit.* He'd sworn never to badmouth Cynthia to the kids. "Hey, son," he said. "Just a problem with timing, I'm sure. But I have some flexibility right now. So I figured I'd take a long weekend and come out here." He turned back to Cynthia, baring his teeth in what should've been a smile. "I've got hotel reservations for a couple of nights. I'll take the kids; they can show me their new city. I'll have them back to you Monday night."

"Um." She looked over his shoulder. "I don't know if they'll want to miss the movie premiere. And the horseback riding on Sunday."

"There'll be other chances," Torey said stoutly from behind Mark. "I want to spend the time with Dad."

That's my girl.

"Marcus?" Cindy pressed. "You're going to play laser tag with the baseball team."

Mark shrugged one shoulder awkwardly. "It's no big. He flew all this way. It's almost Thanksgiving. I guess I don't mind hanging with Dad this weekend." John would have been more depressed by the lackluster tone of that, if he hadn't spotted the stuffed backpack sitting by the boy's feet. *He's already packed.* John held back a more honest grin.

"Then it's settled," he said. "Ten minutes to pack for a couple days, and we head out. The limo awaits."

"A real limo?" Torey asked, looking toward the front door.

They really have changed social groups. "No, baby, sorry. Just a kind of boring rental car. But it comes with a driver who's willing to go anywhere you tell him. So it's sort of like a limo."

Her "Daaad!" was long-suffering.

He smiled. "That's down to nine minutes for packing now, squirt."

"Nine minutes!" It came out as a pained shriek. "Dad, I can't pack my stuff that fast."

"Try."

She scurried up the stairs and he heard her footsteps hurrying overhead.

Mark glanced at him from under his bangs and gave the first hint of a smile. "Want to bet she can't do it in under a half hour?"

61

John stuck out a hand, and clasped his son's long fingers in his own. "You're on." God, he was going to enjoy this weekend.

****

When the airport shuttle dropped John off in front of his house three days later, there was just the faintest hint of pink in the early morning sky. He paused, bag at his feet, to stretch and look around. An overnight flight was not kind to someone his height, especially when it was packed full. He decided that when he headed to work, he'd make his first job a hike around campus. He could check some of the mulching he had the crew doing yesterday while he was gone. A hard walk would get out some of the kinks.

No one walked in LA, apparently. The kids had looked at him like he was crazy when he'd suggested it. Thank God for GPS in rental cars.

He'd let them choose what they wanted to do. It hadn't been perfect. After all, a girl of twelve and a boy of almost fifteen can hardly agree on what day of the week it is, let alone what to do with a free afternoon. But they'd managed. When Torey had begged for shopping, he'd managed to fit it in by dropping Mark off at his baseball team's end-of-season laser-tag party. That way, Mark didn't miss the time with his friends, and John got to sit around in a mall watching Torey try on clothes.

Torey. God, she was growing up before his eyes. Wearing a bra, for Christ's sake. Which apparently it was now okay to let show under your clothes, because when he down-checked a shirt for showing her straps, she'd rolled her eyes. He'd given up on the fashion commentary early. A mother, watching her daughter go in and out of the same changing rooms had offered some advice—*if it's really too tight or too low-cut, you either tell her it makes her look a little heavy or the color doesn't do good things for her. But use your veto wisely.*

The third time he'd come out with, "The color doesn't do good things for you," Torey had about died laughing. But they'd found a few pieces they both liked, without him having to put his foot down officially. And later, after the movie, he'd given Mark a bonus, letting him drive the rental car slowly around the dark vastness of the mall's remote parking lot.

It had been Ryan's suggestion, when he had begged for tips about where to take the kids in LA. Along with a list of attractions, he'd suggested driving for Mark. Apparently Ryan's older brother had let him take the wheel when he was twelve and got his first growth spurt. Ryan claimed the resulting hero worship had taken years to wear off.

He hadn't planned to follow through with it. Letting a kid drive without a permit was totally illegal, and a terrible precedent. But there'd been a core of sadness, something rigidly solitary about Mark. Like he was holding himself aloof from the world. In desperation to break through that barrier, he'd offered to turn over the wheel, there in the safe empty space. And it had worked on Mark too. The kid had sat up out of his slouch for the first time, and paid rapt attention.

They'd done some of the tourist stuff the next day, letting the kids show him their city. They got off on correcting his errors, so he'd pulled out a few wild guesses, speculating at random for them to set him straight. Truly, he hadn't known stuff like the origins of the HOLLYWOOD sign. By the end of the weekend, his credit cards were about ready to burst into flames, but the early distance between them had vanished. He got goodbye hugs from both kids when he dropped them back home. And Mark had said he liked his early birthday gift.

They were LA kids now. Clothes, vocabulary, activities. But they were still *his* kids. They both wanted to come back to York at Christmas. Cynthia had promised, and John would hold her to it this time. As fun as the weekend had been, he wanted to see them back here, running up those steps, leaving that yellow door open so he could yell at them.

He felt a warm glow as he picked up his bag and headed up the walk. He liked this house, he realized. Really liked it. He'd felt pressured by Cynthia when she made him buy a bigger place. He'd gone out and gotten the biggest one he could afford. But somehow it had grown on him over the past year.

It welcomed him home. The porch light was on by the door and a lamp shone deep inside, brightening the front window. Probably from the kitchen. He glanced at his watch. Yep, six thirty a.m. Ryan would be up, yawning, pouring his first cup of coffee.

Ryan was usually up before him, and moving around in the kitchen when John straggled in closer to seven. The coffee would be brewed in the old thermos. John would pour himself a cup, and give Ryan a hard time about doing it wrong. Just because. In fact it was hard to do drip coffee wrong.

Ryan would be at the table, eating a bagel and a banana. If he had a quiz, there might be a book propped up against the tissue box in front of him. If the subject was hard, there'd be a little crease between the guy's dark eyebrows as he concentrated. But he'd look up and smile when John came in.

He'd been surprised to find himself missing Ryan's company in LA. Every now and then, he'd wanted someone adult. Someone who would get his worst puns, or roll his eyes in sympathy when his kids gave him pure teenager disdain. And Ryan knew LA. He would've been a help when they got confused in the downtown streets. Maybe sometime Ryan would want to visit his brother, and they could combine trips.

John dumped his bag in the hall by the stairs, and headed for the kitchen, drawn by the scent of coffee. And there was Ryan, leaning against the counter waiting for the toaster. He was wearing loose PJ pants and an old T-shirt. His black hair was rumpled and damp from his shower. He looked perfectly at home. And when he saw John, his smile was sweet and warm.

"Hey, look what the cat dragged in."

John took one step forward and stopped. What was he going to do? Shake hands? Hug the guy? He'd been away for just three days, for Christ's sake. He converted the motion into a pass at the coffee thermos. Which was, after all, why he'd gone in there. Yeah, that was good. He sipped and rolled the dark liquid on his tongue. "Three days without the good stuff. I was going into withdrawal."

"Did you eat anything? I could toast you a bagel."

He shook his head. "I ate some kind of vending-machine crap at the airport. I don't think my stomach is ready for real food."

Ryan wrinkled his nose in sympathy. "Hate those red-eye flights. So, tell me about your weekend. Was it worth the trip?"

"Hell yeah." He peered at Ry. "Do you really want to hear about it?"

"Of course I do." Ryan juggled his hot bagel onto a plate and dug in the refrigerator for the butter. "I feel like I know your kids already. And after all, if they come to visit, I'll have to live with them."

"Oh. Yeah. Cynthia promised they'd come out here in December. She said it in front of them, so I hope this time she'll follow through. Which means you'll have to share a bathroom with two teenagers, unless you decide to use mine."

"No sweat." Ryan licked a smear of butter off his thumb and set down the knife. "I grew up sharing a bathroom with three brothers, I can handle just two."

John blinked. "Three brothers? I thought you had two brothers." At the look on Ryan's face, he quickly added, "None of my business. I just…"

Ryan was shaking his head slowly. "I had three. Andrew, who's in San Diego with his family. Brent, who's now in Boston. Then me. And David was the baby, a year younger than me. He died ten years ago."

"I'm sorry."

"I don't talk about him much."

"You don't have to…"

Ryan looked up at him. "No, you know. It's kind of fucked up that I don't talk about him. Like, he's dead, so it's like he never existed. I tell people I have two brothers. Like he's not important."

"Maybe he's too important," John suggested softly.

"Maybe I just don't want to have to explain." Ryan leaned back against the counter, green eyes gazing at nothing. He had that little crease between his eyebrows. His fingers pleated the dish towel hanging beside him into tight folds.

"You don't need to explain to me." John wanted to bring back that sunny smile Ryan had given him when he walked in. "You should eat your bagel before it gets cold."

Ryan didn't look at him. "David always wanted to be a firefighter. From when we were little, you know? I wanted to be a doctor, or maybe a paramedic, and he wanted to fight fires. When I went off to college, I went into pre-med. David skipped college and took the firefighters' service exam in New York. He passed, he did the training, and joined a crew."

Ten years ago in New York? "Oh God," John breathed. "9-11?"

Ryan gave him a twisted smile. "Nope. He would've been there. Lots of guys he knew were. But six months earlier, his fiancé got an offer to do a bit part in a sitcom in LA. He followed her out there, went to work for the LAFD. When 9-11 hit, that was the only scrap of good news in all the bad, that David wasn't there, inside those towers coming down." He blew out a breath. "The flags were still all at half-mast when we got the call."

65

Ryan turned to look out the picture window, at the dim expanse of lawn and trees. His fingers were white on the edge of the counter. "It was a stupid little house fire, some idiot smoking in bed. The house had a basement. I mean, this was LA. How many houses out in California have basements? But this one did, and the teenage daughter had her room down there. The fire started in the night. She was supposed to be home in bed. No one knew she'd sneaked out to be with her boyfriend."

"Ryan." John stepped closer, wanting to offer something.

"Davey and another guy went down after her. But of course they couldn't find her. The place was shit built. The floor caved in. David was under it."

Ryan was leaning on his arms, his back bent. John reached out a tentative hand and rubbed Ryan's back, just the barest touch.

"I was in college, starting senior year. I had these med-school application forms spread out on my desk, waiting to be filled out. But I felt like… I don't know… like other people were out there, working and dying to keep us safe, and I was looking at five more years hiding away in school. The LAFD didn't have any openings, but San Diego did. I ripped up those applications, dropped out and flew to the west coast for the funeral. And stayed there."

John rubbed a little harder, slow circles over muscle tight as iron, and just listened.

"I liked being a firefighter. It was hard; it was important. The guys in my crew were like brothers, like a new family. Because my real family was shot to hell. Mom died just three months earlier. Which was maybe a blessing in disguise, because David was her baby, her favorite. Losing him would have devastated her. But Dad was a wreck. Andrew's wife had had a miscarriage, and he was all wound up with her. Brent left the country, went to work in South America for a while. He said every 9-11 tribute made him think of David, who was just as dead and no one cared. He couldn't take it."

Ryan pulled in a long shaky sigh. "So I fought fires. And I was good at it. But something was always missing, and when… when I couldn't do that anymore, I thought I'd give being a doctor one more shot. I'd finished the biology degree on the side, just to be done with it. I had the grades. But I was still lucky to get in anywhere. So now I'm a student again. And I never talk about David. Because it fucking hurts. Still. After ten years." Ryan's voice was getting rougher. "You're older than me, John. Explain that to me. They say everything gets better with time. So why does it still hurt so bad to talk about him?"

"I'm not sure," John said slowly. "I think, maybe, it's partly because it *does* get better. You go along just fine, and you never think of them. You're happy, life's okay, and then when you do get reminded, it's worse. Because you feel like you betrayed them. Like, how could you forget, how could you be okay, when they're gone?"

Ryan froze under his hand, and then turned. Their eyes met. "Who did you lose, that makes you feel like that?"

John could have passed it off. A lot of people had died in his life. But only one who mattered that much. "My son," he said quietly. "I lost my son."

"But..."

"My first boy. Cynthia was pregnant when we got married. We were a little drunk on prom night, maybe a lot drunk. It was my first time. I think it was hers too. We screwed up. But it was okay because I was in love with her. And my dad still had money then, to help us out. Then the baby came early. He was over four pounds, he had a chance. But he got a couple of infections and..." John's throat closed. "He lived three weeks in the NICU. He never made it to his due date. The only time I got to hold him out of the incubator was after..." He tried again. "It's not like your brother. I don't even know what color his hair would have been but..."

"Shh." Somehow Ryan's hands were on John's arms now. "He was your son and you loved him and he died. We don't need to compare. Did you name him?"

"Daniel." John took a deep breath. He could do this. "He would be eighteen this year. And sometimes, when I look at Mark, when I hear that fucking Elton John song, it still hurts."

And there they were, staring at each other. Ryan's green eyes were bright, the dark lashes clumped from unshed tears. They were both breathing hard.

Ryan gave a short laugh. "God, we're pathetic. What do we do now to work off all that? What are the traditional remedies? Cry, run, fight, fuck?"

"I don't want to fight you," John said. His vision had tunneled in to those shining eyes. Like nothing else in the world existed. Ryan was simply looking back at him, not moving. Slowly, John leaned forward and kissed him.

It was meant to be just a touch of lips on lips. Hell, it wasn't *meant to be* at all. He didn't think. But his mouth found Ryan's, and it was like fire rushing through him. They swayed together, arms around each other, lips and tongues and warm, living breath. And then Ryan broke free and was across the room.

They stared at each other. Ryan's chest heaved as if he couldn't catch his breath. John couldn't keep his eyes from tracking downward and yes, Ryan's body had been just as interested as his own in what they'd just done. Both of which scared the shit out of him.

"What the fuck was that?" Ryan demanded.

"I'm sorry. God, I'm sorry. I didn't mean to do that. I don't even know why it happened. I swear, I'm not gay. I've never…"

"Me either." Ryan sat heavily in his chair.

"I didn't mean anything by it." God, he needed to fix this somehow. He was suddenly terrified that Ryan would leave. They'd been so good, so close, and he'd screwed it up. "I won't touch you again. I promise. I'm so sorry. That was wrong."

Ryan shook his head. "John. Stop." He rubbed his forehead. "I can't think about this right now. But it wasn't all your fault. Maybe I've been… too close. I don't know." He looked up. "For a moment there, when you… I liked it."

John took all his courage in hand, and said two words. "Me too."

Ryan stood abruptly. "I need a shower. I have to get to class. I can't… Later. We need to talk later."

"You're not… leaving?" John asked. He had to know. "Can I still give you a ride to campus?"

Ryan gave him a smile that was the ghost of his usual grin. "Door-to-door limo service, or two crowded city buses. Let me think. Yeah, I still want a ride." He looked a little uncertain. "A silent ride?"

"I can do that," John promised.

It was only after Ryan walked out, and the water came on, that he remembered the wet hair. Ryan had already had his shower this morning. John pressed his fingertips to his skull, to not think about Ryan up there under the water. To somehow exorcise the confusing stranger who had taken up residence in his head.

****

Ryan never got much out of embryology lectures, even on a good day. For one thing, the class was right after lunch. The professor turned off the house lights and showed an interminable series of slides. Each differed from the one before it by a tiny amount. The man's voice droned on.

For another, he just couldn't get into the subject. Sure, knowing how a baby developed might help explain certain birth defects. But locating the exact formation of the branchial arches in an embryonic chicken? Not so much. His classmates obviously shared his opinion, since sometimes the only thing keeping him awake was how loud the guy in the next seat over was snoring.

Usually he could lean back, get enough to soak in to pass the class, and let his mind drift. But today his mind was like a fucking arrow. Every time he let loose of it, it aimed straight back at that morning, and John.

What the hell happened?

He was going to have to sit down with John later and say... something. So maybe he should figure out what. Because he really didn't want to move out. He liked John, liked living in the house. It was almost like being back in the fire station. You had someone around to talk to, share a meal with, but you didn't have to cater to them if you weren't in the mood. No one got huffy if you spent the meal with your nose in a book. But they were there to share the funny parts with, to share the chores with, to appreciate it if you made the coffee or took out the trash.

Actually it was better than the fire station. That place was usually high on testosterone and adrenaline, and low on social graces. When you were working, the guys were closer than brothers. When you weren't, well, they were still like brothers. Brothers who might prank you by putting your cell number on an Internet dating service, or borrow your last clean shirt. You could never quite let down your guard.

John wasn't like that. Ryan felt like an equal, just two grown-ups living in a house together. Even though John was bigger, and older, and owned the place, he never gave orders or threw his weight around. If something needed to be done, he'd ask Ryan if he'd mind catching it. Or more likely do it himself. John really did more than his share.

And he was quiet, restful to be around. Considering the amount of coffee and Mountain Dew the guy put away, he should have been a raging maniac. But somehow despite all the caffeine in his bloodstream, John managed to be solid and dependable. Paradoxical drug reaction, maybe? It was like you could lean on him and never fall. *And wasn't that just the thing that got you babbling about David, which got you into this mess.*

So Ryan needed to figure out what to say, to get them back on solid footing. Because he sure wasn't gay, and he didn't think John was either. Every time they were out, if one of them noticed a hot body, it had been a girl. A woman— John didn't seriously look at anyone under thirty. But he *had* looked at some of the older ones. And he could've had any of them. The guy might not be a twenty-something underwear model, but he had the kind of face that would keep getting more handsome as he got older. Those light smile lines just accented his craggy features. He'd be drawing women like flies when he was sixty. John was in great shape too. All those muscles, everything a woman would go for.

So why would he be interested in me?

He wondered if he somehow gave off some kind of gay vibe. He didn't think so. Sure, men had come on to him a few times when he was younger. But not in a serious way. That happened to all men if they weren't ugly, right? And he'd never thought twice about another guy, when there were pretty girls around.

He'd had his pick of the firehouse groupies, the women who hung out and drank with them, in the hopes of picking up a man in uniform. He'd learned early to tell the difference between the ones just looking for hot sex or another badge to hang on their wall, and the ones who wanted to become Mrs. Firefighter. The latter he left strictly alone. The former, well, if both people understood it was only sex from the start, where was the harm in scratching an itch?

He liked sex. With women. He didn't obsess over it, like some of the guys, but he liked it fine. And the women seemed to have no complaints. He'd refined his skills over the years, from the shy, solitary nerd he'd been in high school, jerking off to faceless images of tits and butts. He paid attention to what his partner wanted. He didn't think he'd ever left a woman unsatisfied.

Although really, how could you be sure? A woman could fake it. A little shaking and moaning and who would ever know? Now a man was different. If you were having sex with a man, using your mouth on him or whatever, there'd be no hiding whether he really liked it enough to come. It would all be right there. *Shit!*

Ryan bit his tongue, hard. John had him all messed up. He was so not thinking about that. *Conversation. You were plotting your conversation.*

Right. So he would sit down with the man and he'd say, *John.* And then he'd say…um. Yeah, he probably *would* sit there with his mouth open saying um, if he didn't figure this out. Start again.

He'd say, *John, I really like you as a friend.* Because he did. Already more than any other guy he'd hung with since Corey moved away in fifth grade. *John, I'm sorry if I gave you the wrong impression. I like living with you.* No. *I like living in your house, and I hope we can go back to how things were. I want to stay friends. I'm just not interested in anything else, okay?*

No, drop the okay. Because he had to be firm, cut this off, wherever it was coming from. *We got kind of emotional, and it's no one's fault, and I want to stay friends.* There, that would do it. And then John would agree that yeah, they got carried away with some weird vibe and let's order pizza, and they'd be good. Ryan hoped.

Embryology droned on. His classmate snored. Ryan's brain ran round in circles, imagining scenarios, wondering what John would do, would say. Sometimes in his imagination, John tried to kiss him again. Ryan shied violently away from the picture that made, back to the beginning again. *Go in the door, say, John, I'm really glad we're friends but…*

By the time he walked in the actual front door, he'd reworked his speech a dozen times. Two dozen. He wanted to do this right. He didn't want to hurt John's feelings or make him feel bad. But he had to put on the brakes, unmistakably.

John was in the kitchen, playing with a plate of microwave prepackaged glop. He looked up as Ryan came in. "Hi."

"Hey, John." Ryan slid into the other seat and stretched his aching leg out. *Just say it.*

Before he could get the first word out, John said, "I wanted to talk to you about this morning. Because it was weird. I don't know what happened. I mean, I'm not gay, and you're not either. I guess we just… When you talk about tough stuff like that, you want someone to hold on to, to make it feel better. And there we were, and no one else was available. So… that happened. And it was my fault. But I want to go back to being friends, okay?"

Ryan blinked. *He cribbed my speech.* "Yeah. I mean, I want that too."

71

"I really hope I didn't make you think about moving out. I hate living alone. I mean, if the alternative is living with you. I like having you living here and I'd hate to see you leave. I won't do anything like that again. I hope I didn't freak you out too much."

"No," Ryan said slowly. "I don't want to leave."

"Good," John said firmly. "I mean, are we good now?"

"Sure. We're fine."

John stood up abruptly, dumped his plate into the sink, and then stuck it in the dishwasher. "Great. I have some work to do, so I'm going to go and... work."

Ryan was left staring at his retreating back. He wasn't sure why he felt slightly let down. Clearly they were on the same page. Things were back to normal. So why was he disappointed that his wonderful speech letting John down gently hadn't had to be uttered?

Chapter Seven

Ryan found himself looking at everyone on campus differently. Two guys would come into class together, hair ruffled by the wind, and he would wonder if there was anything there except friendship. He found himself looking at the women, trailing his gaze over butts and boobs, checking his level of interest like some weird sex-o-meter. Feeling relieved every time a woman's body caused his hormones to rise. And yet, it was all hypothetical, like *yeah, big tits still turn me on.* He had no interest in taking it beyond a glance. He didn't want to flirt with those women. He certainly didn't want to get mixed up with dating one.

Dating was a hassle anyway, the small talk, the adaptations you had to make to fit someone else into your routines. Women expected conversation, and flowers and proper attention. You couldn't grunt at them that you were busy and expect to get by without a hurt look and a pout. They were soft and they smelled good, but they were work.

He found himself looking at men too. He'd never done that before, that he could remember. He'd never bothered to check out whether a guy had big arms or a tight butt. He was only doing it now to confirm that he really had no interest in such things. And he didn't. His body didn't react to any of the cute young guys around him. So he wasn't gay.

But he still kept catching himself looking, thinking that this one wasn't as muscled up as John, or that one didn't move with the same grace. It was like probing the space where a tooth had been pulled. He knew it wasn't there, but he kept testing his reactions, kept pulling up images of John next to these guys. And remembering that kiss.

Talk about zero to sixty in two seconds flat. He'd always liked kissing. He'd never been one to fuck a woman's body like the rest of her didn't exist. But he'd also never had a first kiss happen like that. Like someone poured liquid heat between his lips and took over his breath and his heart and his groin, until all he could think about was getting more.

John had obviously put all that behind him. Ryan had started out being really careful. He'd avoided being around John for anything too comfortable, too emotional. At the same time, he'd tried to act like nothing had changed.

Thanksgiving dinner had been weird. By some unspoken mutual consent they'd bought all the fixings, chicken and stuffing and pie, and shared it at the small polished table. But no cooking together, no wine, nothing that put them side by side in the kitchen. The meal had been pretty silent.

John seemed a little depressed. He'd made one or two comments, but drifted off staring into space again and again. Ryan figured he had to be thinking about how different this was from family holidays in the past. He'd have had his wife and kids, maybe other relatives, his father, or in-laws. Old traditions, old arguments, who knew? Something more than this.

Ryan had dug around on the remains of the chicken for a few last morsels, and then worked the wishbone free. He sucked it clean and forced a laugh. "At least you only had two kids. Four of us at home and one wishbone made for epic arguments. One year Mom made two turkeys, just so there would be two wishbones. We ate leftover turkey for a month."

John seemed to come back from wherever his thoughts had been. He gave a crooked smile and then reached out to take one end of the wishbone. Ryan shifted his grip to the other end. For a second they eyed each other. John's hazel eyes were shaded to dull gray, giving nothing away. He glanced down for a second, and then wrenched on the small bone. It snapped cleanly, with the bigger half in Ryan's hand.

John's smile became warmer. "Yours. Don't tell me what you wished for or it won't come true."

Ryan looked blankly at the stub of bone in his hand. He'd forgotten to make a wish. Did it still count if he made it now? He could wish for things to go back the way they were. He could ask for this new uncomfortable awareness of John to disappear. Hell, he could wish for his leg to be healed while he was at it, if he wanted to pretend it was *that* magic. *I wish I knew what I wanted.*

Two weeks later and he still didn't know. He missed the easy way they had been together before... *before he kissed me.* Except that was unfair, because even if John had made the first move, Ryan could still feel the slip of the man's silky hair in his fingers, the press of his hard body. And the way Ryan's own had responded. The way he'd kissed John back.

He thought that if someone offered to turn back the clock and give him a do-over, he would probably take it. Except... except he'd never felt as alive as he had the past two weeks. Sounds were louder, lights were brighter. It wasn't just the girls, and the guys, that he was noticing more.

He saw the lace of frost on a window in the morning, fascinated by the way the curls of ice spread in fractal patterns across the glass. He heard the drum of a woodpecker on the dead tree down the street, in syncopated time. Coffee…God, coffee tasted like heaven.

It was like someone turned the amplifier on his life up a notch. The smell of a bakery as they passed filled his mind with donuts. The smell of formaldehyde was sharp in his nose. He could identify his lab partner at ten feet by her floral perfume, and a couple other people in the class even farther from the hit of their heavy chosen scents, as they walked past with perfume or cologne set on stun. He could smell John's shampoo and clean skin down the hallway in the evening, after he'd showered.

Ryan shook his head hard, and stepped out the door of Bradford Hall, into the clean, cold outdoors. The air promised snow. A hint of smoke hovered, like a touch of autumn past. He had been here just three months. And somehow, he was a different man from the one who sat in that welcome-to-med-school lecture, so short a time ago.

****

Late December meant that there was less outdoor work on campus, at least until the snow came. John's crew was down to the two permanent members. The campus plantings had been put to bed, even the hardiest annuals dug up and the beds mulched, now that a hard freeze had come and gone. They were erecting snow fences where the wind might cause drifting. Wrapping the tenderer bushes, and planning for next spring.

Which left time for a bit of exploring. John lengthened his stride down the next hill. He was pleased that he was breathing easily, despite the steep climb up the back of the ridge. He was getting into amazing shape these days. *Yeah, running away from your problems will do that.* Although mostly he was just trying to wear his problems out.

He and Ryan had fallen back into their familiar routines. Ryan still got up first and started the coffee. John still gave him a lift to campus most mornings. They still shared meals sometimes. They'd even managed a kind of Thanksgiving dinner with a roast chicken from the supermarket. For a few days, Ryan had retreated to the privacy of the parlor to study in the evenings. But now, without comment, he'd returned to spreading his books out on the kitchen table. John made a point of wandering through at the end of the evening, and grabbing a drink or a snack. Ryan would give him a nod or a smile. He'd give Ryan a hard time about whatever wimpy caffeine-free beverage the guy was drinking after ten p.m.

It was just like it had been. Except it wasn't. There was that edge of tension that never went away.

In the past, he might have bumped up against Ryan if both of them headed for the fridge at the same time. Or he would have put a hand under Ry's elbow, if some move shifted Ryan's weight awkwardly onto his bad leg. Because the stubborn bastard refused to use his cane around the house. Now, though, there was a careful few inches of space between them at all times. Yet he was always aware of exactly where Ryan was. And of wanting him.

He'd thought about that kiss. Hell, he'd obsessed about it. All that first Tuesday before Thanksgiving, walking around campus, Ryan had been the only thing on his mind. And he'd decided not to lie to himself. It was no freak impulse, no one-time emotional overload, that had put his mouth on Ryan's. It had been a long time coming, as inevitable as the onset of winter.

Gay or not, he realized he'd been aware of Ryan from the very first moment. He could remember everything from that day— the color of Ryan's eyes when they blinked open, as he lay on the steps in pained confusion; the softness of his hair as John's fingertips cleaned his cut scalp; the muscles of his arm; the bump of hip against hip. And every day since then, in growing intensity, he'd turned to Ryan like steel to a magnet.

By the end of that Tuesday, he'd worked himself up to a panic, wondering how he could persuade Ryan not to run away. He'd figured out his preemptive strike. Before Ryan could open his mouth to say, *maybe I should find another place to live,* John had taken it all back. He'd played the friendship card. The *I don't know what happened but it will never happen again* card.

And it worked. Ryan was still there, in his house, in his life. All it took was pretending that he didn't care.

He'd tried to make it true. He'd gone out a few evenings, and deliberately chatted up women. He'd immersed himself in soft flowing hair, and rounded curves and sweet perfume. And never taken it further than that, because it was empty. One thought of Ryan, and he came to attention, and the woman in his sights faded. And while he was willing to bend himself into pretzels lying to Ryan, he wasn't fooling himself. So he stopped fighting it.

He admitted that all he wanted was Ryan. But he also decided half a loaf was better than none. To be comfortable again, Ryan needed John to back off, to be cool, to be a friend.

He could do it. He could ignore the way Ryan's hair smelled when it was wet, the way his eyes lit up at a bad joke, the way he licked the excess butter off his fingers after preparing his morning bagel. Well, okay, maybe not ignore that. But he could wear loose shirts over his jeans and try not to watch. He could get himself so tired out that by evening he basically just wanted to crash. Because he wanted Ryan around as a friend most of all.

If there was ever going to be anything more, it would have to be Ryan doing the asking. Ry would have to make the first move. Probably it would never happen. Ryan seemed pretty certain of his heterosexuality. But every now and then, John thought there was a spark between them that wasn't just in his mind. He'd catch Ryan's eyes on him, lingering without reason. And so he hoped.

Wearing himself out with physical work had the side benefit of getting to know the campus better than he'd managed in the past two years. The property was big. There were parts of it he'd never visited. Most of it was left wild, but he was making plans for more hiking trails and paths.

He'd found an amazing field of wild raspberry bushes, the scant remaining fruit dried on the branch now, but worth a visit next summer. There was a stream that ran down the other side of this ridge in a series of steps, pretty pools with waterfalls between them. There were wild roses growing south of campus. And…

He paused, staring more closely. In a hollow near the bottom of the slope, there was a big cluster of dead bushes. True, it was December. Most deciduous plants looked pretty dead anyway. But hell, he was a trained professional, and those bushes did not look natural.

Grabbing at the close-growing poplars for support, he slid down the steep incline. By the time he reached the bottom, he could see the cut ends of the small trunks. Someone had brought a dozen scrubby bushes and dumped them here. Which made no sense. He moved closer.

Whoever it was seemed to have tried to uproot them first. The ground had been dug out underneath. But then they'd just cut and piled the brush. In the loose dirt he could see raccoon tracks. But no coon could do that kind of damage. Beavers, sure, but the marks of their teeth were nothing like those straight cuts.

77

The raccoons had been digging, though. He bent and looked closer. They had brought some food, the remains of a small animal, to eat here and... *No.*

He turned away, gagging. Then he forced himself to look again. Those fine, gnawed bones weren't the leg of a mouse. At one tip, there was a flat oval nail, with just a hint of polish. Emerging from the dirt were the tips of other fingers, flesh still clinging to them. And through the dirt beside them, the glint of a woman's ring.

Okay. Stop and breathe.

There was no hurry. That burial hadn't happened in the past hour. Or even in the past day. Despite the creeping feeling at the back of his neck, no one would be out there watching him. *Oh hell.* He spun around, staring through the underbrush. He was alone. He knew he was alone.

He fumbled out his cell phone. One bar was good enough. He pulled in a long breath to steady his voice, and dialed 911.

It seemed to take forever before he heard voices approaching through the trees. *Thank God for GPS.* He wasn't sure he could've found this spot again without a lot of searching. Coming toward him through the underbrush were two town cops in uniform, and Benson from campus security. John walked a few steps to meet them.

"She's under there," he said, pointing. "I tried not to mess up the ground, once I realized..." He swallowed. "She was buried, but not very deep. It's her hand sticking out."

"You're sure there's a body?" Benson stepped around him. "Not just some kind of animal bones or twigs?" He headed for the mound of dirt.

"I'm sure." John turned to the female cop who'd stopped a little ahead of her colleague. "There's fingers with nail polish."

"Okay." She looked past him and yelled, "Hey you, Benson, don't mess up my crime scene."

Benson had knelt down to look more closely. Suddenly he turned aside and vomited.

"Oh hell," muttered the woman. "There goes the forensics." She turned to the other cop. "Mike, call it in, request backup, the coroner, everything. At least we don't have to worry about crowd control out here." She looked back at John and narrowed her eyes. "So. Two hundred acres of wild land, and you just happened to stumble over her?"

"Not exactly. I mean, yes, basically that's what happened."

"I think," she said, "that you'd better start at the beginning."

****

Last anatomy lab before finals, and half a dozen students were still finishing up. Ryan was among them, working late because yes, once again, Kaitlyn had managed to dissect at half speed and yet totally miss the path of the blood vessels they were after.

At the next table, Anita was staying late because… well he wasn't sure. It might just be his ego saying that she was hanging around waiting for him. He hoped he was wrong. He wasn't sure what she saw in him. She was wicked smart, and very pretty. There were plenty of better-looking younger guys in the class eager to put a move on her. And yet she seemed fixated on him. This time, she brought over her anatomy-lab text and asked to look at his dissection.

Since he was pretty proud of the way he'd isolated the main artery and its branches, he let her look. Then he stepped back as she accidentally-on-purpose brushed her ass against him, bending over. Not that it wasn't a world-class ass, but he just wasn't interested.

They were all stressed and short of sleep, and once upon a time he might've considered sex a good antidote, too. God knows, he'd used fast sex to decompress after a shift, plenty of times. But not now. She was too young for him. Too demanding. Too something.

As he casually circled to the other side of their cadaver, on the pretext of getting a better view, their classmate Ron wandered over to join them. He gave Anita a wolfish smile. "Hey, pretty lady, want a strong guy to walk you home after you're done with lab?"

She gave him a scornful look. "Which strong guy? Do you see a strong guy? Anyway, I think I can cover five hundred yards to the dorm by myself, thank you."

"Don't be too sure," Ron said. "You might get murdered, like that girl they found today."

That got everyone's attention. "What girl?" Anita asked suspiciously.

Ron preened, enjoying the attention. "Well, I heard that the cops found the body of a dead girl out in the woods on campus."

"Who says she was murdered, though?" Anita demanded with a flick of her hair.

"Trevor told me about it. He said she was buried in a shallow grave. They arrested some guy, too."

"The killer?" Sharon asked.

"I don't know. That landscaper guy who does the flowers and shit."

"They *arrested* the groundskeeper?" Ryan demanded.

He didn't realize how loud he'd said it until Ron took a quick step backward. "It's just what I heard. God, chill. I mean he's just the gardener."

"John Barrett?"

Ron shrugged. "I didn't hear the guy's name. The gardener. But I don't know if they think he did it or what. Trevor said he saw him in a cop car." He turned his attention back to Anita. "If he's not the right guy, then there's still a killer out there, prowling the campus. You should let me walk you home."

"In your dreams." Anita turned to Ryan. "Maybe I should have *someone* walk me home, though, just in case."

He didn't have time for this. "Call a campus escort if you don't want to take Ron up on his offer." Her mouth twisted angrily at the dismissive brush-off but he couldn't bring himself to care. "I'm outta here."

It had to be some kind of mistake. After all, there were several guys in the grounds crew. Surely it was one of them who'd been arrested.

Ryan pulled on his jacket, grabbed his cane out of the corner, and headed for the bus. As soon as he was out of the building he speed-dialed John. The phone went straight to voice mail.

Which means nothing. He opened his jacket to put away the phone and caught a whiff of himself. *Ugh. Eau de anatomy lab.* He'd go home for a shower, he decided. John would probably be there. Certainly by the time he got out of the shower. And if he wasn't, well, time enough to figure something out then.

Two hours later he stood staring at the front entrance to the central York police station. This was dumb, taking the bus all the way down here, on the off chance John was actually here. On the chance he needed Ryan's help. But maybe, if it was a matter of an alibi… They'd spent all last night in the house. He could vouch for John's movements until almost midnight. And again after six thirty this morning. It might help.

He'd make it clear that he couldn't vouch for midnight to six, though. So no one would get the wrong impression. But he could tell them John would never hurt anyone. He just wasn't like that. Ryan knew the guy well. As a friend.

He was still standing on the steps when the door opened. A pair of women came out. Behind them, tugging on his jacket, was John.

Ryan stepped forward, smiling in relief. "Hey, guy."

John stared at him. "What are you doing here?"

"Looking for you?" Ryan said, stung. "Thinking that maybe you needed an alibi or a character witness or something. Rumor on campus was that you were arrested for murder."

John laughed humorlessly. "Great. Just what I needed." He turned toward the parking lot.

"I take it you weren't." Ryan fell in alongside.

"No. I found the body, out in the woods. They asked me to come in here to give my statement, because it was cold out there and they wanted to secure the scene."

"So you're not a suspect."

John snorted and opened his truck. "I wouldn't go that far. I don't think they have a lot of leads yet. I somehow stumbled over her body in two hundred acres of forest. That has to look suspicious." He swung himself up into the seat. "On the other hand, she'd clearly been buried out there to keep her from being found. So it doesn't make much sense that I would do that, and then turn around and lead them to her."

Ryan looked up at him. "They just don't know you, or they wouldn't even consider it. They'll find someone else soon."

John stared out the windshield. After a moment he said, "I assume you need a ride home. Get in already."

Ryan circled the truck and hauled himself inside. He pulled his door shut and clicked the seat belt. "Did you know her?" he asked gently.

"I don't know. I didn't see who… it was just her hand sticking out when I found her. I don't know who it is… was. And can we not talk about this?"

"Sure."

After driving for several minutes in silence, John said more quietly, "Not that I'm not grateful to you for coming down. I mean, if I *had* been arrested, I'd have been glad of the support."

Ryan relaxed in his seat. "Hey, I figured I'd tell them that a man who makes coffee like you do can't possibly be a killer."

"Yeah, that would settle it."

They didn't talk on the rest of the drive home. Because if he wasn't supposed to talk about *that,* then Ryan's mind was blank. Small talk seemed disrespectful, somehow, and their personal shit was *not* the right topic. John's tense grip on the wheel wasn't encouraging.

Ryan had left the porch light on when he headed out, and it glowed warmly as they pulled up. "So," John said, clearly reaching for their normal routine. "Exams next week. I assume you'll be hip-deep in the books for a while."

"Something like that. Maybe neck deep." Ryan slid out. "We should still think about getting a Christmas tree this weekend, for when the kids get here. They're not coming until after the holiday, so you won't have a chance to do tree shopping with them. We can set it up, get it decorated, before I leave. Make the house festive."

"Yeah, sure. That'd be good." From John's tone, Ryan figured he might have proposed a wild newt round-up and gotten the same response.

They went in, kicked off their shoes, and hung jackets. John whirled and made a beeline for the kitchen. He was moving so fast, he didn't turn back to pick up his jacket when it slipped to the floor. Which was totally unlike the man. Ryan paused, put John's parka back on its hanger, and then followed him more slowly.

John stood washing his hands at the kitchen sink. The water was running hot. Ryan could see the steam rising. He paused to turn up the thermostat on the wall and then went to lean on the counter beside John.

John soaped his hands, his motions fast and choppy. Then again, with more soap, and a third time, reaching for the nail brush. He brushed his fingertips, and under his nails. When he began scrubbing at his knuckles with the stiff bristles, Ryan reached over and took the brush out of his hands.

"I need to get clean," John said roughly.

Ryan took one big, wet hand in both of his and turned it over, inspecting the short nails and callused palm. "Looks clean to me."

"I didn't touch her. I don't think I touched her."

"Either way," Ryan said, "you're clean now." He let go. The feel of John's hot skin seemed to linger in his hands. He turned to the fridge. "Can I get you something? A soda, coffee? We could go out for a beer." They still didn't keep beer in the house, even though John drank in moderation outside it. Surely if any occasion called for a drink this was it.

"I don't want to go anywhere."

"Okay." Ryan went back and stood in front of him. "Do you want to talk about it?"

"No." John's eyes were dark, the hazel faded to gray. "Don't want to talk about it, think about it." He looked up at the ceiling, brows knitted angrily. "Who would do a thing like that?"

"The cops will find out." Ryan reached out and put a hand on John's arm, suddenly aware that he hadn't touched the man in... what, a month? Not since... *and maybe there was a good reason for that.* John's eyes met his suddenly, gold heat rising in them. Then John looked down. But he didn't step away.

Suddenly it was hard to breathe. Ryan was only aware of having swayed toward John when a big palm landed on his chest, hot and hard, keeping them apart.

"Don't," John said.

Ryan whispered. "Don't what?" This was crazy. This was so wrong. And yet, for the last month he had woken more times than he could count with the imagined taste of John's mouth on his own, and his body humming in remembrance.

He'd sworn it wasn't happening again. He'd even borrowed the truck and gone on a date with Rhonda. Who turned out to be as bored with him as he was with her, and just as glad to be dropped off at her front door with the briefest of kisses. John wasn't boring. And despite that let's-be-friends speech, Ryan had felt John's interest, banked but not gone, all this time.

"Don't start anything," John said, his voice just as soft. "Don't do anything because you're sorry for me, or want to play on the queer side for a minute."

"I'm not playing," Ryan said recklessly. "And sorry is the last thing I feel for you."

"Then what?" John's arm was like iron between them.

"I don't know," Ryan admitted. "I don't know what I'm doing. All I know is… I've been thinking about you. All the time. I'll be doing something else and there you are in my head. I know what you sound like, what you smell like. You walk in the front door and I come on alert like a bird dog pointing a pheasant. And maybe I'm just tired of fighting that."

"It'll change things." But John's hand was sliding downward, letting them move closer. "We're friends now, best friend I ever had. I don't want to mess that up."

This was so backward. When Ryan had thought about this, which he had done too many fucking times, he'd imagined being seduced. He'd figured John would decide enough was enough and make some move. And then he… just wouldn't fight it.

But instead, it was him moving in, sliding his hands up John's arms. It was his eyes that sought and held those golden-hazel ones, looking for some kind of sign. It was his mouth that leaned forward, upward, seeking John's wide, mobile lips.

And then there was just heat. Different from what he remembered from that first kiss. Better, because there was less surprise, less holding back.

Kissing a man wasn't the same as kissing a woman, but it wasn't that different either. He tilted his head, changed the angle to make it hotter, deeper. And now finally, *finally,* John's arms came around him and he was held in an unbreakable grip. He drove his tongue into John's mouth, tasting, demanding, and John opened sweetly for him. And God, he needed to breathe, but he didn't want to stop.

He eased back and looked up. John's eyes were bright. He was breathing hard too, his lips a little reddened from Ryan's mouth. *So kissable.* Ryan brushed his fingers up the arch of John's neck, cupped the back of his head, and pulled him down again. And for a long time, there was nothing else but the taste of John.

"Holy shit," John whispered, minutes later. "When you decide to go for something, you don't hold back."

Ryan leaned away, enjoying the secure arms around him. "You get all the benefit of my years of experience."

"With girls."

"Well, yeah."

"So now what?" John's eyes were quizzical, but his hips pressed into Ryan's, his interest made pretty blatant. Except Ryan was more shaken than he'd thought, because he wasn't sure what he wanted now.

He dropped his hands to the small of John's back, holding them close together, but barely managed a laugh. "I don't know. I want more but... I don't have a plan here."

"We can go very slow," John offered.

"Oh really?" Ryan ground himself against John, feeling the hardness of their erections rubbing against each other. His body wasn't saying slow.

John's laugh was a groan. "Didn't say it would be easy."

Ryan opened his mouth to say *what the hell, how about less clothes, more bed*, but he was cut off by the ring of John's cell phone in his pocket.

"Don't worry," John said. "That's no particular ring tone. Let it go."

Still they froze as the phone pinged a voice mail.

John leaned forward and brushed his lips lightly over Ryan's. "So, where were we?"

The phone rang again, a different tone. "Damn," John muttered. "That's Marcus." He pulled out the phone and flipped it open, stepping well away from Ryan as he did so.

Ryan tried not to feel abandoned. Obviously, it would be odd to talk to your son while holding your male... *what? Lover?* He swallowed, listening with half an ear to John's conversation.

That became both ears, when John snapped, "You're *where?*" in tones of disbelief. "No. No, I didn't... She didn't call... Yes, I'm sure. No that's okay. Of course I'll be there. As soon as I can. Yeah, see you soon." He flipped the phone shut.

"What?" Ryan asked, his stomach dropping.

"The kids are at the airport."

"They're *where?*"

"That's what I said. It seems Cynthia had a change of plans, and decided to send them for the week before Christmas, instead of the week after."

"Without asking you? Without *telling you?*"

"Mark said she sent me an e-mail."

"Which you didn't see because you haven't been on the computer in two days," Ryan realized. "Christ, doesn't she know you well enough to know that's not a good choice? She should have called."

John sighed. "The me she knew in my corporate days checked my e-mail multiple times a day. I would never have missed seeing it. I guess she thought… I don't know what she thought. Maybe because this way I couldn't ream her out or tell her no?"

"You have to go get them, now."

"Yeah." John's face looked stricken. "Ryan, God, I don't want to leave it like this."

"No." Ryan dug his hands into his pockets to keep from reaching for John. "Maybe this is good. Like you said, it would be hard to go slow. This way we'll have to."

John whispered, "I'm scared you'll change your mind."

Ryan was afraid he might, too. *Would his nerve hold, if he didn't go through with this now?* He stepped to John and tilted his face up. "Promissory note."

John kissed him simply, keeping it soft.

"I swear," Ryan told him. *Told himself.* "When the kids are gone… except, fuck, they're here for a week?"

"That's what Marcus said."

"I head home in five days."

They stared at each other.

"You could share my bathroom, instead of theirs," John suggested. "We could find a way."

"No. Not now. Not yet. So, okay, when the kids are gone *and* I get back from Christmas, I promise we'll take up where we left off."

"I'll hold you to that." John's eyes were hot.

"I'm counting on it."

Chapter Eight

"It looks different," Torey said suspiciously, as they pulled up the drive in front of the house. John put the truck in park and turned off the engine.

"It's too dark to see anything, moron," her brother growled.

"I guess I see better than you do, stupid."

"Jeez Louise," John said. "Give it a rest, guys." Several hours on their best behavior for the flight must've burned out all their self-control, because they'd been bickering non-stop for the whole hour-long drive.

"You cut down the swing!" Torey said. "I knew something was missing."

"The swing?" He thought back. "That was two years ago, honey. Remember? The branch died and it wasn't safe."

"Told you." Mark jumped out of the truck and headed for the back.

"Wait up," John called. "Let me get that." He cleared the cover off, and lifted down their suitcases. "Oof. Feels like you brought enough stuff."

"Most of that's Torey's," Mark said disdainfully. "She brought, like, everything in her closet."

"Because my old stuff that I left here won't fit. Because I'm growing. Unlike some people."

John could visibly see that shot hit. Mark was still barely over five feet tall and sensitive about it.

"Wait till your brother hits his growth spurt," he put in. "You might want to be nice to him now."

Torey huffed. "Anyway, you brought your guitar, stupid."

"I want to practice."

"You want to show off."

"Kids!" John let his voice sharpen. "You want to stand here in the cold squabbling or get inside where it's warm?" He picked up two bags and led the way up the steps.

Ryan was sitting in the kitchen. He stood up and came into the hallway as they hung up coats and sorted out bags. "Need any help bringing things in?"

John shook his head. "We got it." He tried not to look at Ryan, not to pay attention to…ah, shit. He gave the guy a warm smile. "So, Torey, Marcus, this is my roommate that I was telling you about. He's renting the spare room. Ryan, these are my kids, Mark and Torey."

"I've heard a lot about you," Ryan said easily.

"Dad doesn't talk about you much," Marcus returned. "What do you do again? Are you a gardener too?"

John opened his mouth for a reprimand, startled by his son's rudeness, but Ryan gave him a quick headshake. "I'm a medical student," he said calmly. "In three years, you can call me Dr. Ward, but for now it's okay if you call me Ryan."

"What happened to your leg?" Torey chimed in.

"I was a firefighter before I was a med student. Something fell during a fire and it damaged my knee. It didn't heal right."

"That sucks," Torey said. "So is it ever going to, like, heal?"

"That was over a year ago. So I think this is all the better it's ever going to get." After a moment's silence, he added, "But hey, that's okay. I mean, I want to be a doctor. So I'll need good hands, eyes, ears, a good brain. But knees? Not so important."

"I guess. Being a firefighter is cooler."

John cleared his throat. "Why don't you kids take some of this stuff on up to your rooms. I'll bring the rest. We can end up in the kitchen and have a hot drink or something." When they hesitated, he made a shooing motion toward the stairs. "Go on."

Under the cover of their footsteps clattering upstairs, he turned to Ryan. "I'm sorry, man. They're not usually that rude. I don't know what got into them."

"I'm in their space," Ryan said. "They got sent off here by their mom on short notice, you weren't expecting them, and there's an intruder squatting in their house and taking some of their dad's attention."

"Not as much as I'd like," John said softly.

"Stop that." But Ryan smiled. "It figures that they might be a bit hostile. It's probably good I'm just your roommate right now."

"I guess so." He wished otherwise, but Ry was probably right. "I just hope a little rest and food puts them in a better frame of mind, or it's going to be a very long week." He scooped up the two biggest bags and headed upstairs.

Ryan was standing over the kettle, waiting for it to boil, when John got back down to the kitchen. John allowed himself a two-second fantasy of walking over and kissing the back of his neck. *Stop. Don't go there.* He needed to get his mind back into Ry-as-roommate mode or the kids were going to notice. He *really* needed to get his body back into roommate mode.

"Coffee?" he asked.

"And hot chocolate. What do you think the kids would like?"

"We have hot chocolate?"

"I made a quick grocery run while you were at the airport. We were pretty low on everything."

Torey clattered down the stairs and into the kitchen. "Dad, do I have to use that old princess comforter? Don't you have anything less dorky?"

"You picked that one out," John told her.

"Well, yeah, when I was, like, ten. Dad, I'm not ten anymore. It's so juvenile."

"I'll trade with you," Ryan suggested. "I've got plain green, if you like that better."

Torey gave him a look. "Like you'd use the princesses."

89

"Hey," Ryan said, spreading his hands. "I'm secure in my masculinity." John coughed and drew a glare from those green eyes.

"I have an old red plaid in the closet," he told Torey. "We can get it later. And then maybe next week we can buy you something better."

"Well, okay." She sniffed the air. "What smells good?"

Ryan raised his cup. "Hot chocolate." He pointed at John's mug. "And coffee. Want something?"

"Coffee?" John could see that Torey was pleased at being asked.

Ryan shrugged. "Either one."

"I might try some coffee," she said consideringly.

Ryan nodded. "Your dad makes it pretty strong. It's better with some milk and sugar in it, for those of us who still have a stomach lining." He gave John a mock sneer. "Or you could put half coffee into some hot chocolate. Like a mocha."

"Mocha, I guess," Torey said.

"Coming right up." Ryan took down another mug and began concocting.

Upstairs, the sound of a guitar started up. Ryan glanced up as he handed Torey her drink. "That your brother?"

"Yeah. He plays that stupid thing all the time." She took a cautious sip. "Hey. This isn't bad."

Ryan gave her his best smile. "Thank you, my lady." He looked at John, with a nod to the stairs. "The boy's pretty good on that thing."

John tried to remember the last time he'd heard Mark play. It hadn't sounded like this. "I didn't realize."

"He wants to be in a real band," Torey said. "I tell him not in a million years."

"Oh, I don't know," Ryan said. "He's better than some I've heard playing for money."

"Yeah." Torey smiled wickedly, showing a dimple. "But I'm not going to tell *him* that."

Ryan laughed. "I have two older brothers. They need to be kept in their place."

"Exactly." Torey eyed him with more approval. "So, are you really living here?"

"Upstairs. Spare room. Check it out."

"Like, I could go in there? You wouldn't care?"

"If you want." Ryan shrugged. "Pretty boring though. Mostly books, books and more books. A couple of free weights. Actually, the princess comforter might improve it."

"Why are you living here?"

"I needed a room. Your dad needed money to support you and your brother in the manner to which you have become accustomed. And he hates to do dishes. So it's a win all around."

"You pay rent?"

"He wouldn't take green stamps."

"Huh?" Torey said.

Ryan smiled at John. "Never mind. Old-people joke."

John returned the smile, feeling warmth flooding through him. This was going to work out.

****

Ryan struggled to shut the zipper on his suitcase, sitting overstuffed on top of the bed. He didn't want to repack, but he was getting frustrated. Which had been pretty much his standard state for the last five days. Frustrated, and also horny, and yet content underneath it.

The kids turned out to be mostly human, once the effects of their long flight wore off. They'd picked out a big Christmas tree together, and spent a nice

Sunday afternoon decorating it. The kids had argued about which ornaments went where, of course, but it'd sounded more like habit than serious fighting.

Torey was a cute kid, bright and fun, trying so hard to grow up fast. Ryan was amused to see how often John had to bite his tongue, wanting to keep her a child. It probably wasn't as funny from a father's point of view, but there was no real harm in her pining for the clothes and styles of her peers. Ryan secretly agreed that Cynthia's refusal to let Torey get her ears pierced until she was sixteen was overprotective. Although out loud, he and John had backed his ex-wife up, for solidarity.

The way to Mark's heart was his music. Ryan had been pleased to find that all his own skills hadn't rusted away, in the year since he'd picked up a guitar. He couldn't match the kid's fast rock licks, but Ryan still could pick a mean classical line. He'd even been able to show the boy a couple of chord progressions.

Mark was quieter, more subdued and introspective than his sister. Ryan worried that the kid might even have some depression issues. More than once, he'd caught the boy staring blankly out a window, and his responses seemed flat and disengaged. Fifteen was a hard age, especially if you were small and not athletic and plagued by acne. Unlike Torey, Mark hadn't talked about calling his friends back home, or even mentioned having any. But he came alive in his music, so at least he had that. And hopefully he'd open up to John, who so obviously cared about him.

The zipper on Ryan's suitcase snagged in bulging fabric again. Ryan cursed, trying to tuck it in, then bit off the end of the phrase, remembering there were children in the house. Which was a good thing, as Torey said from the doorway, "Want me to sit on it?"

"Couldn't hurt."

She came over and balanced herself on top of the bag, sitting cross-legged. Ryan wrestled the zipper the rest of the way around. "That helped. Thanks."

She hopped off nimbly, and eyed the bag. "You pack like I do."

"I guess. Although a lot of this is presents. I have two nephews."

"Will they be there for Christmas?" Torey asked diffidently.

"Yes, at least for a few days. We'll all go to my Dad's in Oregon—me, my two brothers, Drew's wife and the kids."

Torey went to the window, looking out. "The whole family together."

"This year. Some years we've had to miss out." Last year, he'd still been in rehab, unable to travel.

"I miss having everyone together," Torey said.

"I bet." *What to say?* "But your Mom and Dad don't get along well right now, so it's better to have two separate holidays."

"Mom's having another baby," Torey told the windowpane. "That's why she sent us away."

"Oh, honey." Ryan went up to her and touched her back. "She didn't send you away. She'd promised to let you visit your dad, and earlier just worked out better than later. You'll go home in a couple of days."

"She was sick and grumpy with the new baby," Torey muttered, still looking out. "She said if we were going to be loud and unruly, we might as well go bother John for a bit."

That sounded like a quote. Ryan sighed silently. "Well, do you think you can be loud and unruly again, like in January? Because your dad and I would love to have you back soon."

That got him the ghost of a smile. "Really?"

"Of course. Although there might be a better way to do it than making your Mom angry."

From below, John called up. "Hey, Ryan. Get your butt down here. The shuttle's waiting."

Ryan gave Torey a quick squeeze around the shoulders. "I have to go. I'm sorry you won't still be here when I get back. You visit again soon, okay?"

To his surprise, she turned and hugged him back. "Have a good Christmas."

"Yeah. You too. Listen, can I tell your dad? About the baby?"

"You really won't tell him if I say no?"

93

"It's not my business, exactly," Ryan said cautiously. "But I think it might make things easier for him to understand, if he knows."

"Okay."

"That's good. Thank you. You have a nice holiday too." Ryan headed down the stairs carefully, lugging his full suitcase. All he had to do was make it out the door without tripping over his bags, say goodbye to John with his children watching, and tell the man that his ex-wife was pregnant. Piece of cake.

****

Bars in airports were all basically the same, Ryan decided. Too bright, too quiet, and filled with people sitting alone trying to get sloshed before their flight. Although he was getting sloshed *after* his flight.

He should've been on the shuttle by now, on his way back to the bosom of his so-called loving family. No, that wasn't fair. They *were* a loving family. Which was part of the problem.

For a year now, Dad had had this strained cheer whenever he talked to him. That fake voice when someone is trying to cover up a disaster. Like, Dad couldn't admit he was worried, so he had to pretend everything was going to be perfect, because he also couldn't admit things were never going to be okay.

Which was bullshit, both ways. The leg would never be perfect. But Ryan *was* okay. He'd figured out what he wanted to do next, and gone for it. He was back on track. He didn't need to be treated as fragile.

He took a long swallow of his drink. The scotch rolled smooth and smoky over his tongue and down his throat, and he had a moment's flash of John, sitting at a table in the Stein, drink in hand. He slapped his glass back down roughly. The dregs were low enough not to spill.

He slid off his stool, adjusted his cane and grabbed the handle of his damned bag. He was tempted to just leave it, but if someone walked off with the kids' gifts it would put a damper on Christmas. In the bathroom, he leaned the bag in a corner, finished up, and then stared at his reflection in the mirror. Dark hair, green eyes, nothing he hadn't seen a thousand times. He'd stood like this often enough, combing his hair and wondering whether the girl *du jour* liked what she saw enough to say yes. Shouldn't he somehow look different now? When he had a *guy* liking what *he* saw?

The farther he got from John, the more unreal that moment in the kitchen seemed. The person who'd stood there passionately kissing another man was someone Ryan didn't recognize. He leaned closer, looking himself in the eyes. His return stare was blurred by fatigue and alcohol, but not… gay?

He suddenly missed his mother with a sharp pang. Someone to talk to who would just plain be on his side. Someone without hang-ups and agendas, who'd let him talk this thing out. He left the bathroom, but paused in the dim hallway. His phone was in his pocket. He leaned his shoulders against the wall, angled his cane against his leg and pulled it out. And then hesitated with his fingers on the screen.

He could call John. But if the kids were around, it would mean hushed voices and cryptic euphemisms. And anyway, talking to John wouldn't help him figure out where he stood in his own mind.

His friends from school were still casual acquaintances, the relationships built on study sessions and sharing class notes and agonizing over cryptic exams. He couldn't think of one of them he'd even say the word "gay" to. His buddies from the firehouse had been closer than kin, but the distance between them had widened. And they were not the type to talk about feelings with. Except…

He found the right contact. The phone rang twice and then a woman's sleepy voice said, "This better be important."

"Um, Andrea?"

There was a second of dead air. "Ryan? No, can't be. Ry Ward lost my phone number. He never calls. I get little say-nothing e-mails about the weather from him."

"I've never e-mailed about the weather."

"Last one you sent, and I quote, 'We're having an ice storm.' End quote."

"That's not weather. That's like a natural disaster."

"Only if you break a bone or wreck your car." Andrea's voice warmed. "It *is* you. How are you doing, Ry? It's good to hear your voice."

"Likewise." His throat tightened for a moment. Andrea had been the lone woman in the firehouse. As such, she'd worked hard and played even harder, holding her own among the guys. She was a hundred and thirty pounds of pure muscle and attitude, and they'd been pretty close back when. "I've missed you."

"Well, if you hadn't moved a thousand freaking miles away, you wouldn't have had to. Or if you'd picked up the phone now and then. I was beginning to think you'd forgotten I exist."

"If I crawl on my hands and knees and beg your pardon, will you talk to me?"

"I'd think about it."

Ryan tilted his head back against the wall. Andrea's familiar voice wrapped around him. "Tell me about yourself, about all the guys. Catch me up to date."

"What? You have an hour? I'd need that just to go through Harry's harem."

"Hit the high points."

Her chuckle was still the same. "You mean the low points?" But she willingly rattled off a string of news. A couple of babies, a wedding, a messy divorce, a winning basketball team, a half dozen new regulations that made no fucking sense, a batch of chili so hot even Miguel wouldn't eat it. He let it all seep in.

Eventually she paused. "What about you, Ry? I'm doing all the talking here."

"I'm good. I'm fine. Classes are going well."

"You seeing anyone?"

Not at this precise moment in this damned airport. "Not really." He took a breath. "One odd thing happened. Um, Andrea, do you think I look gay?"

"You? Jesus, no. Why, did some guy hit on you?"

"Something like that."

Andrea snorted. "Well he's either a fool or a complete optimist. Relax, Ry, you don't look gay. We all know how much you appreciate the ladies."

"I've never had a long-term girlfriend, though."

"Have you ever wanted one? I thought you were the king of the hit-and-run."

"Something more settled might be nice."

"Well, halleluiah! I wondered if I'd ever see the day. Did you have someone particular in mind?"

"No," he said hastily. "Just thinking."

"Well, you go on trying to do that. Maybe you'll get the hang of it someday."

"Bitch. I'm spilling my guts here and you're making fun of me."

"I somehow missed the spilling-guts part. Unless you do have a girlfriend."

"No." He went for a half-truth. "Closest I've come lately is the guy who hit on me."

"You should ask him if he has a sister." Andrea's voice sobered. "Seriously, Ry. You're a nice guy. Some girl will take a look and realize you're worth wading through all the bullshit you put out there."

He grunted noncommittally.

"Ryan, you appreciate women, you talk to them like you care about more than the double-D bust line. You went from girl to girl and took what was offered, sure, but I always figured you'd find a nice woman someday and settle down. You're that type."

"Maybe." He sighed. "It's a pity you're in a different state, hot stuff."

She laughed. "We make great friends, but we'd be lousy lovers. Together I mean, because when you're not around, I'm awesome."

"And if I don't agree with that, you'd hit me."

"If you were within reach, you bastard. Listen, I have to go. But call me soon. E-mail is just not the same thing. And hang in there. The girl who finally lands you will be a lucky woman. Shit, there's my alarm. I have to go on shift."

97

Ryan closed his eyes. He could almost see her, getting ready in the evening dusk. And the other guys, straggling into the firehouse, joking with each other, topping each other's tales of who did what during their down-time. "Say hi to the guys for me."

"I will. Bye."

He stood there another minute, listening to the silence on the phone. So it wasn't some gay-bi vibe he'd always had. Not that Andrea was necessarily the most perceptive person in the world, but she'd known him better than most. And she'd never seen… He needed to finish that drink.

His half-empty glass was still on the bar. Andrea would've scolded him for leaving it unattended, but he'd never had to worry like she did. He drank, rolled the last sip around in his mouth, and wondered if he needed another.

He would go home soon, back to the family who had no fucking clue. Not about what worried him, what hurt or scared him, nothing but the very surface of what he'd been doing for the last year, or the last week. He needed some kind of cushion, some way to squeeze himself back into being the Ryan they expected to see. Because he wasn't ready to show them anything else. He might never be ready.

The bartender was busy at a table. Ryan tipped the shot glass, watching the last drop roll around in the bottom. He wasn't drunk yet, far from it. He needed one more. Or maybe two. Or… he looked around the bar. At the tables, several couples sat together, laughing, leaning in. They seemed at ease and comfortable.

Or maybe what he needed was… to get laid. It'd been way too long. All those pent up hormones were probably screwing with his brain. He liked John. Of course he did. Liked him a whole lot, but still, Ryan wasn't gay. He never had been. He'd always appreciated big tits and a tight ass. He liked a woman's lips, her hair, her soft voice, her scent, the way women moved and looked. Like that blonde over at the end of the bar.

Maybe he'd been going too fast. Maybe he owed it to himself *and* to John to think this thing through. He caught the blonde's eye, gave her a small smile. Wheel of chance. If she blew him off, he'd go home. If she came over… Her return smile was bright. With an eye on him, she picked up her glass and slid down the bar.

"So, coming in or leaving town?" she asked.

"Just got in. You?"

"I work for United. I'm unwinding, end of the day."

"You look good, unwound," Ryan told her, with his best boyish grin. *Aren't you too old to be going for boyish*, the voice in his head asked. So his best material was a little rusty. So sue him. He tried to make the smile more real.

"Well, thank you," she said, showing a dimple.

Ryan held out a hand. "I'm Ryan."

"Melissa."

"Can I buy you a drink?"

She raised the glass in her hand. "Got one. And that's my limit. But they do a mean quesadilla. I should probably eat something, to soak up the drink."

Ryan looked around, nodded left. "There's a table over there."

Half an hour later, Ryan was thoroughly sick of himself. He sat back somewhere in the deeper recesses of his brain and watched Ryan Ward operate on auto-pilot. And operate was the key word. Med student, firefighter, fucking hero, he had all the lines.

Melissa was definitely interested. Her calf pressed against his under the table. Her eyes were fixed on him. All the usual female comebacks— rapt attention, smiles in the right places, little tidbits about herself and then she'd turn the conversation right back to him. *Guys like to talk about themselves.* He wondered what magazine she'd read that in.

He could have her, he thought. If he worked it right, she would take him home to that apartment she shared with her flight-attendant friend, who was conveniently out of town. The brightness of her eyes, the way she played with her hair, told him she was interested. Even his cane, that had made her flinch at first, was excused for an injury in the line of duty. In that context, it was some kind of freaking badge of honor. He could almost see the wheels turning in her head.

He could probably lay her on a bed, put her on her knees, and get what he needed, what he liked. Or let her take over and do him. Except... he didn't want that. He thought about her naked, and his body responded. But it was a tepid interest, like muscle memory. It was a reflex that bypassed his brain. Whereas remembering just one kiss with John… *fuck!* Voice, smell, touch, taste. He was instantly hard enough to drive nails.

He shifted in his chair, and tried to get his attention back on Melissa. But he just didn't care. His mind was home in Wisconsin. He wondered what John was doing now. Were the kids getting ready for bed? Was Mark holed up with his guitar, pulling comfort from those strings? Was Torey angling for one more bag of microwave popcorn? Or texting her friend back home for the two-hundredth time that day?

And John. Was John thinking about him? Was he sitting somewhere in that big warm house, eyes closed, remembering, anticipating. Was he in the shower, water streaming down those long, hard muscles until the last drop of heat was wrung from the water tank?

Ryan looked over at Melissa. She hesitated in her narrative, catching his expression.

"I'm sorry," he said. "You're very pretty, and fun to talk to. But I might have someone back at home. And as screwed up as it is, I'm going back there in a week, and I'm going to give it a try."

"Huh?"

"Never mind." He stood, fishing on the back of the chair for his cane. "Thanks a lot for the company. Have a good holiday." She was still staring after him as he limped out of the bar, hauling his suitcase toward the elevators. Ahead was family Christmas, one more week to be the old Ryan. At least on the outside. Because after that, he was going home to John.

Chapter Nine

There were still lights on in the house, as the shuttle turned into the drive. Ryan wasn't surprised, just… pleased. Because with one delay and another, his eight o'clock arrival had become midnight. Now it was after one, and John would've had every right to have given up on him and gone to bed. Especially because Ryan hadn't phoned to explain the delay. Which he hadn't because… he didn't know why.

But the hall light came on too, as he was getting out, and then John was there, taking his bag out of his hand. "Let me get that. You must be beat."

Ryan gave the shuttle driver an extra big tip, for waiting so late, and turned to John as the van rolled away. "I'm not *that* tired."

And there it was, that coiled heat inside him, just like the past fifteen days had never happened. "Come on," John said. "Let's get out of the cold."

Snow squeaked under Ryan's shoes as they climbed the stairs.

"Sorry, I should have cleared those off again." John swiped at a riser with the side of his foot.

"Since when, twenty minutes ago?" The steps had a thin dusting of white, compared to the deep blanket covering the lawn. A few flakes still spiraled down, glittering in the porch light. Ryan pulled the door open, and inhaled the familiar scents of sawdust and coffee. It smelled like home.

He leaned his cane in the usual corner. "My family admired your work." He pointed his chin at it. John had taken the commission and carved him a stick of twisted, entwined tree trunks, with the faces of small creatures peering out from between the curves. It was intricate and beautiful. People who noticed it were so busy checking it out they forgot to check him out. It was brilliant. "I told them I was renting a room from an artist. They were impressed."

"What else did you tell them?" John headed for the kitchen.

"Not much." It had been weird, his first time home since the accident. His father and Drew had made a point of not watching him, not helping him. His dad looked older. Brent had missed the visit altogether. Thank God for Drew's boys. The adults had all made sure the holiday revolved around the children. Ryan's problems had been allowed to go unmentioned. And the changes in his life that weren't problems... well, he hadn't been ready to mention those either.

"Can I get you something?" John said. "Water, juice?"

"Nah. They kept serving drinks on the plane to keep us busy through the delays. I'm about drowning in soda."

John nodded. "So."

They stood looking at each other. "I wish you'd called for me pick you up at the airport," John said softly. "You'd have been home half an hour sooner."

"Right. After an hour in the truck, sitting next to you, not touching you." Ryan felt the heat ratchet up a notch. Not that he needed it. He'd spent most of the flight with a magazine over his lap, anticipating, dreading, wondering... something. "I didn't want to do this at a public airport."

"Do what?" John's voice was hoarse.

Ryan let himself smile. "This." He stepped forward, and ran his hand slowly up John's arm, over his shoulder, and behind the man's neck. He cupped the base of John's skull, and pulled him down.

"Thank God," John whispered against his mouth. Then John kissed him. Ryan had wondered if his memory had exaggerated the feel of John's mouth, but if anything, this was better. John kissed him softly, with his eyes closed, and all of his attention on just that one thing. Ryan opened his lips to a probing tongue, and stepped in closer.

Warm and soft became hot and frantic. Ryan wrapped his other arm around John as they pressed together. John's hands cupped his ass, fingers digging in hard. He found himself rutting against that tall body, wanting more, wanting closer. John's moan vibrated against his mouth.

"Let me." He fumbled between them. John pulled back a few inches, to make room for their hands. It was clumsy and awkward, buttons and zips, as they still kissed, unwilling to break contact. Ryan slid his mouth to John's neck, sucking hard, feeling the slick of skin under his tongue. John must have shaved for him, recently. His hands slipped down past the waistband of John's boxers. Familiar unfamiliar sensation. He had a man's hard dick in his hands and it wasn't his own. And then callused fingers closed on his erection in turn.

He squeezed, pumping firmly. Slick precome coated his fingers and he spread it, fisting over John's unfamiliar length. Soft sac, firm round balls, hard velvet shaft, curved head becoming slippery.

"God, Ryan," John breathed. "We can…"

He caught John's mouth in a punishing kiss. He pushed the man back against the counter, hands frantic. No waiting, not this time. He *wanted*.

John went with him. His fingers were just as busy on Ryan. The sensations like heat and ice ran through Ryan's groin, building. He kissed John's mouth again, plunging his tongue deep. He wanted to undo this man. Wanted to feel him come apart.

John's hands fell away. His head went back, eyes half-closed. Ryan sucked on his neck, biting. John's hips jerked, thrusting hard into Ryan's hands. Ryan laughed against his skin. *Yes. Shit, yeah!*

Then John groaned, his body shuddering. Jets of spunk slid through Ryan's fingers, spattered against his jeans. John grabbed for the edge of the counter. Ryan leaned forward. His hard dick pressed into the angle of John's bare hip where he'd tugged those boxers low. The sensitive head dragged over hot skin and rough curls. He moved in tighter, panting, thrusting hard. Then John's arms wrapped around him and kept him from falling as he came. Came against John, on him, in a blinding rush that took his breath, and forced his eyes closed.

"Holy, holy shit," he whispered. John's shoulder was right there, and he laid his head on it for a moment. "Wow."

"Are you okay?"

Ryan breathed a laugh against his neck. "Stupid question."

"Good." John's arms kept their warm hold, a hand gently rubbing Ryan's back. He bent and kissed the top of Ryan's head.

"Don't waste 'em." Ryan put up a sticky hand and pulled John down to reach his mouth again.

This kiss was different, slow and sweet. He touched his tongue to John's teeth, traced his lower lip. John sighed against his mouth.

"What?"

"I was so scared you wouldn't want to, after having all this time to think."

"Oh, I've been thinking," Ryan said. "It's a good thing my nephews aren't telepathic, or they'd have gotten a real early education."

John kissed his jaw, his cheek. His eyebrow.

Slowly, Ryan became aware of the chill on his thighs. "We're kind of wet."

"I guess." John's arms dropped away reluctantly, and he stepped back. "Here." He dampened a paper towel and passed it over. For a minute they pursued cleanup, not looking at each other.

"You're probably tired," John said tentatively. "You'll want a shower and sleep."

Ryan pulled his jeans into place and deliberately left them unbuttoned. "John. Every single soda I drank in the last five hours had caffeine in it. Fuck sleep."

John's slow smile was a gift. "You have something else in mind?"

"You, on the bed, naked," Ryan said firmly. "Your bed, because it's bigger than mine."

"We could do that." John led the way upstairs. Ryan's mind was racing a million miles an hour. So far, he'd stuck to his plan. He was still damned if he knew what he was doing, but this time he had a plan. John's room was warm. The big bed was neatly made, pale blue sheets, dark blue comforter. Ryan reached out and stripped the covers back in one motion. He felt great. He felt like a god.

"Get those clothes off."

John raised an eyebrow. "Bossy, aren't you?"

"Is that a problem?"

"Not in this case, no." John's fingers went to hem of his sweater. Slowly, he raised it, and pulled it over his head. His auburn hair fell tousled into his eyes. He tossed the sweater on a chair. Staring into Ryan's eyes, John began to methodically unbutton his shirt. Inch by inch, the edges fell open, exposing his chest. Lamplight glinted off a scattering of copper curls, between the hard planes of his pecs. Ryan had always thought a woman's breasts were beautiful. So why did his breath come so hard in his throat at the sight of a man's flat nipples?

John dropped the shirt on the chair and slid his hands to his jeans. "Let me," Ryan told him. He moved in close, twisting the metal button out of its hole. The zipper slid down with a whisper. Cotton briefs, damp from the first time, barely contained this man. Ryan shoved all the bunched fabric downward. As he dropped awkwardly to one knee to finish the job, John's erection bobbed beside his cheek, jerking to the man's pulse.

"Ryan?"

He looked up into John's eyes. "Lie down on the bed."

John did as directed, sliding up on the pillows to look at him. "Are you going to undress?"

"Eventually." *As late and as little as possible.* He crawled up the bed toward John, straddled him, and leaned in for a kiss. John ran his hands through Ryan's hair.

"Let me." Ryan wanted to explore, to look and taste. John lay back, eyes half-closed, stroking Ryan's neck and shoulders as Ryan took his time. Licking, tasting, touching his lips to eyelid and jaw, neck and throat. He swirled his tongue around John's nipple, loving the way the bud tightened to his touch. He bit it, lightly, and John jerked under him.

"Lie still."

He moved lower. He still didn't know exactly how he wanted to do this. But he'd been on the receiving end often enough, and he'd imagined this. More than often enough. A dozen times he'd typed *"gay sex video"* into his browser, and as many times he'd erased it without looking. He hadn't wanted this first time to happen with the image of any other man on his mind.

John's dick was bigger than his own. The skin was one shade darker than on the pale groin, the head was wide and flaring. John's curls were soft not wiry, and a little sparse. Ryan moved down, kissing below John's navel. "Hey," he whispered against that flat stomach. "You're a true redhead."

John laughed. "No kidding." He cupped the back of Ryan's head and pulled. "Come back up here."

"Not yet."

Ryan slid his hand around the hard shaft, raising it. John drew in a sharp breath. A drop of precome formed at the tip, rolled down. Ryan bent and kissed the silky skin beside the slit. Then he touched the flat of his tongue to that droplet, swiping across the flared head.

"Shit," John hissed. "Ry?"

Salty, a little bitter, not that bad. It didn't taste like his own which, yeah, Ryan had tasted, wondering, planning this all through the last week. John's flavor was just like him, better than expected. Ryan licked again, harder, and another drop rolled across his tongue.

"You don't have to."

Ryan blew a breath over wet skin. "Told you I have plans."

"I never argue with a man who has my cock in his hand."

"You've had experience with that?" Ryan asked, taking a long slow lick from root to tip, tracing the raised veins.

"Unh. No, just you." John's length jerked in Ryan's fist.

"Good." Ryan closed his mouth on the dark plum of the head. John groaned. Slowly, experimenting, Ryan licked and sucked. He wrapped his fist tight around John, and leaned in, taking the head in his mouth, slowly pushing down to meet his hand. *Not too bad.* At least he hadn't choked himself. He pulled back, sucking hard.

"Oh, ah, Jesus," John babbled. "Jesus God, Ryan. I'm not going to last if you do that. God, I can't." His words became hoarse groans as Ryan dipped his head, speeding the motion, fast plunge, and long slow suck upward.

John's hands fisted in Ryan's hair. His hips took up the rhythm, jerking upward. Ryan tried to slide his hand and mouth together, letting John control the speed.

"Oh, Ryan, oh, Ryan, oh, man."

Ryan's mouth filled with slick cum and he jerked back, gagging a little, letting it dribble out onto John's belly as he kept up the pressure and rhythm up John's length with his hands. John shot again, across his chest and abdomen, slick and white with the smell of sex. Ryan stroked until the last shudders were done, and then reached over for a tissue and wiped his lips. And another for his hand, and John's stomach. Clearly some practice was in order at the end there. But he had the general idea.

John's grip in his hair guided him up the bed, and down against a sweat-damp shoulder. Ryan laughed with satisfaction, then took John's kiss, sharing the flavor. John moaned and shuddered again.

"Good plan," he breathed eventually into Ryan's hair. "Well thought-out, well executed."

"Thank you."

John's arms tightened around Ryan's shoulders. "Give me a minute to get feeling back in my legs and it's your turn."

"I'm fine."

John's hand slid down and over Ryan's hard dick, drawing an involuntary sound from him. "You're excellent. And gonna be better."

Okay. Planned for this too. Ryan rolled onto his back beside John on the bed. He lay flat, letting his weight press him into the mattress, as John eased up on one elbow and wiped himself off. That electric grin on his face was hard to resist, as he flicked the tissue in the direction of the trash, then slowly opened Ryan's shirt, and unzipped his jeans.

John's mouth tickled across his skin. "You need to lift up a bit." His fingers slid into Ryan's briefs. "So I can get these off."

"I like it like this," Ryan returned. "You naked, me half-dressed. Sort of a master-slave thing." When John paused, he added. "What? Too challenging to work around a little clothing?"

John kissed him slowly. Mouth, neck, chest, nipple, stomach, navel, hip. And there he paused and looked Ryan in the eyes. "What do you think I'm going to say when I see your leg?" he asked gently.

Ryan could feel the heat of his blush. *Busted.* "I don't know." He worked for a light tone. "The last person I was naked in bed with said, *ew, gross!*"

"Dating fifteen-year-olds, were we?" John asked calmly, kissing his belly.

"She was twenty-four."

"Damned immature for twenty-four." John licked back over his hip and looked up again. "Ryan, I'm thirty-seven. I've seen dead bodies. I saw all three of my children born. I'm not likely to be bothered by a few scars."

A few scars. Ryan sat up, staring John in the eyes, pinning him in place. He yanked off his shirt, dragged down his jeans, his underwear. Everything went on the floor. Then he rolled over, naked, and buried his face in the pillow.

John said nothing, not an intake of breath, not a sound. After a moment, Ryan felt warm fingers on his back. They traced slowly downward. Ryan knew what they were outlining, although half the time he couldn't feel the touch.

The burning beam that fell on him had been scorching and heavy, and he'd been pinned with his suit ripped. His shoulders weren't bad. Just a few patches of paler skin where the grafts hadn't matched. But from his left hip, downward and inward, the real mess began. Deep ropes of scars, gaps in his thigh and calf where the dead, cooked flesh had been removed. His skin was fish-belly white, where it wasn't red or silver-gray. On his ass, on his right thigh, the sites where grafts had been harvested showed their own scars, neat and surgical.

John said nothing, just trailed his fingers over the mess. Ryan couldn't take the silence. "Pretty, huh?"

"Must've hurt like hell."

"Wasn't fun."

John slid a fingertip around Ryan's left knee. "Looks like you had a bunch of surgeries."

"One more than the insurance would pay for."

"Well, they got you walking. That had to be a minor miracle."

"More like a major one." The tightness in Ryan's chest was easing. "They didn't think I would keep the leg."

John just bent and kissed Ryan's left ankle. The one he would have lost. "Roll over, Ry."

Ryan turned. The damage was much less visible from this side. Although if you knew where to look, the scars from the surgeries and grafting sites were scattered across him, and the deep burns wrapped around below his knee.

John began at his ankles, kissing his way up Ryan's legs. "If anything hurts, tell me."

"Will you kiss it better?"

"I might."

Ryan pointed at his hip. "There." A soft brush of a kiss on skin.

His stomach. "There." Warm lips, a rasp of teeth.

"There." And oh, yes, John's mouth where he wanted it, John's hands, John's tongue. Ryan closed his eyes, lay back, and abandoned himself to sensation.

****

John gathered Ryan in against his side and pulled the covers up over them. Ryan made a soft sleepy sound and curled tighter. The man had to be exhausted. John was wide awake.

It had taken everything he had to not react to Ryan's scars. When Ry rolled over… God! He hadn't imagined anything that bad. He thought he'd done okay. That tight, false tone in Ry's voice had faded. And there was no doubt about how hard Ryan had eventually come, with John's first-ever blow job. He'd swallowed it all down, too, even though he'd been worried about that part and planned to pull back. When the moment was on him, he'd wanted to take anything Ry was giving him, just wishing he could take the pain with it.

He didn't need the details to imagine Ryan, pinned to the ground in some burning hell, as the fire ate into his leg. He brushed a kiss over the sleeping man's hair, silky dark strands against his lips. He wondered how close he'd come to never meeting this man. It seemed inconceivable. But Ryan could have died. He'd lost his career, but not his life. Was it selfish to be glad that his lover would never again have to walk into another burning building?

Ryan murmured something against his chest.

"Hm?" John hadn't quite made out the words.

"I said, you're awfully good at that. For a novice."

"Native talent." *And research.* "You're not too bad yourself."

"It's not that different from doing oral on a woman. More fun though, and a lot more to play with."

"Cynthia didn't really like me doing that. I'll take your word for it."

"What about your other girlfriends?" Ryan asked, his voice clearer.

109

"Are you being nosy?"

"Maybe."

John laughed contentedly. "Doesn't matter. There were no others."

Ryan rolled up on one elbow. "None? Ever?"

"In high school, I was obsessed with Cynthia for years before she consented to go out with me. And after the divorce... I don't know. I dated some but... it just never went that far." He just hadn't wanted a new relationship enough to be worth the effort. The last years of his marriage, there hadn't been much sex. He'd gotten used to going without. Or he thought he had. Current evidence might contradict that. He slid his hip against Ryan, lightly, nudging him with a growing erection.

"Again?" Ryan laughed softly. "What? Are you taking Viagra?"

"With you around? Who needs it?" John rolled on his side, pulling Ryan close on top of him, already rocking, thrusting.

"Oh God." Ryan's mouth came down on his again, and they were lost in the heat of friction, and the press of body on body.

****

John woke to the sun shining in his eyes. He squinted. There was a gap in the curtains that he had never noticed. Probably because he had never slept in until...holy crap, eleven thirty! Against his side, Ryan still lay like a dead man.

John nudged him. "Wake up."

"Huh?" Ryan burrowed his head into the pillow.

"Wake up. We've already wasted half the day."

Ryan opened one eye and gave him a wicked grin. "Wasn't wasted."

John laughed. They'd slept in snatches, waking to turn to each other, thinking it would be for a kiss, a touch. And then the flaring heat had taken over, again. Shit, he was actually sore from too much friction. Happy, but sore.

He shoved Ryan harder. "Get up. Eat breakfast. Or maybe lunch. Buy groceries."

"But then we'd have to get out of bed."

"Ry, I've done all the bed my elderly body can handle. I need a shower and some food."

"Share the shower?"

"God." The image of Ryan in the shower, his skin wet, made John's cock twitch, even after last night. But only twitch. "It would be wasted on me this morning. But hold that thought."

He slid out of bed and stretched, raising his arms toward the ceiling and twisting.

"Now that's a nice view," Ryan murmured, curled on his side in the bed. "Nothing elderly about it. At *all*."

"Up." John reached down and ruthlessly pulled off the covers. "I'll let you have the first shower."

"You'd better. There'd be no hot water if you go first." Ryan rolled out of the bed and stood, one hand on the mattress for balance. He glanced at John cryptically, and then bent to pick up his clothes. His back was to John. The bright light of morning played across those scars clearly. John figured that might be the point.

He took his shirt and snapped Ryan's butt with the soft side of the hem. "Leave the dirty clothes. I'll throw them in the laundry. Get your sexy ass under the water. I want my turn."

Ryan was smiling as he turned. "Ten minutes."

"I'll start the coffee."

It was nice, but a little strange, sitting at the table with Ryan, having brunch, like it was still last month and they were barely roommates.

"What?" Ryan said, his mouth full of bagel. "You're looking at me weird."

"Sorry." John drank a slug of black gold. "I guess I don't know what comes next."

"Next comes dishes. And then we do need to buy groceries."

"So, do we, what, go grocery shopping together? I've never lived with anyone but Cynthia. I'm not sure I know how to do this."

"Puts you one up on me," Ryan said. "I've never lived with anyone." He shrugged. "I don't see why we have to change things too fast. We never shopped together before. Put up a list and one of us can make the run. We don't have to do all the couple-type things."

"What if I want to?"

Ryan stared at him.

"Ry, this isn't just about sex. Not for me. Yes, I like the sex. Okay, I'm crazy about the sex. But because it's you I'm having it with. I'm not simply horny. I don't think I'm even all that gay. I'm just crazy about you."

"I..." Ryan swallowed and tried again. "Yeah, me too. I mean, I'm not checking out other guys on the street. But with you, God, that was so hot."

John was caught by a wash of disappointment. *Fool. Why would you be disappointed that Ryan finds you hot?* But somehow he wished Ryan had phrased it differently. "We'll go slow," he offered.

"Last night was slow?" Ryan wiggled his eyebrows.

"We can do the sex as fast as you like. We'll do the rest, the becoming-a-couple thing slow. If you actually want to."

"I don't know. I hadn't thought beyond getting you into bed."

I got as far as planning the next twenty years. John bit his tongue. He knew he was out ahead of Ryan on this whole thing. He needed patience. He didn't think Ryan would've been in any man's bed if it was just about sex. But he knew his hopes would take time. If they could even get there at all.

Chapter Ten

A week later, Ryan still didn't quite have the rhythm of their new relationship. On the outside, things hadn't changed much. They shared a ride to school each morning, went their separate ways, usually met over the dinner table. Evenings were for work and study, or occasionally an hour of TV. But then at the end of the day, they went to bed together.

That they were getting good at. Ryan found he loved the taste of John, the feel of hard flesh in his mouth. He was even learning to swallow without gagging. Ryan loved watching John come undone under his hands, under the press of his body and his mouth. And at night, Ryan slept better than he had in over a year, with John's warm body next to his own.

But their days felt unfinished. As if there were steps they were still waiting to take. Which of course there were, in bed and out of it. Ryan just wasn't sure when he'd be ready for anything more. *If* he'd ever be ready for anything more. He wished school would hold off, and give him time to figure out his life. But the new semester had opened with a load of new coursework and new classes. Ryan had to dig in, work like a maniac, and find his bearings again.

He looked up from his books, scattered across the dining room table, when the doorbell rang that evening. From the workshop, John called, "Hey, Ry. Could you get that?"

"You expecting someone?" he called back as he hauled himself up and hobbled to the front door. He'd been sitting wrong and his leg had stiffened up. Or maybe he'd pulled a muscle chasing John around the bed last night. They'd found they enjoyed a little roughhousing in with the foreplay sometimes, and John was hard to pin down.

"Not me," John called. "Maybe it's that *Gay Kama Sutra* book you ordered."

"In your dreams. I don't need no stinking textbook."

He reached the door and pulled it open. A tall woman in a blue parka stood on the porch. "Can I help you?"

"Does John Barrett live here?"

"Yes," Ryan said cautiously. "Can I tell him who you are?"

She pulled out a wallet and flipped it open. "Detective Carstairs. York PD."

Ryan blinked. "Sure. Come on in." He led the way toward the kitchen. "Hey, John," he called toward the workshop. "It's the police."

"Who?" John appeared in the doorway. "Oh, Detective Carstairs. Hello."

"Mr. Barrett. Could we have a talk?"

"Sure, have a seat."

Ryan cleared his books over into a pile, to make space at the table. John sat down, seemingly at ease. But Ryan could see the tension in his body despite the leg-sprawled pose. Carstairs leaned against the counter.

"There's coffee left in the thermos," Ryan offered them both. "Best in town."

The detective glanced at him. "That would be good. Thank you. Would you tell me your name?"

Ryan gimped to the counter, and poured coffee into a mug. "Ryan Ward. Do you take cream or sugar?"

"Just black, thanks." She took the mug, cupping it between her palms as if her hands were chilled. "You're Ward? I didn't realize you two knew each other."

"What's this about?" John asked.

The detective turned to look at him. "That body you found. We finally identified her from her dentistry. Her name was Kristin Saunders. Ring any bells?"

John frowned. "I don't think so. Ry?"

Ryan shook his head. "Not in my class anyway."

Carstairs set her mug on the counter. "She was Alice Tormel's roommate."

"Alice?" Ryan said. "Like, fell out of a tree, Alice?"

"Yes." She eyed them, her expression giving nothing away. "You both knew Alice. But you never met Kristin?"

114

"Neither of us knew Alice," John said firmly. "I saw her home one night when she was high. Ryan tried to save her when she climbed the tree, also high. That's all the contact we had with her. If this Kristin was the girl who took her up to her room that first night, or one of the ones trying to talk her out of the tree, we didn't know it at the time. Did she have dyed red hair?"

"Blonde," Carstairs said. She pulled out a photo and passed it to John. He studied it, and then handed it to Ryan. "Either of you recognize her?"

Ryan shook his head. He wasn't surprised when John said, "I've seen her around campus. More last year. She used to rollerblade sometimes. I don't think I ever heard her name."

"Any idea who she hung around with, who her friends were?"

John shook his head. "When she skated, it was by herself. I'm sorry."

"And it's just coincidence that you were there when Alice fell, and you were the one to find her roommate's body?"

"Yes," John said firmly. "It was just coincidence."

"Were there drugs in Kristin when she died?" Ryan asked.

"Funny you should mention that. Not only did we not find any drugs in Kristin's body, we didn't find any in Alice's."

"Then you didn't look for the right thing," Ryan told her. "That girl was definitely on something. Unless she was mentally ill, to the point of hallucinations, but it sure sounded like a drug high."

"According to the two of you."

"Talk to the two girls who were there." Ryan didn't like that skeptical tone. "They'll tell you the same thing. She was trying to be a squirrel-bird and fly when she jumped out of the tree."

"We'll be talking to them again," Carstairs agreed evenly. "We can't test for every possible intoxicant, so we might have missed something. But it was none of the common ones." She picked up her mug, took another sip. "So, how do you two know each other?"

"We're roommates," Ryan said quickly. Anything else was none of her business. "I rent a room. John owns the house."

"I see."

"When did Kristin die?" John asked. "I'd think I would've heard if a student had suddenly gone missing from campus."

"Her stuff was gone too. So everyone thought she couldn't handle what happened to Alice, and went home. She's been gone since a week after Alice died."

"Shit." Ryan frowned. Three months in the earth. No wonder John had been so freaked when he found her. He'd never said much, but Ryan could tell it had been bad.

Carstairs told John, "I'll need a list of everyone who's been working on your grounds crews since September."

"Why my crews?"

"Access to tools, a good excuse for wandering around campus with a shovel? People who might be familiar with the remoter parts of the campus."

"The college personnel office would have the list," John said. "I have names, but not contact details. They do the hiring, I just tell the men where to go and what to do."

"Have you sent anyone out to work in that area in the last year?"

"No. I was checking it out for the first time myself, thinking about a hiking trail."

"Do you remember any instance when tools were stolen, or used and left dirty?"

John laughed humorlessly. "They're gardening tools, shovels. They're often left dirty."

"Help me out here," Carstairs said. "Is there anything you remember that would be worth my time to pursue?"

"No," John said firmly. "Nothing."

"I think you should be looking for the drugs," Ryan repeated. "Because Alice was flying. Figuratively before the literally part."

"Mr. Barrett, are you aware of drugs on campus?"

"Sure," John said. "Lots of pot, probably plenty of other stuff too. It's a college. I don't worry about the pot. If I knew who was selling the hard stuff I would tell you immediately. I don't."

Carstairs looked around. "This is a nice house. Must have cost quite a bit."

"I used to work for a big firm." Ryan admired John's calm tone. "I had some savings."

"There's money to be made selling drugs on campus."

"I'm sure there is. But not for me."

Carstairs drained the mug and set it in the sink. "If I find out either of you knew something that could have helped us, and didn't pass it along," she said, "I'll be back, and it won't be a social call."

"You're welcome back any time," John said.

Carstairs gave him a smile that didn't change the cool look in her eyes. "Your *roommate* is right by the way. Great coffee."

Ryan stepped away from the counter. "I'll let you out."

When he came back to the kitchen, John was still sitting at the table peering into his empty mug.

"How come you didn't get mad when she practically accused you of dealing drugs?" Ryan asked.

John shrugged. "She's fishing. I imagine they don't have many leads. Can't blame them for chasing anything they do have."

"So she can just come here and accuse you?"

"She was looking for a reaction." John looked up at him. "Why'd you tell her you were my roommate?"

"Because I am," Ryan said, ignoring a twinge of discomfort. "Anything else is none of her business."

"Yeah, except she said *roommate* like she didn't buy it. And now she'll wonder what else I'm hiding."

"What did you want me to tell her?"

John said steadily, "I think of you as my boyfriend."

Ryan winced. "I hate that word. It's so… high school."

"If you were dating a woman, you'd call her your girlfriend."

"Maybe. But it's not the same thing."

"What do you think we are, then? Lovers, partners, fuck buddies, friends with benefits, what?"

"I don't," Ryan said desperately. "I don't put a name on it. Christ, John, it's only been a week. I'm still trying to accept the fact that my biggest fantasy these days involves getting another man naked in bed. You're my best friend and we have sex and I don't put a label on it."

"Do you want to hide it?"

"Not hide it." Ryan was aware that John's gaze looked wary, waiting. "I just don't see where it's anyone else's business. We can live our life without... advertising."

"So if I see you on campus I'm allowed to... what? Shake your hand? Is a hug okay, if there's some manly backslapping included?"

"Don't. Don't push me. Not yet."

John nodded. "I'm sorry. I guess I'm greedy. I want it all. I want to have your picture on my phone, and call you for no reason, and kiss you when I see you."

Ryan couldn't imagine it, didn't want to. He had to head this off. He walked over to where John sat, and fisted a hand in his shirt. "You could kiss me now."

John's eyes warmed. "I don't know if I want to do that," he drawled.

"You do." Ryan hauled him upward. John stood slowly, and then bent his head. It took nothing, just the barest touch of their lips, for the heat to ignite. John kissed him like he wanted to eat him alive. He shoved Ryan back against the table, demanding his mouth. Ryan heard a book go flying.

He pulled free to say, "My histology text."

"To hell with histology." John's hands were hard, rough, over Ryan's back and down inside the waistband of his jeans. He bit at Ryan's neck, sucked hard. Ryan leaned in tighter, needing more.

"The bed is upstairs."

"To hell with the bed." John dropped to his knees in front of Ryan, hands fumbling with fastenings. And then Ryan's fingers tangled in that auburn hair, and John's mouth was too full for talking.

****

John juggled the grocery bags as he opened the front door. There was an unfamiliar car in the drive. He wondered if the cops were back again. If they were, he hoped Ryan was keeping his temper. Carstairs had been around campus all week, and she'd made it a point to seek John out more than once.

Ryan was ticked off, but John could sympathize with the detective's frustration. He was the closest thing they had to an angle on the case, because as far as he could tell, they had no leads. Both the college and the community urgently wanted the murder solved, before sensationalist publicity made too many parents decide to send their little darlings elsewhere to school. Carstairs was no doubt getting a lot of pressure to do something, fast.

As he set the bags on the counter, he took note of voices in the living room. Ryan and another man. Conversation sounded cordial. John put the milk and orange juice in the fridge, then wandered in.

Ryan was sitting in the wingback chair. Across from him, another man sat on the couch. He looked vaguely familiar, but John couldn't place him. Dark brown hair, dark eyes, a pleasant face, slightly overweight. He was dressed in a business suit, the tie pulled loose and one button undone.

Ryan looked up as John came in, and he smiled, but it was a strained, pale version of his usual. "Hey, John, I'd like you to meet my brother, Brent. Brent, this is my roommate, John Barrett."

John held out his hand. "Hey, good to meet you. Ryan's told me about you."

Brent's handshake was solid. "Wish I could say the same. But I haven't heard from my little brother in six months. I missed the Christmas family thing."

"I sent you a card," Ryan said.

"Yeah, great, so I knew you were still alive and able to sign your name. Thanks, bro."

"You could've called me."

Brent looked uncomfortable. "Well, I wasn't sure, you know, you weren't very talkative last time."

Ryan looked almost as pained. John said, "So, what brings you out here? This wasn't a planned visit, was it? Not that you're not welcome."

"Oh, I'm not staying," Brent said quickly. "I had a client down this way, had to make an in-person call to straighten a problem out. And it occurred to me it was less than fifty miles out of my way to visit Ryan."

Ryan said, "He blew into town, called my cell and asked for directions to the house."

"Yeah." Brent looked around the room. "You know, this is a cool place. You could do a lot with it. Do you own it?"

"John owns it," Ryan said. "I just rent a room."

"Better than a dorm," Brent said heartily.

"Right."

"So, would you like to have some dinner?" John wasn't sure what was going on with these two guys. Ryan had always talked about his brothers with affection, but you could cut the tension here with a knife. "I bought groceries," he added. "So we actually have food."

"No, no," Brent said, getting quickly to his feet. "Let me take you guys out to eat. My treat. I can expense it. My boss is always giving me a hard time about making his meal charges look bad by comparison. He'll be happy if I spend a few bucks."

"You two should go," John said. "I'm sure you have catching up to do. You don't need a stranger horning in." He wanted Ryan to invite him, to deny he was a stranger, ask him to meet the family.

But it was Brent who said quickly, "No. Really. You should both come."

"You'd better have an unlimited budget if you're offering to feed this big lug," Ryan said, motioning to John with humor that seemed forced.

"I doubt he can out-eat you," Brent said. "At least the way you used to eat. I mean, you look good, so you aren't overeating, clearly." He flushed. "Look, I'll go warm up the car. We can ride in mine, so you can give me directions."

John stared after the man as he headed to the front door. "What's his problem?" he whispered to Ryan.

Ryan's lips twisted sourly. "He doesn't deal well with weakness, emotions, all that shit. I told you, when David died he left the country. When I was hurt, he did the same thing. Suddenly a week later he had a rush job in Mexico that lasted for months. I make him uncomfortable."

"Still? You're pretty normal now. Well, for a maniac."

Ryan smiled briefly. "Thanks, John. Yeah, apparently, still uncomfortable."

"So we'll go out, have a meal. Let him see you're fine."

Ryan nodded unconvincingly.

They chose to go to Luigi's. John found himself in the front seat of the car, directing Brent, while Ryan sat in the back. The drive was quiet. As they pulled in to the restaurant, Brent cleared his throat and said, "Ryan, do you want me to drop you off in front?"

"Huh?" Ryan frowned. "No. I can actually walk quite well now. I even run, climb rock walls, complete a mean triathlon, kickbox."

"Really?"

"No, dumb shit. But I can make it as far as the parking lot."

John reached back and smacked Ryan's arm. "Don't tease your brother."

Brent gave them a startled look, but pulled obediently into a regular parking space. He headed toward the door ahead of them, not looking back at Ryan. "I'll get us a table."

Ryan followed, careful on the icy sidewalk. "Shit," he muttered.

"Shit, what?" John held station, close enough for a catch but casual enough not to look like he was hovering.

"He still won't look at me."

"What?"

"In the hospital, when he would visit." Ryan pulled the door open. "He looked everywhere except at me. And then he left town."

"Maybe you're exaggerating."

The restaurant was warm after the winter air outside. It was modest, but clean and bright, with red chairs and paper tablecloths. A savory smell of tomatoes and garlic filled the air. John breathed in appreciatively. "Well, if he's willing to buy me a great meal, he can look anywhere he wants."

"I suppose."

"Right this way, sirs." The maître d' led them toward a table. Brent went first, and John decided Ryan was right. The extra time it took Brent to get settled in his chair wasn't random. He'd made sure that Ry was fully seated, before he looked up.

They ordered drinks, which amounted to beer all around. When the waiter had gone, Ryan reached down and pulled out his cane. "Hey, Brent," he said.

"You have to see this. I commissioned it from John here. He's some kind of artist."

Brent swallowed as he took it, but then his attention was caught by the intricate carving. He turned it in his hands, checking it out. "Hey, this is great." The man looked less uncomfortable as he lost his pinched expression. "John, this is pretty amazing."

"Thank you."

The waiter brought their beer and took their orders. Brent raised his mug and said, "Listen, little bro. I want you to toast my good news."

"You finally learned how to play that ukulele you bought in tenth grade?"

"No. Asshole. I met a girl."

"Really?" Ryan leaned forward. "A real girl, not a blow-up one."

"That's your specialty, Ryan." Then Brent looked stricken. "I mean, not that you can't find... I mean, I heard about Marla."

"Jesus, that's ancient history. Quit tiptoeing around my frailties, and tell me about this lunatic female who is actually willing to date my brother."

"Her name's Anne." Brent pulled out his cell phone, and brought up a picture. "That's her."

Ryan tilted it so John could see too. "She's very pretty," John said quickly, to head off whatever brotherly comment Ryan might have made.

"Too pretty for you," Ryan said. "You sure this isn't some kind of fantasy thing?"

Brent smiled. "I asked her to marry me."

"Hey." Ryan's return smile was genuine. "That's great! Assuming she said yes."

"We haven't set a date, but she took the ring."

Ryan held out a hand. "Congratulations, brother."

John echoed the handshake.

"So, have you told Dad?" Ryan asked. "Has he met her?"

"I called him a week ago. He was thrilled. He said, the way that all I talked about for years was the other guys at the office, he was worried I was turning queer. I told him I was never that desperate. Anne's amazing. I hope you'll meet her sometime."

Smiling down at his phone, Brent probably missed the look Ryan and John exchanged. John held his breath to see where Ryan would take this.

"I'll see her at the wedding, if not before," Ryan's tone was perfectly level. "I assume I'm invited?"

"I'll even let you bring a date, if you can find one." Brent stopped, and flushed bright red.

"Brent, listen up," Ryan said firmly. "I'm fine. I gimp a little, but I'm doing well. I'm even dating. Not everyone is as superficial as Marla. You need to quit worrying."

"I'm sorry," Brent said. "I'm just... concerned about you, I guess." He glanced at John. "Kid brothers. When you're not beating them up, you have this instinct to protect them. What happened to Ryan... We all feel like we screwed up."

"I'm an only child." John let his voice drawl. "But I think Ryan's big enough to take care of himself." He took a long draught of beer to drown his frustration. Ryan was being very careful with his dating pronouns, or lack thereof. Clearly this was not going to be meet-the-family night.

"So, this dating. Do you have anyone special?" Brent asked Ryan.

And sure enough, there was Ryan saying, "Not that I want to introduce you to."

"Afraid she might like me better?"

"No, I'm not worried about that."

John couldn't resist running his finger around the rim of his beer mug and saying, "Oh, I don't know, Ry. Your brother's a good-looking guy. Some people might find him very attractive."

He winced as Ryan's foot connected with his ankle under the table. And yet even that contact raised his spirits. *Barrett, you're pathetic.*

The food came and they ate, mostly listening to the latest nephew stories from Brent. He and Drew obviously stayed in close touch. Ryan added a couple of family items from Christmas. John would've felt more neglected, except that halfway through the meal, Ryan's hand landed on his knee under the tablecloth. The strong fingers inched their way upward, while he tried not to react. Luckily, Ryan could only reach so far. John concentrated on listening to Brent, and not getting up from the table with a hard-on.

Brent dropped them off at the house, saying something about a hotel reservation and an early flight. Ryan didn't even make a token protest. Once they were inside with the door shut, he blew out a breath and relaxed visibly.

"Were you that scared he might find out about us?" John asked.

"Huh? No. Not that. It's just, when he looks at me, he's remembering the hospital, and thinking about me as his crippled younger brother. And he makes me remember how it felt to have everyone hovering and worrying. And I fucking hate it."

John stuffed his own issues away and put his arms around Ry. "I promise I won't protect you. In fact I might wrestle you to the bed, and forcibly have my way with you."

"Queer sex? Are you that desperate?"

Clearly, Ryan was a little hung up on his brother's reactions. "Desperate." John nodded. "Yeah. Ravenous. Demanding. Insatiable."

Ryan softened in his hold. "Wait. I thought that was me."

John kissed him. "Shall we go to bed and find out?"

Upstairs in their room, with the door shut, it was just him and Ryan. John took a kiss, hot and wet, as he struggled with the buttons of his shirt. Ryan was naked first, and he dropped to the bed, watching John with an expression of heated impatience. So John drew his undressing out slowly.

He was playing with the waistband of his briefs when Ryan reached over, hauled him close, and stripped the shorts off his ass in one smooth move. "You're a tease, Barrett," he growled.

"A tease is someone who won't put out," John protested, stepping out of the shorts and running his hands down Ryan's fine chest. "I plan to put out real soon."

Ryan bit John's stomach, nibbled his way over to his thigh, and sucked on one hip bone. He looked up. "How soon?"

John shivered at the feel of Ryan's mouth, the touch of his hand sliding down between John's thighs, deeper, as he spread his legs for that touch, a finger stroking around and behind his balls. They hadn't yet gone there, but he'd been thinking about it. A lot. "Let me run to the can, and then I'll show you."

When he came back out, Ryan was propped on his elbow in the same spot, waiting, his expression carefully blank. John bent to open the bedside drawer. After that first night, he'd invested in some good lube. He pulled it out. Then he reached back in and pulled out the unopened box of condoms.

Ryan froze. John looked steadily into Ry's green eyes as he sat down and set the box on the sheet beside them. *I don't know if I can do this.*

He'd rehearsed it, planned it, done his research. He'd tried it out in the shower several times, testing himself with a finger, then two, even three, thinking about Ryan touching him, stretching him. He'd gotten himself hot enough to melt steel, and then chickened out each time he thought about mentioning it to Ryan. Not tonight, though. He cleared his throat. "Ry. I want you inside me."

He could see the jolt of reaction in Ryan's body. But Ryan's voice was soft as he said, "You? Are you sure?"

"I think so." *Now that's passionate.* "I mean, if you like. If you want to."

Ryan reached out and ran a warm hand slowly over John's thigh. "I've done it a couple of times with women. When they asked."

"Did you like it?"

"Oh yeah."

His voice was hoarser. "Did they?"

"They seemed to. No complaints."

John nodded. "I'm asking." He stretched out, trying to look confident.

Ryan bent over and kissed him, soft and sweet. But John didn't want soft. He clamped a hand behind Ryan's head and opened his mouth. The kiss went from soft to desperate in five seconds. Ryan's tongue was *way* down his throat and John couldn't hold back little whimpering noises. Ryan's hand found his dick, and then stopped.

"Christ, don't stop."

Ryan pressed him down into the bed and rose over him. "Don't worry, man. You're gonna get fucked. But we're doing this my way. By the time we get there, you're not just going to be asking. You're gonna be begging for it."

125

John shuddered. Ryan closed one fist over his cock, stroking firmly, while the other hand slid lower, now lubed and wet. John spread his thighs apart, tilting his hips up. Ryan worked him, rolling his balls, pressing behind them, running a finger around his hole. Then one fingertip pressed in, slowly. It felt weird, but it didn't hurt. Prickly heat burned through John, arcing from his ass to his dick. He was leaking hard. Ryan slid his palm over the dripping slit and added the slick fluid to the slow hand job.

Two fingers in his ass now, and the stretchy burn hovered near pain. Then Ryan slid down lower on the bed, and took John's dick in his mouth. A white-hot arc of need made John's eyes cross.

"Holy crap, Ry. Don't! I don't want to come yet. Not yet."

Ryan hummed around him, as he pressed in deeper with his fingers, stretching John's tight opening. All John could focus on was the vibration of Ryan's tongue on his cock head, and the overwhelming need to thrust, or pull back, or do something. John knew he was gasping nonsense, but it was out of his control. He was out of control. He arched upward, wanting more pressure, more touch. Ryan pulled his fingers back out of him, and ripped open a condom. His other hand still slid rhythmically over the base of John's hard, aching length.

Then John watched, his breath coming short, as Ryan slid the thin latex down his own erection. "Roll over," Ryan told him.

John followed orders. Ryan tucked a pillow under his stomach as he turned. John's erect dick pressed into the fabric, and he fought not to hump it like a dog. Ryan's hands spread his cheeks open. The bedroom air was cool on his overheated, lube-wet, waiting crevice. He clenched, involuntarily, and tried to breathe evenly.

"Jesus, John," Ryan whispered. "That's so hot. You're so hot." He bent and kissed the base of John's spine, his hip, the top of his ass. Ryan's thumbs pressed him wider. "Ready?"

John was vibrating between need and fear. "Yeah, ready, please, I'm ready. Just… go slow?"

The touch of latex was just odd at first, then there was building pressure, then pain as his body fought against it. He struggled to relax. He could hear Ryan's rough, fast breaths. Then suddenly his body consented to be taken.

Ryan slipped inside with a groan, and stopped moving. "You okay?"

"Only if you don't fucking stop there," John grated through clenched teeth. Ryan felt huge and hard inside him. He slid a hand underneath himself, needy and shaking, to touch his softened dick. His first stroke made him shudder. His ass still hurt, but in an odd way that didn't stop the craving for more. He jacked himself hard, and the friction spiked into him, pain fuzzing into an itchy, building need.

Ryan pressed in an inch or two, slowly, and then drew back.

Jesus God, that was freaking amazing. He'd never thought that pain went with sex, but this mix of sensations was beyond anything, the edge sharpening the pleasure. "Do that again," he begged.

Slow slide of pressure, sharp drag outward. The sound he made had no words. He fisted himself urgently.

"Yeah, John," Ryan groaned. "Touch yourself."

John had to brace, as Ryan's hips moved harder, each drive a little deeper, each pull a little faster. Ryan's hand clamped onto John's right hip. Ryan's thighs lay heavy against his own. John gasped, again and again, as Ryan drove him up and up, pain swamped by the heat. The sounds from Ryan's mouth were ones he'd never heard before.

Then suddenly the last resistance of his body was gone. Ry sank deep, and brushed hard against John's prostate. John arched, convulsed, coming in waves that rolled through him, spurting into his cramped hand. He heard Ryan cry out, but could feel nothing more over the black velvet relief that darkened his vision.

A moment later, Ryan collapsed on John's back, breathing in rasping shudders. Ryan's thighs brushed his sweaty, chafed skin, and Ryan's chin dug into his shoulder. John couldn't have moved if the house was on fire. He lay boneless, feeling Ry's breath hot against his neck.

"Wow," Ry whispered. "I think I broke something."

"Not literally?"

"No." Ryan bit his shoulder lightly. "Moron."

"I don't think you're allowed to insult me while you're still inside me," John said, and shuddered. His body tensed hard, riding the aftershock, and then slumped again. His ass was beginning to feel too full, but it added welcome reality to this floaty newness. *Ryan is inside me. We did... that.*

Ryan pressed a kiss to his neck. "Should I move? 'Cause I'm not sure I can."

"Not yet." He could feel an ache beginning. He was going to be sore. But for now he was warm and content, and replete. He reached a hand back to press Ryan's ass down over his own. The weight was sweet. The ripples of scars under his fingers were just Ryan. His Ryan. *This is right.*

Ryan's mouth moved softly over his neck. "It never felt like that before. Either you have the hottest ass in creation, or it's just that much better when it's you."

Warmth spread though John. "I'm thirty-seven. You guess."

Ryan's teeth scraped his skin. "Hottest ass. Definitely."

Eventually Ryan reached down to hold the condom and pulled out slowly. John whimpered, trying not to show the pain as his body released the last inch of flesh. Yeah, that was going to smart for a while. He felt itchy and oddly loose and sticky. But so worth it. Ryan dropped the condom into the trash, and turned to him.

Ryan touched John's jaw, and up to his cheek, fingers tracing over his features, like a blind man learning his lover's face. "Tell me you're okay. Because I'm going to want to do that a lot."

John kissed a wandering fingertip. "I'm a little sore, but it's a good sore. It felt... so right. Give me a day or two."

"Let me know when." Ryan lay down and pulled John into a spoon. "Not that all the other things we do aren't awesome too. But... wow."

John chuckled. Maybe Ryan wasn't willing to tell the world about them. Yet. But John figured he was in no danger of losing the man any time soon. *Patience.*

Chapter Eleven

Ryan cursed softly, his voice echoing in the basement laundry room as he wrestled with wet fabric. But he was too content to put much heat into it. Even though John's washing machine was prehistoric and temperamental and deserved to be insulted.

He bent over and dug deeper. Ah, there was the problem. No matter how carefully you loaded the damned thing, it would end up unbalanced, with the clothes in a wad on one side. Then it would start banging like it wanted to take out the back of the house. If John was around, he would wander down eventually and fix it, but Ryan couldn't hear that noise without moving fast to make it stop. John had seen him charge downstairs once, and the next day both staircases in the house had a second railing installed on the other side.

Ryan dragged out the mess of wet fabric. This time, one of John's sweatshirts had somehow wrapped its arms around the comforter, pulling it into a big strangled ball. Long sleeves had knotted around thick quilted fabric. Ryan teased the knot apart, and smiled, because it was his fault they were washing the comforter. He'd been in too much of a hurry last night to pull it down before shoving John face down on the bed.

He shook out the sweatshirt, and wondered if those sleeves were stretched beyond redemption. Although, maybe John's arms really were that long. Sometimes that was the best part, afterward, when John would pull him in close and hug him up tight, and he'd feel that steady heartbeat against his back. And those strong arms wrapped around him.

A faint sound caught his attention, and he dropped the laundry back in. The noise came again. This time he identified the doorbell. With a sigh, he closed and restarted the washer, and climbed slowly upstairs. Whoever it was would just have to wait for him. He made his way to the door and pulled it open. The porch light wasn't on yet, but in the fading daylight he recognized the backpack, the guitar, and the boy.

"Marcus!" Ryan pulled the door wide. "What are you doing here? Come on in."

Mark ducked his head and stepped inside, his hands full. Ryan reached for the pack and hefted it, eyeing Mark more closely. The boy looked rumpled, and tired, and chilled.

"Where's your jacket?" Ryan asked. "You must be freezing."

Mark shrugged. "I was in California. A parka kind of stands out there."

Ryan opened his mouth and shut it again. *Let it go.* "Is Torey here too?" He peered out into the dusk.

"No. Just me."

"Well, come on in and have something hot to drink. Just dump your stuff." Ryan led the way to the kitchen and grabbed the kettle. "Coffee? Tea? Hot chocolate?"

"Coffee, I guess."

He got the bag of fresh grounds out of the freezer. "Did your dad know you were coming?" John hadn't said a word about it.

Mark's voice was low. "No."

Ryan blinked. "Does your mother know where you are?"

For a minute Mark stared out the big kitchen window. "Probably not."

"She must be going crazy!"

Mark shook his head. "I bet she hasn't even missed me yet."

Okay, not my place to get into the middle of this. Ryan wanted to push for more information. But it was John's job, not his. He poured water over the grounds, and got out milk and sugar. "You want some food with this— cookies maybe? We'll have dinner when your dad gets home." *And didn't that sound domestic.* But not a ripple passed over the boy's face. *He has his own problems.*

"No, thanks."

Ryan doctored the coffee heavily with milk and sugar without asking, and handed it over. The boy wrapped his fingers around the mug and stared into it. He had big hands, Ryan thought. Mark might still be on the short side, but Ryan bet there was a growth spurt coming. The boy's voice was deeper, more settled in its register, even after just a couple of months. *But he's still only fifteen.*

"Are you hurt, at all?"

Mark's eyes flew to his face. "Huh? No."

"Okay." Ryan poured himself a cup and sat too. "I'm going to call your dad." He hesitated a beat until Mark nodded. John's phone went straight to voice mail, which probably meant he was in his truck. "Hey, John, it's Ryan," he said, more formal than usual with the boy listening. "I hope this means you're on your way home. If not, I'd appreciate it if you would come as soon as you can. We have a… situation that needs you. Not a disaster, just… soon." He flipped the phone shut.

"You didn't tell him it was me."

"No point in getting him worried and driving too fast. You sure you don't want some cookies? Don't worry, neither of us baked them."

Mark's lip twitched. "I guess."

Ryan fetched down the Oreos and some chocolate chip ones, and tossed the bags on the table. "You're family, you don't need them on a plate, right?"

Mark dug out a cookie and stuffed it in his mouth.

"Guess not." Ryan reseated himself and took a mouthful of his coffee, wondering what to say. *When in doubt, say nothing.* He slid a notebook closer and pretended to study. The boy ate another cookie, and finally began to sip his own drink. He looked a little less strung out.

Ryan paused at the thought, and eyed Mark covertly. But he decided no, the boy was just tired, maybe scared. No tremors, skin tone normalizing, midrange pupils, steady gaze. He breathed a small sigh of relief.

The sound of the front door made them both jump. John's voice called out, "Ry? You home?"

"In the kitchen with company," he called back, before John could say anything indiscreet.

John appeared in the doorway and did a visible double take. "Mark?" But an instant later he strode forward and pulled his son up into a hug. "It's good to see you. You've grown since the last time you were here." Only after a minute did he pause and set the boy back to look at him. "Why *are* you here?"

Mark squared his shoulders and looked his father in the face. "Can I stay with you?"

"Right now?" John asked slowly, "Or forever?"

Mark flushed and looked down.

"I think we need to talk," John said.

"I can go and study in my room," Ryan offered, although his curiosity would about kill him.

"You live here, so this'll involve you. Unless Mark needs you to go?"

Mark shrugged. "I guess he can stay."

John leaned against the counter and looked at his son. "So tell me."

The boy's eyes tracked left and right, as if looking for a way out, but eventually he said, "I can't live there anymore. With them. All we do is argue and fight. And then Mom cries, and *he* says it's all my fault. I can't ever measure up, and school is awful and… I want to stay here."

"You're always welcome here, son," John said. "I promise. But your mother has custody. You know that. If you want to change things, we need to talk to her. Did she know you were coming to see me?"

"No."

"You ran away without telling her? She'll be terrified!"

"No!" Mark gripped the edge of the table. "I told her I was spending the weekend with a friend. And then going to school straight from his house today. It's two hours earlier in California. She won't be looking for me yet, or not much."

"Right. I'm calling her now." John pulled out his cell and dialed with one eye on his son. "Cynthia. It's John. Do you know where Marcus is right now?" He waited. "Well, that's because he's here, in my house... Yeah, in Wisconsin... No, I don't know but I'm going to find out... No, I don't think that's a good idea right now." He winced and held the phone a little farther from his ear. Ryan could hear a woman's shrill voice but not the words. "Cynthia," John said firmly. "Listen. He's fine. I'm going to call you back when you've calmed down." He paused. "I assume you *do* know where Torey is?... Good. I'll call you." He shut the phone.

"Was she really mad?" Mark asked.

"She was worried." John sighed. "Okay, yeah, mostly mad. But she'd have been worried if you'd been gone much longer."

"She hadn't missed me, had she?"

"You can hardly complain when you set it up that way."

Mark shrugged. "I knew she wouldn't check up on me. They'd be too happy to have me out of the house for a while."

"How did you get here?"

"I used her credit card and bought a train ticket. The Zephyr, the Empire Builder. And then I hitched."

John winced. "You hitchhiked?"

"Yeah." Mark's gaze was defiant.

"Okay." John blew out a breath. "Mark, I will always come get you if you need me. *Always*. Anywhere. Don't freaking hitchhike."

"I didn't want to answer any questions on the phone."

"Uh-huh." John rubbed at his forehead. "So, when you say you argue, it's with Brandon?"

"And with Mom. He mostly wants to know why I'm such a screw-up. Then she gives me hell for not listening to him. And he yells at me for upsetting her, in her *delicate state*. And over and over."

133

"He considers you a screw-up?" John asked, obviously working to keep his voice mild.

Mark sighed. "I am. I can't do anything right. I hate school, and my grades suck. He says I could do better if I try, which is so not the actual truth. So he grounded me from band practice. And the band got another lead guitar. So I got mad, and basically stopped doing anything much. Then he got a call from the school. Which drove him absolutely bonkers, because you know, Loyola Prep. It's his old school. He thinks they walk on water or something. He was one of the A list, with the money, and the looks, and the football letter. He doesn't know what it's like when you're not one of those."

"You were on the baseball team."

"Yeah. And I liked it. But I'm not great. I went 0 for 12 my last four games, and we didn't get close to making the playoffs. So I'm a failure there too. He got mad, because he wanted to coach me and I said no. So obviously I have no interest in improving myself, or contributing to the team. I want to suck the rest of the team down to my level."

"Mark."

The boy's voice rushed on, pitched higher. "All Mom talks about these days is how we have to keep him happy, and he makes all this money for us, and I should try harder. And she's all wrapped up in the new baby coming. She's *knitting,* like, Mom, actually knitting! Half the time, she has this glazed look in her eyes, and she doesn't even hear what I'm saying."

"Hey, hey. Take a breath. I'm listening now." John frowned. "How's Torey doing?"

Mark shrugged, his tight shoulders dropping a little. "She's not happy, I guess. But she gets good grades, and she's a girl, so Brandon doesn't get on her case half as much. He doesn't have this agenda for her to measure up to. And she's kind of looking forward to the baby. A couple of times, she's talked about coming back here to live with you, but I don't think she was really serious. Brandon mostly ignores her."

John leaned forward. "Mark," he said carefully. "He doesn't hit you, does he?"

134

Mark shook his head slowly. "No... not really. He can be pretty scary when he gets mad, but mostly he just yells. He grabbed my arm a couple of times, when I tried to walk away from him, but he's never hit me." He looked up at his father, eyes wide. "I'm more scared that I might hit him. Because of the stuff he says. He knows all my sore spots, somehow."

"Mark—"

"He makes it seem like my fault that I'm short and slow and clumsy, and not as smart as Torey, and have bad skin, and everything. Like, if I just do what he tells me, think what he tells me, fucking eat what he tells me, then I'll somehow become a carbon copy of him and life will be wonderful. Only not quite as good as him, because after all I'm not a true Carlisle. But at least he could mold me so I'm not a fucking disappointment and a loser and a failure."

"Dammit," John grated, then visibly clenched his teeth together.

"You're not any of those things," Ryan put in, because he didn't think John could talk right now. "Well, okay, you're short, but from the size of your hands that's gonna change, without any special diet. And I've had conversations with you and Torey, and you don't need to worry. You have very different minds, but both of you can think rings around most people."

"He hates my music," Mark said, but his tone was less desperate.

Ryan blew a loud raspberry. "There. See? A guy like that, you *know* he has no taste, so why worry about anything else he says?"

John took a smack at Ryan's arm, but his expression was grateful. "Trying to have a serious conversation here, Ry."

"Well, I think we need some serious dinner." Ryan pulled himself to his feet. He figured the emotional level needed to ratchet down a little. "Mark, when did you eat last? Real food, I mean."

Mark looked startled, then uncertain. "I'm not sure."

"Then it's past time. If you're gonna hang out here, you can wash up and then get out some salad greens. I figured I'd make pasta. John, you have half of the campus under your fingernails. Go shower."

John blinked up at him.

"Shoo." Ryan flapped a hand at him. "You're not going to solve everything in the next five minutes, so get clean, we'll all get fed, and look at this again after dinner. Right, Mark?"

"Okay." The boy jumped up, went over to the fridge and began pulling out salad fixings. Ryan figured he was hiding his face in the open door and catching his breath. Which was fine, for now.

Reluctantly, John headed for the stairs. "I should call Cynthia back."

"After dinner?" Ryan suggested. "'Cause if you don't make it back down before the spaghetti is cooked, you'll have to eat yours cold. Go." He met John's eyes and gave the man his best supportive smile, since a hug would clearly be too much. How long would it be before he could safely give John anything more intimate than a smile? Ryan forced himself to turn away and get down the big stockpot.

"Mark," he said. "Before you start the salad, why don't you put the small table away and get out the big one again, and another chair. If it's going to be three of us here, we'll need the space."

****

That evening, John hesitated outside the door to Ryan's room. It was closed. Did that mean he should keep out? Was Ryan mad at him? From down the hall, Mark's fast, angry guitar licks echoed through his own closed door. John's head throbbed like a drum, and he just needed... he needed. He knocked lightly.

Ry pulled the door open. "Hey." His smile was gentle and friendly. Maybe he wasn't angry. He grabbed John's arm. "Get in here."

As soon as the door closed, Ryan pulled him close and kissed him. But it was more sweet than hot. Ryan's thumb brushed over his forehead, soothing him. "You look like hell."

"Headache," he admitted.

"Did you take something, or are you trying to be a martyr?"

"Took some. Hasn't kicked in yet."

136

"Come sit down." Ryan led him to the bed and pushed him onto it. John didn't have the will to resist, but he scooted back until he was sitting up against the headboard.

"Things didn't go well with Cynthia, huh?" Ryan sat beside him, their hips touching, and tipped his head back against the wall, eyes drooping shut.

It made talking easier, not having to meet anyone's eyes. "Not particularly." She had accused him of brainwashing their son, of bribing, of coddling, doing anything and everything to get Mark away from her. He'd snapped and accused her of allowing her new husband to psychologically abuse the boy. You might say it hadn't gone well.

"She'd have sicced the law on me for breaking the custody agreement, except that Mark told her flat out that if she forced him home, he'd just run again. And maybe not run to me."

Ryan laid a hand on John's thigh, rubbing gently with his thumb. "That's pretty scary."

"Yes."

"So he's staying with us?"

"For now." John hesitated, unsure where to start. "I guess I sympathize more now, with you not telling your brother about us," he offered tentatively.

"This isn't the same thing."

"No. But, Ry, I can't tell him. Not now."

"Of course not!" Ryan sounded surprised. "That's what I meant. This isn't just you not being ready to let someone know about us. He needs you to be his safe, familiar dad right now. I get that."

"You do?"

"Idiot. The last thing that kid needs tonight is to deal with finding out his dad is gay, or bi, or whatever the hell we are."

"I'm scared that if I try to explain, if he thinks I've been lying to him about important stuff and stops trusting me, he's going to take off. And God knows where he'd go."

"John." Ryan cupped his cheek and turned their faces together. His lips brushed John's softly. "I moved back into this room because he's a troubled fifteen-year-old boy, and I'm thirty and settled. I can wait while he gets his life together." He kissed John again, harder. "Not that I'll like it. But we're officially back to being roommates *without* benefits, until you think he's ready."

John pressed his forehead into Ryan's neck, inhaling his scent. "God, that bed's going to seem empty without you. And I do want to tell him. I want us to be out in the open, to everyone. But… it could be a while."

"If he stays, he'll surely be in school sometimes. Or at the movies. Or something."

"It's not the sex I'm thinking about," John said. "Or not only. It's all the little stuff, day to day. It was just starting to feel right, like natural. I don't want to give up kissing you over coffee in the morning. But I don't want him to see."

"Considering that half the time it ended with one of us on our knees in the kitchen," Ryan teased gently, "we'd better take a pass."

"I can't send him home."

"I don't want you to. John, I like the kid and he's your son. If he's that miserable at home, he should stay here with us, if there's any way to swing it. Hell, I always wanted kids. Anyway, it's not forever. In three years, he'll be off to college."

"I just want to get through the next three days."

"One day at a time." Ryan rubbed his thigh reassuringly. "Tonight he's here, he's safe, and warm and fed. Tomorrow, we'll go on from there."

John leaned his head back against the wall. "I'm just really glad that Cynthia *didn't* know he was gone until I called her. Can you imagine going through the last two days, *knowing* the kid was out there in the wind somewhere?"

"No what-ifs," Ryan said firmly. "We go on from here. What do you want to do with him tomorrow?"

"He can tag along to work with me," John decided. "Earn his keep with some shoveling."

"I've got a jacket in the closet he can borrow," Ryan offered.

John rolled his eyes Ry's way and raised an eyebrow.

"He came with just a backpack, no gloves, no coat."

"Shit, I didn't notice." What kind of father didn't notice that his kid had no winter coat in February? A sharp pain in his thigh made him yelp. Ryan had pinched him! "Hey, what was that for?"

"No wallowing. You're a good dad, and you didn't notice because he was indoors when you got home. Quit blaming yourself for mistakes you didn't make. There'll be enough real mistakes to go around."

"No doubt. I haven't been a full-time father since he was ten."

"Ten is nothing like fifteen. Maybe we just have to start from scratch."

"We?" John liked the sound of that. It didn't look so insurmountable if he could share the job.

"Sure. I'll help as much as he'll let me. Sometimes a kid talks better to someone who's not their real parent."

John thought about people who were not the real parents. Like stepfathers. He was worried about Torey. He'd insisted Cynthia let him talk to his daughter. She'd sounded subdued, but all right. But how could you tell from two thousand miles away? Anything could have been happening and he wouldn't know it.

"Do you think something happened he's not talking about?" Ryan asked, echoing his thoughts.

"How can I tell? If that bastard did do something to Mark, I'm going to—" Ryan silenced him with a hard kiss.

"We have to focus on taking care of Mark here first. Don't borrow trouble."

"Right." To distract himself, he looked around the room. Ryan's clothes had mostly still been in here, although they'd slowly been migrating piece by piece into his room. But he recognized the robe that had hung on his door yesterday, the novel from his nightstand. The bookcase was overflowing. "This room is really small."

Ryan laughed, and kissed him again, hot and dirty. "Now that's just pathetic, if you're feeling guilty because I have to stay in my tiny, dank, dingy little room all by myself."

"Are you insulting my house?"

Ryan's eyes held a wealth of heat. "Go back to your own master bedroom, big man, and go to sleep on your nice, big, soft bed, while I lie here cramped and uncomfortable."

"Only one reason you'll be uncomfortable." Against his will, John's eyes tracked downward, and yes, that did look uncomfortable.

Ryan shoved him over and smacked his ass firmly. "Git. Before we forget our resolution." He cocked an ear toward the music in the hallway. "I think that's the end of the song."

Right. It was really hard to walk away from Ryan when he had that glow in his eyes and the growl in his voice. But John went to the door and let himself out.

"Sleep well. Don't let... anything bite." Ryan's words held a quiver of laughter. John closed the door, and adjusted his pants. Two doors down the hall, Mark's guitar had fallen silent. His door was still shut, and when John gave the handle a surreptitious turn, it was locked.

He knocked lightly. "Hey, Mark?"

After a moment there was a begrudging, "Yeah?" from inside.

"You need anything?"

"No."

"Okay." He hesitated. *You're the dad here. Don't wimp out.* "House rules, son. No loud music after ten p.m. Ryan's up at six thirty. There's breakfast if you want some. We leave for the campus at seven thirty. Dress warmly tomorrow. You can come with me and earn your keep."

A hesitation and then, "Can't I just stay here? I'm pretty tired."

He probably was, but instinct said not to leave him alone to brood. "Get a good night's sleep then. If you don't want breakfast, you can get up just early enough to be dressed for seven thirty."

140

He held his breath, because really, what would he do if Mark said no? But eventually he heard some kind of affirmative grunt. At least he would assume it was affirmative. "Good. Sleep well, son," he said firmly.

His room was warm and quiet. The Tylenol was kicking in, and his throbbing head was down to a dull ache. He went over to the window and looked out.

The field behind the house was dark. The light from his window and from Ryan's reached the nearby ground, making the fresh snow glisten. Enough white stuff had fallen over the weekend to keep his two winter crewmen busy on campus for a couple days. He'd be able to give Mark a valid job to do. Physical work was always good, to take the mind off one's troubles.

And off other things too, which was why he'd be glad to be out there with them shoveling tomorrow. As his head eased, he became more aware of his body. His ass was a little sore. Ryan had been wild last night, dominating and impatient and passionate. John wasn't complaining. Being with Ryan was already way out beyond anything he had done with Cynthia. It was sex ramped up to eleven, when Cynthia had been more like a six. He just hadn't known the difference. He wondered suddenly if this was what she'd found with Brandon. If so, her leaving was easier to understand.

Looking back, he thought his love for her had been naive. A picture of the perfect life, more about the idea of her than who she really was. They'd married so young. He'd been obsessed with her from a distance all through school, and then paralyzed with delight when she finally noticed him, and let him have her. He'd never looked twice at anyone else. And then there was the baby. He'd loved her being pregnant. Loved the thought of a child of his growing inside her, adored the children when they were born. But he'd never been as easy and as close with Cynthia as he already was with Ryan.

Now she was carrying another man's child. He was surprised to realize that the only thing he felt was mild irritation. He'd been hurt, betrayed, but also crazy jealous, when she'd first told him about Brandon and asked for the divorce. But maybe that had been more because this intruder was getting the life John had built for himself— wife, children, house, and all— and less because the man would be sleeping with Cynthia.

Now if *Ryan* ever dated someone else... A rush of heat and pain swept over him. Well, he'd just better not. That man belonged in this big bed, and no one else's. The barest thought of Ryan naked in bed had him stiffening, and he slid a hand into his pocket, brushing himself lightly through the fabric. *Ryan's just down the hall. Kids sleep soundly.* But he knew he wouldn't do it, wouldn't take the chance of Mark hearing or seeing something. Not until he could make his son really understand.

He tried out phrases in his mind. *I'm in love with Ryan. I'm sleeping with another man, but it doesn't mean I didn't love your mother. I'm gay.* He hadn't said that out loud yet, but he was pretty sure it was true. Ryan might still be pussyfooting around the word, talking about having sex with him like it was a different thing. And hell, maybe it was for Ryan. He couldn't be certain how someone else felt. But he was gay.

Having another man's mouth on his, another man's dick in his hand or in his ass was just plain right. Loving another man satisfied him, at a level that loving a woman never quite had. Well, not any man, but Ryan, for sure. He was more turned on by Ry's male body than he could remember ever being, even in the days when he was young, horny, and stunned by the wonder of making love to Cynthia. It explained why he hadn't really looked at other women after the divorce, why his half-hearted dating attempts hadn't felt worth the effort. He was gay. He just didn't know how he was going to explain that to his fifteen-year-old son.

Chapter Twelve

Early the next morning, the cab of his pickup truck felt crowded with the three of them. Mark was squeezed into the middle seat, drowning in Ryan's old parka. Ryan, riding shotgun, looked tired. John wondered if Ry had slept as badly as he had.

"I've been thinking about buying a car," Ryan said, breaking miles of silence. "I was being all economical and ecological and other virtues, riding the bus. But I'm a lot less virtuous now that the temperature gets down near zero."

"You were never virtuous," John quipped, and then bit his tongue.

Ryan gave him a mock glare and then whined, "Maaark, your dad's picking on me."

Mark snorted. "How old are you guys anyway?"

"Old enough to know better, but not old enough to care," Ryan said.

John shifted in his seat. He was horny as hell, and everything Ryan said this morning seemed to have a double meaning. Moving around the kitchen in the pre-dawn dimness, it had been hard to avoid brushing up against Ryan accidentally-on-purpose. Hard to remember not to look where he wanted to, touch what he wanted. Mark's stumbling entrance had them jumping apart guiltily, even though they was already two feet of space between them. Going back to being platonic was going to be a hell of a challenge.

Ryan had fed the boy, joking with him lightly. Gradually Mark's monosyllabic grunts had expanded to actual sentences. John had watched, feeling a little jealous of both of them.

"Speak for yourself," John said. "I'm a mature, responsible adult."

"So, Mark," Ryan asked. "If I go car shopping next weekend, do you want to come with me?"

"I guess." There was reluctant interest in the boy's tone. "What kind of car do you want to get?"

"Well it has to be used, because I'm broke. What I really *want* is a Corvette. But since I'm buying it to drive in Wisconsin in the winter, I'll have to be more practical than that."

"You're, like, old," Mark said. "Why don't you have a car already?"

"I did," Ryan said easily. "A classic Mustang, actually. Which is part of the reason I'm now broke, 'cause maintenance was expensive. But the 'Stang was a stick shift, and I couldn't drive a clutch after I got hurt, so I sold her."

"Oh. Right." Mark looked down.

"So I need an automatic, but there's no reason it can't be a fun car. Maybe a Miata."

"In Wisconsin. In winter. In a household with three people," John said.

Ryan grinned. "Mark wouldn't mind riding in the trunk, would you, kid?"

Mark turned to John. "You know you're renting a room to a crazy person, right?"

John hid a smile. Mark and Ryan had hit it off well at Christmas, and Ryan seemed to have the right touch to get them back in that easy relationship again. "His money's as green as anyone's."

They turned onto campus, and John pulled over in front of Brennan Hall to let Ryan out. Ryan wrestled his backpack out from behind the seats and hefted his cane.

"Watch the ice, guy," John told him lightly.

"See you tonight."

John lingered long enough to see Ryan find his footing up the front steps, and then pulled around to the staff parking lot. His office was in the basement of Croft. He found Juan and Kwame waiting for him, and introduced Mark to the guys.

Juan was tall, bulky and quiet, with pale gray eyes in his tanned face. At near fifty, he had been around the campus a long time and knew it well. At first, John had tried to consult with him on decisions, soliciting his opinion. But he'd had found that what Juan wanted was to be given a task and left in peace to do it. He would eventually answer a direct question but in the fewest possible words. Detective Carstairs had probably not enjoyed her interviews with him.

Kwame was short and stocky, with mahogany-dark skin and sad, world-weary eyes. He was a whiz with things mechanical, but he was squinting today, which usually meant he was hung over. And while he never shirked his work, he did noisy jobs slowly on his bad days. John assigned him to apply ice-melt on all the building stairs, and told Juan to drive the temperamental sidewalk plow for a change.

John had the feeling Kwame drank to forget, not to party, and he could sympathize. He'd been there himself often enough in the year following the divorce. As long as Kwame never came to work still drunk, or ditched the job, John could make it a little easier on him.

John got shovels out for himself and Mark, and led the way to the rose garden. This spot was one of his favorites. A series of paths wound through flowering bushes and climbing arbors. This part of Wisconsin was really borderline cold for growing roses, and John had to use all his skill to keep them healthy. The last thing he wanted was to have the motorized plow dumping packed ice on them. But that meant doing the job by hand.

He got Mark started at one end, showing him where the path went, and where he wanted the excess snow. Then he started at the other end. He could watch Mark while he worked. The kid was going at it with a will. He was trying to follow directions and use his knees not his back while shoveling. John could see when he forgot and started bending, and then remembered and tried to squat and lift. He was working hard.

That was part of what bothered him most about Mark's complaints last night— Mark admitting that he'd stopped working at school, stopped trying. Because Mark was the kid who'd never needed to be pushed.

Torey was a different story. Things came so easy for her, she often didn't see why she should make any big effort. It took a firecracker to pry her away from her books or the TV to do her chores. Mark was the one who would remember to clear the dishes or take out the trash, and do it without being asked. Mark had been known to do his homework days before it was due. If he'd quit trying, then something important was broken.

John thought about his conversation with Cynthia. She'd ridiculed his concerns about Mark. She insisted that Mark was jealous of the coming baby, that he didn't want to work hard enough to meet the standards of a rigorous school. That he just needed more discipline. John heard Brandon's influence in everything she said. As if she'd given up control of Mark to her husband. He ground his teeth, and pitched snow off the path with a will.

Before he realized it, he was bumping his shovel into Mark's. He looked up. The kid had managed to do close to half of the work. It was pretty impressive. *My son does not need more discipline to be made to work.*

Mark looked up into his face. "Are you really mad at me, Dad?"

"Huh?" John realized he was scowling. "No, son. I'm mad at..." At the last moment he substituted "Brandon" for "your mother". He forced himself to relax. "I gave that guy the two most precious things in my life to take care of— you and your sister. And he messed it up. So I'm pretty angry with him."

"It wasn't *all* his fault," Mark admitted.

"No," John agreed. "You own a piece of this mess, and your mother does. I'm at fault too. You were here for a week, and I didn't notice you were that unhappy, and you didn't feel able to tell me. That's on me." He felt a twinge of guilt. *If I hadn't been so obsessed with Ryan at the time, would I have paid more attention to Mark?* He shrugged for Mark's benefit. "But I'm kinda fond of you and me. And I even still care about your mother. So it's easier to be mad at Brandon Carlisle."

Mark cracked a small smile.

"Come on," John said. "Warm-up break." He led the way into the utility room of Robinson Hall, and pulled off his gloves. He'd been sweating with exertion, but his fingers were chilled. He blew on them. Beside him, Mark unzipped his jacket and pulled off his borrowed gloves. John spotted a red mark and caught his son's hand for a closer look.

"That's a pretty big blister you've got there," he said. "You should've told me."

Mark inspected it with a shrug. "I didn't even feel it till now."

"Still, enough shoveling for you." John rummaged in his pocket. "Here's a twenty."

"Dad, you don't have to."

"Don't turn down free money," John quipped, and then hesitated. *Is that the right message to give a kid?* "If it really is free. I mean, usually if someone's offering what looks like free money, there's a catch in it somewhere and… you're laughing at me."

"Dad, you don't have to be Yoda, font of all wisdom. Give me the money."

"Go get yourself a snack," John told him. "You know where the student center is. Then go to the library. And you know what you *can* do for me? Make a list. All the things you liked about living in California, and all the things you don't. Then what you're hoping will change by moving here. Tonight we have to have a serious conversation with your mother, and it'll help to have ideas written down."

"I can try."

"You have your cell phone?"

"Yes."

"I'll text if I need you. Set it to silent in the library."

Mark sighed. "Yes, Father."

John took a swipe at his kid's head. "Go away now."

Mark's grin was almost his old familiar one.

By lunchtime, John had made a good start on the secondary cleanup, the less used doors and steps, and the rougher paths where the plow couldn't go. The college had a separate plow service for the roads and parking, so he didn't have to worry about those. Except when the service pushed snow from the lots up onto his newly cleared sidewalks. *Damn.* He paused to re-shovel an obscured path.

He met with his crew, gave them directions for the afternoon, and sent them on break. When his office was clear, he glanced at his watch. 11:55. Ryan would be done with Histology lab. John really needed a hit of Ryan's presence in his life. He took out his phone.

"Hey, you." Ryan's voice was warm.

"Hey. Done squinting through microscopes?"

"Absolutely. I'm going cross-eyed here."

"Up for some lunch?"

"With Mark or without him?"

147

"Um." It took a second for that to compute. Then John felt embarrassed. *What kind of dad forgets about his kid?* "I don't know. I'll call him in a minute. I sent him indoors to keep warm."

"How about at The Gong?" Ryan said. "Mark might like the music. Unless, I forget, is it karaoke day?"

"Nope. Acoustic Tuesdays."

"So I'll see you there?"

"You want to come to my office first?" John asked, not sure if he was really serious. "I could lock the door."

"I have a one-o'clock class."

"I can work fast."

John loved Ryan's laugh. "With our luck someone would knock at just the wrong moment. I'll see you at The Gong."

John tried Mark's phone but it went to voice mail. *Probably still in the library.* He texted the lunch invitation. For a selfish moment, he hoped the kid wouldn't spot it. He wanted to sit and talk with Ryan without Mark as an audience. Even in a room full of other people.

The Gong was in the basement of the student center. It was student-run, through a co-op, and served an eclectic mix of food. It also served music. There was a small stage tucked in one corner. Students could line up to perform for ten-minute sets. Beside the stage was a gong, though, and if you weren't popular, your set might last a lot less than ten minutes. The audience never knew what they would hear, but some of the kids were very talented.

John went down the wide staircase to the lower level, and looked around. Ryan was just coming out of the elevator, and his face lit up as he caught sight of John. John let himself just watch Ry walk over to him. That crooked limp was just part of Ryan now, and the slow, deliberate, rolling steps he used to mask it brought other encounters to mind. *Damn, that's one good-looking guy.*

Ryan stopped in front of him, cast a quick glanced down John, and then back up. "Hungry?"

"Damn you."

Ryan laughed. "Come on, let's find a table. Is Mark coming?"

"I don't know. I sent him a text."

The Gong was crowded at this hour, most of the tables full. John was scanning for an open one when Ryan said, "Hey, that's Mark."

John looked up. Ryan was staring at the stage. Three students were playing— a tall blond kid on flute, a shorter, stockier guy using a tub as an improvised drum, and sure enough, Mark on guitar.

"He didn't bring his guitar this morning," John said, puzzled.

"That's not his, unless you've been spending a mint on him. Sounds good in his hands, though."

They made their way over near the stage and listened. The music was vaguely familiar. The boy on flute got a clear, soaring sound from his instrument that formed a unique counterpoint to Mark's playing. The drummer had little range with his instrument, but did a lot with it. They played un-gonged through a full set, and got loud applause as they finished. John and Ryan edged closer, as the boys left the stage, making room for a pair of violinists waiting behind them.

Mark carefully handed the guitar to the drummer "That was amazing," John heard him say, his tone brighter than it had been since he arrived. "God, I've never played anything that sounded like that."

"And never will again, until your dad hits the lottery." Ryan spoke up from behind him. "Hey, Mark, you guys were hot up there."

Mark turned in surprise. "Ryan, Dad. What are you doing here?"

"I thought we were getting lunch," John said, "But apparently we were listening to you play first. Do you know these guys?"

"We just met," the guy holding the guitar said. "Mark saw my Martin—" He stroked a curve of the instrument. "—and he was really into it, so I let him try a few notes while we were waiting, and hot damn, he was doing too good to stop. I'm Calvin, and this is Patrick."

Mark turned to Calvin. "Thanks a bunch for letting me play with you. It was sweet."

"You're good," Calvin said. "Better than good. In fact, I was wondering if you're getting tired of whatever band you're in, because we're looking for a lead guitar, and you're better than any of the guys who've auditioned so far."

"Really?" Mark's face lit up.

"Yeah," Patrick put in, "although some of them were pretty bad, worse than Calvin." Calvin punched his arm, and he flashed a grin. "We're getting desperate."

Ryan gestured away from the stage. "How about we take this to a table, if you're serious. We're blocking the view."

"Sure," Calvin said. "I'm serious." He went over to a battered case leaning on the wall, and tenderly stowed the guitar away.

They found a table just being vacated and sat. Onstage, the violins were playing something spiky and dissonant. Calvin pulled out a card and passed it to Mark. "That's us. CrossCut. Although we're thinking about a new name, because the cross part makes some people think religion, or anti-religion and we're not. Patrick plays flute and recorder and harmonica and some sax, Gordon, who's in class right now, is our actual drummer, I'm mostly a bass but I've been playing lead since our front man quit."

"Have you played any actual shows?" Ryan asked.

"A few. We've been changing things up since Joe ditched us. He was the one who started the band and he picked the music, but the rest of us want to go a little edgier now, fewer standard covers, maybe write more of our own songs."

"I write, a little," Mark said. "I'm better with the music than the lyrics."

"We practice around four, most days," Calvin said. "Except Thursdays, because Patrick has philosophy." He made a barf-face at Patrick, and then turned to Mark. "If that fits your class schedule, it would be cool if you could come by this afternoon, and meet Gordon and jam with us, see how it goes."

"Um, I don't really have a schedule," Mark said. "I mean, I just moved here."

"And he's still in high school," John said, biting back the *"he's only fifteen"* because he figured it might make Mark want to kill him. "Although four in the afternoon might be workable, even when he starts school again."

"We use a practice room in Kline Hall," Calvin said. "Whichever one we can get. Whoever arrives first signs us in with the band name, so you can look at the sheet. You should really come by later." He glanced at his phone. "Shit. Calculus." He got up and tilted his head toward Mark. "See you later?"

"Yeah." Mark's face was bright. "Later."

Patrick nodded to them and followed Calvin out of the café.

Mark turned to his father. "Can you believe it? I was just hanging out, and his guitar was so sick. I asked if he would play a few notes, to hear the tone close up, and then he asked if I played, and then… wow. That was just cool." He hesitated. "Would you let me join the band, if they ask me? I mean, when they hear me audition they'll probably want someone older and better, but if they do?"

"I suppose so." John would've needed a hell of a reason to destroy his son's sudden enthusiasm, even though things rarely worked out that easily. "You know, I hope you get in but they might find someone else, or you might not like the music they play." *Or you might not get to stay here.* He was ready to fight for Mark, if he had to, but… "You shouldn't count on it."

"But you should go for the audition," Ryan put in. "You'll never know until you try."

"Right," Mark said. "That's what I think. I've got to try."

"Right now you've got to eat," John told him. "You can't audition on an empty stomach, especially after hours of hard labor."

Mark pressed a fist against his stomach. "I don't think I can eat. I'm so freaking nervous. What if they don't like me? What if they do like me and I can't measure up? What if I screw up the audition?"

John got to his feet. "You have four hours to work yourself up over it. I'm getting food. Ryan?"

"Bring me a sandwich? Roast beef on rye?"

"You're asking me to buy it, as well as carry it?" Carrying a tray in a crowded café was not one of Ryan's favorite activities, so he'd taken to hijacking space on John's tray. John was more than willing to carry Ry's lunch. He just liked giving the guy a hard time about it.

"Cheapskate." Ryan fumbled in his wallet, and passed over a few bills. "Keep the change. Tip for delivery."

"Out of three bucks. I'm overwhelmed. Mark? Anything for you?"

His son looked up at him, face anxious and pale. "What if I can't find Kline Hall and I miss the audition completely?"

John fought back a laugh. "I think you'll manage." He left his son to his quiet panicking, and headed over to the food.

****

The next Friday afternoon, Ryan eyed the flight of steps up to Kline Hall's glass doors with annoyance, actually considering going round to the side door ramp. It'd been a long week. At least the sun had melted the last ice off the ground today, and he wouldn't have to watch his footing.

Having lab at the very end of every week was someone's idea of sadistic scheduling. It meant three hours standing and bending, and only rare hope of using a lab stool. He felt it in every inch of his leg. On the plus side, he'd traded Kaitlyn for Greg as a lab partner this term, so the work no longer took four and a half hours. *Onward.* Shifting his cane to his other hand, he took a firm grip on the railing to climb the steps, one careful riser at a time. He'd learned his lesson about the choice between pride and flat on his ass.

Kline Hall was one of the newest buildings on campus. Named after an alum in the recording industry, it housed the music faculty and the arts. The lobby was all glass windows and white tile. It made Ryan think of a hospital. Without the smells. *And hey, hey, with John over there, which made it one of the nicest sights all day.* A week and a half since Mark had come to stay, and the sight of John still hit Ryan right in the gut. Maybe even more, now that he couldn't do anything about it.

"Hey, big guy," he said warmly. "I didn't figure you'd wait for me. Didn't you want to hear your kid practice?"

"Mark doesn't really want me around while he plays," John said. "You can come and back me up." They didn't touch, but Ryan felt the warmth of that slow smile. "Finally done taking corpses apart?"

"Just call me a zombie. *Want brains, braaains.*" Ryan shrugged. "One of the guys had to go puke when they demo'd how to open the skull to access the nervous system."

"Yeah, that would've been me, too." John led the way to the elevator. "Practice rooms are in the basement."

"So, you're going to be nice to the band kids, right?" Ryan said as they waited.

152

"I just want to meet these people. Is it overprotective to want to meet the twenty-year-old guys who're spending hours a week with my teenager?"

The elevator doors opened and they stepped in. "Of course not." Ryan took advantage of the small private space to kiss John's jaw. "You want to make sure they're not doing drugs or getting drunk or whatever you're imagining. Although for what it's worth, Mark talks about the music a lot more than about the guys. I think they really practice, not mess around. It's been a week and a half, and he's playing more obsessively than ever."

The doors dinged open just as John turned, and his return kiss had to be aborted. "Right," John said. "And it's reasonable for me to want their phone numbers and stuff, like to call them if Mark's out sick or something."

"That's your story. Stick to it."

The basement continued the white-tile, white-wall theme, but without the windows. A row of closed doors with numbers marked the practice rooms. *Like the mental ward of a hospital.* Ryan bit his tongue and tried to get his tired brain looking on the positive side.

There was a sign-up list posted on a bulletin board. John stepped over and checked it. "CrossCut, room eleven."

Eleven was the last room on the right. As they passed the doors, the faintest trickles of sound could be heard from other rooms— here a piano, there something in a brass instrument. It was hard to pick out the actual music though.

"Good soundproofing," Ryan commented. He knocked firmly on door eleven.

After a moment it was pulled open by an unfamiliar Asian guy six inches shorter than Ryan. "We have ten more minutes..." he began, but from behind him Mark said, "Dad?"

"Can we come in?" John asked.

"Um, sure." Mark took the other kid's place and pulled the door open. "Is there a problem?"

"No problem."

Ryan leaned against wall beside the door and let John explain himself.

153

"I just wanted to meet the guys in the band, get some contact info and such. You start school next week. I wanted to have a better idea how it's all going to work with homework and practice."

Ryan saw the pained look on Mark's face. *Doesn't like the guys reminded of the difference between them and him.* He spoke up, "And we wanted to hear you play. I'm just curious, so I butted in." He held out a hand to the unfamiliar guy. "You must be Gordon. I'm Ryan. I rent a room in Mark's house."

Gordon hesitated as if the gesture was unfamiliar, but then smiled wider and shook hands. "Oh yeah. Mark says you play guitar too. I'm the drummer."

John said, "I'm Mark's dad."

"Hey." He walked back to his drum kit, and eyed Ryan. "Do you really want to hear us? Because we should run through this new piece a couple of times before we lose the room, so we don't forget it. But it's pretty rough."

"Go for it," Ryan said. Beside him, John reached out, snagged a tall stool out of the corner and shoved it at him. Ryan perched his butt on it gratefully.

The guys turned back to their instruments, with a brief discussion about an acoustic bridge. Mark was clearly self-conscious, glancing their way. But when the others got set, he picked up an old electric guitar and took his place.

The song was… interesting. At first Ryan kind of squinted his ears, but as they went on, the eerie sound of the flute wound through the guitar line in closer harmony, like it was creeping up on true music. The short, brown-haired kid, Calvin, began to sing in a voice that combined true pitch with a breathy rasp. The words were plaintive. When they reached the end, Ryan was caught up in the sound.

"Wow," he said into the silence. "That sounds like it won't work, and then it does. You guys aren't just derivative off-the-shelf, are you?"

The tall guy, Patrick, flushed with obvious pleasure. "Thanks. Mark did a lot of the music for that. I mean, I had the tune and words but it was just flat and Mark, like, found the hook with the flute that pulls it together."

"Nice work," Ryan told them. "Not gonna bring you success as a dance band though."

"I think we'll pass on the dance-band thing," Calvin said. "One more time, guys?"

It was even better the second time. Mark's playing was more fluid, and the song grew on you with familiarity. Ryan glanced at John, whose eyes were glued to Mark's flying fingers. *Must be odd to see your kid grow up in front of you.*

Calvin nodded when they were done. "Nice work, Patrick. And Mark, you nailed it. Let's pack it in on a high note." Patrick blew a tweet at the top of the flute's range, and Ryan laughed.

The guys began stowing away their instruments.

"You don't have to lug that drum kit back and forth, do you?" Ryan asked Gordon.

"Nah." He pulled on a cover and patted the snare. "This isn't mine. A bunch of the rooms here have resident instruments, like the drums or a piano. Makes practice easier. And there are lockers for guitars and shit."

"When you get a gig somewhere," Ryan volunteered, "I'll play roadie, if you need the hands." *Gimpy roadie, but it's the thought that counts, right?* "And John has a truck."

Calvin looked over. "Hey, thanks. And thanks for saying when, not if."

"Gonna happen."

"Ryan," Calvin said. "Mark told us you play. Wanna show us?"

"Not tonight. I'm not in Mark's league, and anyway, I'd leave your guitar smelling like formaldehyde. I just got done with three hours of dissection. I'm wiped."

"You're a med student?" Patrick said. "Oh, hey, you're that med student with the cane."

Ryan kept his voice steady. "Didn't realize I stand out that much." *Dammit.*

"No. It's just, I knew Alice. You're the one who went up the tree after her." Patrick came over and held out a hand. "I always meant to say thanks."

Ryan took it briefly. "No offense but...I didn't save her."

"Yeah, but you tried." Patrick's blue eyes were steady. "Alice was good people. I don't know what the fuck happened with her, but you were the one who went out on a limb to try and save her."

Ryan relaxed. "Kind of literally."

"Yeah. And I figured, you know, she died anyway, so probably no one said thanks. I heard you were, like, forty feet up and almost fell trying to grab her."

"Something like that." Ryan could see Mark staring at him. "It was no big," he minimized. "I was a firefighter once and you don't forget the moves." Change the subject. "How did you know Alice? Did you know her roommate, Kristin?"

"I work in Dr. Crosby's lab, like Alice did," Patrick told him. "We hung out some. I didn't really know her roommate, though."

"Have you talked with Detective Carstairs yet?" John asked.

"Oh yeah." Patrick raised his tone sharply. "What drugs did you give Alice? Who was her supplier? Musicians all do drugs. You must know where she got them."

"He's definitely met Carstairs," Ryan told John. He turned to the others. "It wasn't personal. She does that to everyone, even implied John bought his house with drug money."

"It's so whacked, though," Patrick said. "Because Alice *didn't* do drugs. I mean, medicine, sure, but never recreationally. She was pre-med and serious about classes. She would barely drink a beer."

"She was high that day," Ryan said cautiously.

"I know. I talked to Laura and Mandy. They were there and they said the same thing. She was tripping. But I knew Alice. Maybe someone slipped her something."

"It wasn't the first time," John said. "I met her at the beginning of term, walking around with a candle, really out of it."

"I don't know," Patrick muttered irritably. "I mean sure, you can never tell. But Alice was almost anal about doing things right, recording results, no spills, no mess, no flexibility. It just doesn't sound like her. I almost wonder if her roommate was giving her stuff, trying to get her to loosen up, you know. And then maybe she felt guilty when Alice died, and she killed herself."

"Hard to kill yourself, and then bury yourself," John noted dryly.

"Yeah, that's true."

"Could she have been exposed to something in the lab?" Ryan speculated. "A spill or some chemical mix-up?"

"I don't think so," Patrick replied. "Like I said, she was pretty anal. And we're careful. We plate bacteria that are minor pathogens."

"Speak English, bro," Gordon said.

Patrick turned irritably. "We grow things that cause diseases, like strep or staph, but not bad disease, like Ebola or something. But we do gown and mask and glove for stuff. Absolutely no eating or drinking in the lab. It'd be hard to expose yourself to anything. And anyway, Dr. Crosby is working on developing an antibiotic. There's no psychoactive drugs around." He turned to Gordon. "That's recreational goodies, to you."

Gordon punched his shoulder. "Speak for yourself."

"Detective Carstairs was all over the lab," Patrick said. "At least as much as she could be without catching strep herself. She didn't find anything."

John sighed. "Two girls are dead. I hate not knowing why."

"Yeah," Gordon said cheerfully. "It sucks." Patrick's next punch was obviously harder, because the short drummer gave an aggravated wince and said, "What?"

"We should get out of here," Calvin put in. "The next guys will want to get their turn. Did you come here for something else, Mr. Barrett?"

"Just phone numbers, for contact," John said. Ryan was relieved that John seemed to have relaxed around the band.

"Let's go out in the lobby and we'll get those for you."

As they filed out, Mark whispered to Ryan, "Will you tell me what that shit was all about? 'Cause I'm betting Dad won't."

"Sure," Ryan said out of the corner of his mouth. *The brief and censored version.* "Catch me later."

Upstairs in the lobby, they stood around exchanging phone numbers and contacts, which involved passing their phones back and forth. John didn't object when Ryan, knowing how the little keyboard frustrated John's big fingers, took his out of his fumbling hands and did the honors. Mark stood waiting, empty-handed.

"Don't you have your guitar?" John asked.

"Mine's an acoustic," Mark said. "I don't bring it to practice. I borrow that electric from Calvin."

"Do you need your own electric?" John asked. "Because from what I heard down there, you guys are doing serious work. You should have the tools to do it right."

Mark's face lit up like a Christmas tree. "Seriously? You'd buy me one?"

"Of course. I don't have money for big luxuries, but your music is important. Tomorrow's Saturday. Maybe you can figure out where we should go shop for a good one."

"I could do that." Mark's tone was an effort at blasé, but his eyes shone. And Ryan had a feeling it wasn't just the promise of a new guitar.

"Nice work, Dad," he whispered to John, as they trailed behind Mark toward the parking lot. "Taking him seriously. You made his day."

"They sounded...good. Am I wrong?" John whispered back.

"Nope." Ryan gave a mock sigh. "You should practice weight lifting. Some of those amps are heavy, and I have a feeling we have a future in equipment transportation."

Chapter Thirteen

Ryan stirred the remnants of the oatmeal in his bowl and decided he was done with it. He'd woken to a cold, icy Saturday morning, after the storm that roared through last night. He'd thought a hot breakfast was warranted, especially for John.

Ryan had been roused in the early morning hours by the wind and sleet, and made his way downstairs. John was down there already on the phone to his crew, who lived closer to campus, directing them to start salting the walks. He'd have to go in as soon as it got light, to check up on the success of their work and make clean-up plans. At least they'd get time-and-a-half pay for the weekend. He'd flashed Ryan an apologetic look, while finishing his conversation.

They'd stood close, side by side in the dim kitchen, gazing out the window and listening to the wind. Ryan felt the magnetic pull of that warm body beside him. It would've been so good to press together, to lose the chill in the heat of flesh on flesh. He was so close to feeling John's touch, he'd shuddered when John stepped back as he turned to him.

"Yeah. Shit." John's voice had been soft. "I'm going upstairs to my room behind a locked door now. Damn. I have to leave before eight, but it's Saturday. You don't have to get back up."

A kiss would have taken only one step. "I'll see you at breakfast," Ryan had made himself say.

So, early rising and oatmeal. But he'd maybe overcooked it some. Thank goodness for brown sugar.

"I won't be able to take Mark guitar shopping this morning," John said, as he rinsed his own bowl in the sink. "Maybe you should just go with him."

"Nope." Ryan tasted the last bit of brown glop on the end of his spoon. Definitely overcooked, and no longer hot. "In the first place, I'm not taking

159

my new car out on the icy roads until the city crews have done their thing. In the second place, the guitar is important to Mark, and you should be there."

"I should be done on campus by two. As long as it doesn't start up with freezing rain again, maybe we can go out after."

"Be careful out there. I'll be thinking about you while I sit at home here with hot coffee and a good book."

"You'll feed Mark when he comes down? But not this oatmeal."

"Ungrateful bastard," Ryan mock-growled.

"Hey, I ate it." John relented. "It was okay. Just a little sticky. But nice and hot."

Ryan couldn't help the smile. He got up to clear his dishes.

The sound of Mark's guitar upstairs changed to a new piece. The boy had gotten up early too, and jumped right into practicing. "He's damned good," Ryan said. "I'm glad he's found someone to work with."

"I'm still not sure I like it that they're all so much older. I keep wondering what they want with a fifteen-year-old."

"That," Ryan told him, pointing up. "Age is irrelevant. It's the art that matters. If you can call it art when it's a rock band. Talent, anyway. Be happy for him."

"I guess." John picked up his bag. "You're sure you don't want to come in to campus?" He glanced up the stairs, and then put a hand on Ryan's arm and lowered his voice. "Since you don't have any classes, we could hang out all day. Find a secluded spot. Maybe neck in the truck."

"In twenty-degree weather," Ryan said, moving closer. "I don't think so."

"I miss being with you," John whispered softly. "Sometimes I miss it so much I can't breathe."

"I know." Ryan looked into those hazel eyes, dark with desire. "John, I do know. We just need patience. It's too soon."

John nodded. "I should be the one saying that. I'm the parent."

"We both want what's right for Mark." Ryan cocked his head, listening to the strings overhead, and then put his arms around John for a moment. "Maybe we'll send him to a movie some night."

"Soon," John breathed. He glanced upward too, and then bent and kissed Ryan. The kiss was short and hard, and then longer, mouths melding, tongues sliding over each other. He nipped at Ryan's lip and then kissed him again, softly. "See you tonight, Ry." He grabbed his bag and headed down the hallway.

Ryan heard the door close, the truck start and pull out of the drive. He sighed. *Twelve-second romantic interlude over.* Time to crack the histology book. He turned and froze. Mark stood on the stairs, staring at him from the shadows. Above them, the sound of the guitar played on.

For a long moment they just stared at each other. Then the boy whirled and ran up the stairs. *Shit, shit, shit!* Ryan hovered indecisively. By now, John was on his way to campus, his phone turned off for the slippery drive. Twenty minutes there, maybe thirty with the ice, a painful phone call, thirty minutes back with John worried and sliding around in the truck. *God, John will go crazy, getting back here.*

No. You broke it, you try and fix it. He followed the boy up the stairs.

Mark's door was locked. No surprise. Ryan knocked firmly. And then a second time, and a third. Finally Mark yelled, "Go away."

"Let me in," Ryan insisted. "I need to talk to you."

"I don't want to talk to *you*."

"Look, Mark," Ryan tried, "I can call your dad home from work to discuss this, but I'd rather tell you some things myself."

"I'd rather you go fuck yourself," Mark said through the door. "No, wait, I bet my dad's doing that for you, isn't he?"

"Let me in."

"Go to hell."

Ryan sighed. "I'm just going to sit out here until you open the door. If you don't come out until your dad gets home, then you can take it up with him. I just think that's going to be even harder."

"Fuck harder."

Despite the pounding of his heart, and his damp palms, Ryan almost smiled. "I don't think you meant to say that."

161

After a long moment, the door was yanked open so violently the handle hit the wall. "Okay," Mark snapped. "Come in and say your piece. You're going to tell me what? I'm mistaken? I didn't see what I thought I saw? There's an explanation for all this?"

Ryan went in, leaving the door ajar, and leaned on the wall. "If you thought you saw me kissing your father, then you're not mistaken."

Mark turned to his CD player and cranked the music up. "This is so freaking wrong!"

Ryan held still and let the kid rant.

"He's gay! My father is fucking gay! He lied to me, he lied to Mom. Hell, his whole life is a lie!"

"Slow down," Ryan said. "He may be gay but he's not a liar."

"No? Then what do you call pretending that you're renting a room?" He put on a falsetto voice. "Oh, Ryan's just my roommate." He dropped the tone. "What do you call marrying my mother and having kids with her, when he likes to… be with men?"

"I *was* renting a room," Ryan said, trying to speak clearly over the booming guitar. "When you were here at Christmas, we weren't anything but roommates yet."

Mark spun to click the stereo sound off, and the silence echoed. "And what about now?"

"Now we're… lovers." That sounded strange, but he couldn't think of a better way to say it. "We have been for about a month. Since after New Year's, but we've put it on hold since you got back here. We haven't been lying to you, exactly. We just didn't want you to have to deal with too many changes right away. I think, even if I'd been a woman your dad had just started dating, he might have kept it under wraps while you were getting settled in."

"How am I supposed to deal with this?" Mark demanded. "Am I just supposed to be okay with it? Pretend that I don't care that my dad is some kind of *fag*?"

"No. But it would be nice if you could calm down a little and listen to me. Who your father is… dating, it has nothing to do with you."

"Bullshit. I'm here, and you... And what he did to my mother? That has nothing to do with me either?"

"You have to ask John about your mother," Ryan said. He took a calming breath. "Actually, I think he's bi, not gay. When he talks about those early days with Cynthia, when you kids were small, there's this happiness in him, you know? I think he truly loved her."

The catch of Mark's breath underscored how important it was to get this right.

Ryan was far from a fan of Cynthia's, but John must have seen something special in her. "I think your father's one of those people who cares more about what's inside a person than the shape of the outside. He loved her then, and now he's with me. But he doesn't lie. He's with the person he's with, one hundred percent."

"What about all the other men he's been with?" Mark demanded.

"There weren't any."

"That he told you about," Mark sneered.

Ryan firmly quashed the little voice in his head that was wondering if the kid was right. He knew John better than that. "Mark. He didn't seriously date anyone after your mother, until me. And I dated a lot of women before him, but no men. This is something new for both of us."

"So you're experimenting."

"No. We're building a life." *And God, weren't the pearls of truth just coming out in this fucked-up conversation.* Because a life was what he was hoping for. However much he pretended this was something superficial, temporary, alien to his true nature, in his heart he wanted it to last.

"And you're graciously going to let me fit in a corner of that life? If I can stand to be around it?"

"We want you to be part of it. However we can make it work."

"This year sucks, you know?" Mark paced angrily. "I keep thinking it can't get worse, and then it does. Now I get to choose between Mr. Brandon You-can-never-quite-measure-up Carlisle, and a pair of fags. Maybe I should just drive off a cliff. Except I can't even fucking drive yet."

Ryan nodded. "It's hard when everything changes." He paused. "You have to look at it like a rebuilding year. Like when a team loses all its good players, and you have to start from scratch and make something new out of it. It does suck."

Mark snorted. "What the hell would you know about it?"

Ryan stared at him. "Jesus Christ, kid. Get your head out of your ass and look at me."

Mark turned.

"This has been my rebuilding year. A year ago I had it all. I was a firefighter. I had a job I liked, a dozen good buddies, the latest hot girl going out with me, everything. And then, a day later, I was in the hospital. Leg almost gone, job gone, girl gone because she wanted to date a fireman, not take care of a cripple, my buddies all awkward around me because they didn't like the reminder of how fast it could all cave in. My dad standing there looking like someone kicked him in the gut."

Mark looked a bit sheepish, but still mostly angry.

"So yeah, I understand hitting bottom. I wanted to quit. But I just couldn't. So I had the surgeries, did the drudgery to get back in shape. I took the MCATs flat on my stomach with a special administrator because…" *my ass was still raw from harvesting the skin grafts. TMI.* "Because I couldn't sit. Traveling to the interviews sucked. I got accepted into one medical school, came out here, met your dad, fell in love."

Mark stared at him, the flush of anger paling. Ryan nodded. "Yes, in love. Not lust, not like. I love your father more than anyone I've ever been with. And if that makes me gay, I guess I'm gay." His throat closed for a moment. He'd said the words out loud, and there was no taking them back.

This is about Mark. You do what it takes. "A hell of a lot of pain and changes, in my rebuilding year. But I wouldn't trade what I have now for anything, not even to get the leg and that old life back." *Jesus, another truth.* He put a hand out to steady himself, but kept his gaze on Mark.

"I don't *have* an old life to *want* back," Mark said bitterly.

"No?" Ryan hitched his hip on the dresser, trying to look calm. "You're not wishing you were a kid again, with Mom and Dad and Sis, and everything easy?"

"Yeah, that's not happening."

"No, it's not," Ryan agreed. "So now you have to decide what you want, that you can actually have."

"I can't have *shit*, apparently."

"You can go back to California with your mom, and stepdad and sister, and the baby that's coming. Your mom loves you. If you tell her you need to change things, find a different school, hopefully she'd listen."

"No way," Mark contradicted. "She listens to *him*. And he's stuck on Loyola Prep. He thinks it's the greatest, and it's all my fault I don't fit in."

"He wouldn't let you try somewhere else?"

"He says that's quitting. And quitters never win, and winners never quit. He has a quote for everything, so he never has to listen to me."

"How about this quote?" Ryan suggested. "'The definition of insanity is doing the same thing over and over, and expecting different results.'" He surprised a laugh out of Mark. "You've already tried that school for what, a year and a half?" Mark nodded. "Okay, so if it's not getting better yet, maybe it's not going to. Time to try something different."

"Tell him that. He likes talking about *my kids at Loyola*. Hah. Like it takes anything except money to get in there." Mark looked up, his eyes shiny. "He likes it more than he likes me. We're not really his kids, of course, me and Torey. So it's no surprise we can't meet his standards. Now the new baby, it'll have those good Carlisle genes."

"He said that?"

"He thinks it." Mark's expression was bleak.

"Or you could stay here."

Mark just looked at him.

"You're John's son. You're always welcome. We'd work like hell to persuade your mother. I'm thirty, and in love with a man. John's kids are the closest I'll probably ever come to having kids of my own." For a moment Ryan paused, blindsided by yet another truth. That one had hovered in the background, where he didn't have to look at it, in a mist of *there's always time later*. Except if he was committed to John, later would be... different.

Mark was still watching him with shuttered eyes. *Where was I? Oh, yeah, convincing him he can stay.* "We'd really like to have you. You could try out the school here, like you planned. If that doesn't work, we can maybe consider home-school or online classes or something."

Mark looked skeptical. "But…?"

Ryan leaned forward. "But if you stay here, you'll be living with your gay dad and his boyfriend. No apologies. I won't give up your dad for you, and I sure as hell hope he wouldn't give me up either." He kept his tone confident, despite the inner voice saying, *John moved three times, and gave up a job for his kids. What if he has to choose?* "At least, he won't walk away from me just because you don't like the gay."

The expression on Mark's face became flatter, harder to read.

Was that too strong? He already has a step-dad he hates, taking his place with his mom. "You know your dad loves you, no matter what. That'll never change. But he loves me too. You don't have to like me. You certainly don't have to let me be a second father to you. But you'd have to be civil, you'd have to accept that I may hug your dad or even kiss him in front of you."

Mark was gnawing at the corner of his lip. Holding back more slurs? Just overwhelmed? *What else needs to be said?* "Unfortunately, it sucks but I can't promise, if we come out down the road, that there won't be insults, and intolerance of us as a couple. And of you, as John's kid, from narrow-minded people out there. You might hear some of it. It probably comes with the deal."

"People will think I'm some kind of faggot too."

Ryan let the language slide. He had the feeling it was deliberate provocation. "They may. There's no end to the ignorance. Most won't, but they might still give you a hard time for the supposed sins of your father. It won't always be easy."

"They'll think you and Dad do, like… pervert stuff. *He* says gays are all pedos. That's what people think."

"I hope not." Ryan paused, trying to decipher Mark's expression. "You're not worried, are you?"

"Of course not." But Mark wasn't looking at him.

"Mark, Jesus, your father's the same guy he always was. When you thought he was straight, you weren't worried he would molest girls, were you?"

166

"*No.*"

"Then he's no more likely to molest boys just because he's bi." *Lighten it up.* "As for me, well, I'm sorry, Mark. You're a cute kid and all, but, um, look at yourself and then look at your father. You need about ten years and a hell of a lot of gym time to come close to matching him. I'm not into kids."

"I *know* that! That's what *he'll* say, though. This is so fucked," Mark kicked the leg of his bed. "Why couldn't Dad fall for a girl, like a normal guy?"

Ryan managed a laugh. "I'm not getting a sex change, even for you."

Mark snorted, and when he looked up his expression was warmer. "You'd really be okay with me living here?"

"Sure. I like you. I enjoy listening to you play guitar. I can't wait to see what you're going to make of your life. And if you're here, and happier, then your dad's happier too. That means a whole lot to me."

"Yeah?" Mark tipped his head, hair falling into his eyes.

"Yeah. Enough to share the leftover pizza, and maybe even live with your dirty socks on the floor."

"I don't know." At least Mark's tone was more pensive, less bleak.

Ryan eased down off the dresser. Mark was a thinker. Now that he'd quit freaking out, it might be best to give him space to do that. "You can't decide now, anyway. Call your mom and talk to her. Maybe your stepdad is more flexible than you thought. Give it some time. You can change your mind later, but this'll determine your course for at least the next few months. No need to rush into things."

Mark nodded slowly. When he looked up, his voice was shy. "You really like my music?"

Ryan popped him lightly on the arm as he went past, putting as much conviction as possible in his tone. "Come on, Marcus. You don't need me to tell you you're damned good. Now you just need to decide what to do about it."

Mark shut the door firmly behind him, but there was no sound of the lock clicking over. The music of an acoustic guitar resumed. Ryan recognized

167

Mark's own touch this time, with the occasional error as he picked out a new piece. His playing sounded more pensive than angry.

Ryan made his way down to his own room and pulled out his phone. *God, John only left twenty minutes ago.* It felt like hours. He waited, pacing, until he was positive John would have arrived. Until he was certain the man wasn't still out driving on the ice. Then he speed-dialed.

"Hello?"

"Hey, babe," Ryan said softly. "You got a minute?"

"Sure."

"You sitting down?"

"Okay, why do I get the feeling I won't like what's coming?"

"Remember a little while ago, when you kissed me goodbye on your way to work?"

"Yeah?"

"Well that was a CD playing in Mark's room. He was standing on the steps watching us."

"Oh hell." There was a brief silence. "What did he say? Do you want me to come home? I should probably come home."

"No, I don't think so," Ryan told him. "I talked to him, calmed him down. I think it may be good for him to be alone for a bit, to get used to the idea."

"You think? Shouldn't I come back and face him?"

"I get the feeling he needs to wrap his mind around it before he's ready for that. But later, you will need to have a real conversation."

"What did you tell him?"

Ryan swallowed. *You said it to the boy, now say it to the man.* Why was this harder? "I told him that we were lovers, but only since January. I told him that this was something real, not just sex." He took one more breath. "I told him I love you."

There was a long pause. "Really?"

"John, I love you."

"God, I wish I was standing there when you said that." John's voice was rough. "Did you tell him I love you too?"

Ryan's heart felt tight. "I might've mentioned it." The moment echoed across the space between them. *Why is something so perfect also so fucking complicated?* "You'll have to talk to him about Cynthia. I told him a person can be bi, can love a woman and then a man, and not be lying either time. But he's upset about that part. So it would be good if you can figure out what you're going to say."

"It'd be even better if I had time to figure out the whole truth myself, about Cynthia. I did love her. Not like you, though."

Ryan hid the rush of his emotions with a dry drawl. "Well, if there ever was a moment for introspection, this is it. If you come home when you planned, you have about six hours to think. Use them wisely."

"Ryan."

"Yes?"

"Thank you. I'm so sorry you're the one that had to deal with this first, and thank you for talking to him."

"No, I think it was good it happened that way." Ryan thought about John catching the brunt of Mark's immediate anger, and winced. "He would have been a lot more emotional with you. And hey, on the bright side, now I can kiss you when you get home."

"I'll be thinking about that."

"Don't rupture anything."

John laughed. Ryan heard the rasp of something that wasn't humor.

"Listen," he said. "Call me when you're leaving work, okay?"

"Definitely."

"Be careful out there. Watch out for the ice."

"I love you." John hung up before he could answer.

Ryan sat listening to the dead air over his phone. So, that was that. Bridges burned. *I'm gay, I'm in love, and I've said it out loud. And his kid knows the truth.* Surely it would all be downhill from here.

Smooth and easy. Like fitting an angry teenager and a gay sex life in the same household. Like deciding what to do in a couple of years, after medical school was over and he had to find an internship. *Like telling your own father about John.* Okay, Ryan decided, there was still a lot of uphill in that downhill.

****

That evening, John let himself into Ryan's room. Ryan was stretched out on the bed, leaning on a pillow, making notes from a fat textbook. His black hair fell in his eyes. One muscular forearm supported the weighty volume on his knees. John stopped and just looked at him.

Ryan glanced up from the bed, and set aside his notebook. "How's he doing?"

John sighed and dropped onto the foot of the bed. "Okay, I think. He doesn't seem to be too homophobic, thank God. But he's confused at how I could change like this. He's still worried that I lied and tricked his mother somehow. And although he won't admit it, he's worried I care about you more than him. I could just feel him hovering on the edge of making me choose between you. He didn't say it, but maybe only because he was scared that I'd choose you."

"Like his mother seems to have chosen Carlisle."

"Yeah. God… no wonder he's so scared and pissed off."

Ryan scooted over to swing his legs off the edge of the bed, and slid an arm around him. The press of his hip and thigh were solid alongside John's. "And how are you, John?"

John leaned into him gratefully. "I'm okay. Scared. I don't want him going back to a house he hated enough to run away from. But I still don't know if he'll be willing to accept us and stay here."

"I don't think you're giving him enough credit. He just needs time."

"I hope so." John closed his eyes and inhaled the smell of Ryan's skin. "It's maybe a good thing I had to work so there wasn't time for guitar shopping today. We'll go out tomorrow, get that guitar. It'll give us something positive to talk about that's not… us."

Ryan's mouth brushed his hair. "Good thought."

"Jesus," John said, fighting not to turn and make that a real kiss. "I want you. I thought it would be easier, now that he knows, but I can just imagine him in there, waiting and listening, wondering what we're doing."

Ryan paused. "Shower?"

"Huh?"

"You always take a shower after work. A long shower. With lots of fan and falling-water type noises."

"And?"

"We could maybe take the edge off now." Ryan's mouth was warm across his temple. "Then tonight we can sleep in separate bedrooms again. So the kid can relax a bit."

John pictured it. Heat and water and naked Ryan. "Think you can sneak into my bathroom?"

"I think it could be arranged."

"Five minutes." John hauled himself up off the bed. He paused in the hall to knock on Mark's door.

"What?"

"Need anything? Because if not, I'm going to take my shower."

The return to loud chords could be taken as a no. John headed down to his room to undress. The bottom of his jeans were soaked to the knees. He hung them on the edge of the hamper, stripped off the rest, thought about what to pick out to wear afterward…

He looked down at himself. *Yeah, you're thinking about clothes, right.* He was stone hard and ready. *Five minutes to get ready.* He went into the bathroom and turned on the fan, leaving the door unlocked.

It was closer to ten minutes before the door handle turned. Typical. Ryan was all about anticipation. At least the times when he didn't just slam John down on the bed. *Oh yeah.*

Ryan came in, dressed but with his feet bare, and locked the door behind him. "Now I like this." His eyes swept over John's naked body. His voice was the hot sex-growl that John had missed.

John plastered himself against Ryan, pulling him close, rubbing his naked dick against rough denim. Ryan took his mouth roughly. Ryan's hands found his ass, digging in.

"God, God, God," John moaned against Ry's lips, around the probing tongue. It came out as wordless groans. He fought to keep it soft.

"Water," Ryan whispered, pulling back. "Turn it on."

John reached into the shower and started it, fumbling with the taps while watching Ryan undress. It was worth banging his knuckles, to see that body slowly revealed. Broad, hard chest, lightly furred with dark hair, fat brown nipples tightening in the cool air, round biceps, muscular forearms, flat stomach, and then, *Jesus, yes,* Ryan was going commando. Black jeans dropped to the floor, leaving him revealed. John swayed toward him.

Ryan's hand on John's chest held him at bay. "Get in the water."

John stepped in, letting the spray flow over his head and down his chest. He blinked water out of his eyes. Ryan eased carefully in facing him. "Kiss me."

This was what he needed, John thought, taking that one small step that brought them together. This man, and this moment. Ryan's mouth, his hands, his touch, even the commands that meant John didn't have to think, just feel. The kiss started slowly, as if they were rediscovering each other. But his lips knew where to go, his hands brushed beloved flesh. It didn't take long for them to be wound together, so tightly not even the water could get between them. Ryan kissed him, and kissed him.

Finally Ry slid a finger down his crack, rubbing between his cheeks, and broke the kiss. "Turn around. Brace yourself."

John turned willingly, and put a hand on the wall, and the other on the safety rail he'd installed, thinking maybe, one day. They'd never done this standing up before. He'd been unsure about how it'd work, and he thought Ryan didn't trust his leg enough to try. But John was more than willing now.

Ryan's soapy hands stroked all over him, rubbing, kneading, lathering him. Streams of white foam ran down his chest, around his erect dick and down the fronts of his thighs. Ryan pressed hard against his back, chest on his shoulders, but not touching his ass. John moaned. Ryan gripped the rail too, his arm brushing John's. Between them, his other hand stroked inward over John's ass cheek, probed against him, and then stopped. "No condoms."

"Do we need one?" John asked.

For a long moment Ryan was silent. He kissed John's ear, his tongue sliding over John's neck, his shoulder. Then he said, "No, I guess not. I've been tested recently. You've been… tested, then celibate. If you're sure."

"I want to feel it all," John whispered. His eyes were closed, and Ryan's chest and hand and thigh on his skin weren't enough. He craved more. "I want just you." It was Ryan's turn to groan.

Slowly, carefully, Ryan began stretching him, damp fingers dragging over his tight rim. John bent, and spread his legs, to ease the angle.

Ryan took his hand away, reached toward the corner, and came back with a handful of something slick. "This better? It's one of the creams for my scars." He eased what felt like two fingers inside, tentatively. "Is this okay? Maybe I should go get the lube."

It didn't sting. John arched as those slippery fingers found his prostate, rubbed over it, moved in and out, deeper, wider. "No… fine… great. G' choice." He couldn't work his tongue around proper words, but the last thing he wanted was to slow down now. There was a little pain, but it got lost in the deep building sensations. Ry's touch inside him shoved him higher, panting and breathless, and he pushed back, wanting more. He whined as those fingers pulled away, and glanced over his shoulder to see Ryan reach for the cream again and take another fingerful. Then the tube dropped unheeded at their feet as Ryan moved in close.

"Goddamn." John felt the hard-in-soft pressure of Ryan's cock head pressed against him. No latex. Skin on skin. "That's amazing." He pushed back and tried to relax, waiting.

Ryan lined up and pushed in with a whimper. There was no other word for that sound. Then he stopped, barely inside John, his hand brushing the stretch where they were joined. "So hot, babe, the way you take me bare. You should see how we look."

John tried to shove his ass back. "Less talk, more action."

Ryan reached for the rail, and his free hand clamped John's hip, holding him still. A slide deeper, a pull. Again. Again. Ryan was going really slow.

It wasn't all that different bare, John thought, at least from his side. Warmer, less slippery, although that might be the cream in place of lube. But it felt more intimate. The heat built nicely, prickly resistance giving way to aching, growing, needy fullness. And then Ryan pulled all the way out roughly, and cursed.

"What?" John pressed his palms on the wall, trying not to lose the mood.

"Damned leg. It's not going to hold for this. Dammit!" Ryan's voice was shaking. Pain or need?

John turned, and kissed him hard. "Get out. Lie on your back on the rug."

"It'll get wet." But Ryan carefully did as he was told, easing down and stretching his legs out.

"Who cares?"

John stepped out of the shower, leaving the water running in the background. He looked down at Ryan, laid out for him on the fuzzy blue mat. Wet skin, dark hair, nice chubby cock lengthening and hardening again as he watched. *This'll work.* He reached back into the shower and found the cream, then sank to his knees, straddling Ryan's thighs. Ry's eyes glowed green. "What are you planning?"

John looked down and smiled. Slowly, he squeezed a white glob out over Ryan's dick, watching it slip down toward his wet groin. Ryan shivered. "Cold."

"Let me warm you up." John ran his hands over the veiny shaft, stroking and squeezing. *Yeah, get hard for me.* He didn't stop until he had Ryan thrusting up into his slicked hands. Then he worked his way forward on his knees, just enough, and guided that firm cock head to his ass. For a moment he stopped, looking into Ryan's eyes. He'd never done it like this, on top. He let his weight come down slowly, watching Ry's pupils widen, as he took that naked length inside him.

His body spread, opened, ready and willing, even though this pressed inside in new ways. He shifted, fixing the angle, taking the burn. Suddenly Ryan's hands closed like iron on his hips, and held him still, half impaled. The muscles in Ryan's arms flexed as he took John's weight. Then abruptly, Ryan bucked his hips upward. John let his body slam down. Pain and pleasure rolled through him in a sweet, dark mix. His vision closed to blackness. He gasped for a breath left somewhere out of reach in the lighted world. Here in the dark, he was full and taken.

For a long moment they held still, bonded deep inside. John opened his eyes, managed to drag in that missing breath, and his vision cleared. Ryan's fingers slid around and dug into his ass. He clenched his hands tight around Ryan's forearms. Then they both eased their grips.

Slowly, almost gently, Ryan flexed and arched, moving inside John. John lifted and leaned forward on trembling thighs, to give him room. Ryan found a pace, slow and easy, heat and drag that was like nothing John had felt. He fumbled for the tube on the floor, squeezed it randomly, and reached between them, his fingers sliding over Ryan's curls and hot silky skin. *There.* More ointment on Ryan, more on himself, and no barrier between them. He stroked with his fingers where they connected, and moaned through his clenched teeth. He flexed his hips lower, and slipped down, feeling his ass stretch wide around Ry. *Oh yeah.* Then he had to move his hands and brace, as they began thrusting together, a driving rhythm that stole thought, stole breath, stole vision, and filled his world.

His climax was almost unwelcome, shaking his body out of that heat. Or so he thought, until it hit again, and he was coming in thick jets on Ryan's chest, Ryan's face, while blood roared in his ears and the relief of it flashed through him. Dimly, he heard Ryan grunting, coming. The new liquid heat in his ass was part of it all. When his arms gave way, he slid forward into the sanctuary of Ryan's hold.

Ryan's mouth moved silently against his temple.

"I love you," John whispered, below the threshold of true sound.

"Waterproof lube for in the shower, definitely," Ryan murmured.

John had to laugh, his body shaking until Ryan slipped free of his ass, and he twitched again, involuntarily.

Ryan held him close. "What, you maniac?"

"You," John sputtered. "Me. Us. Romance. Lube. Oh God."

Ryan kissed him. "I love you too, John Barrett. And not just for your ass."

John could have lain there forever, basking. But somewhere outside those closed doors, his kid might be wondering just how long his dad could shower. "Up," he told himself.

"We need another shower," Ryan said, wiping a glob of cum off his chest as they peeled apart.

John's laughter threatened to erupt again. "Fast one. It'll be cold."

"Yeah."

They stepped in together, sharing tepid water and handfuls of soap. John cleaned himself carefully, half wincing and half turned on by the sloppy wetness of his ass and the afterburn of using the cream. So worth it. He wouldn't change one minute of what he and Ry had done. But he *was* going to invest in more lube for the bathroom. The water had gone cold as they got out, and John shut it off. Ryan tossed him a towel, and grinned. "So, how long do you think that'll that hold us for?"

John looked at him, his chest so tight it hurt. "Half an hour?"

Ryan snapped him with his towel. "Go make dinner, you insatiable fool. It's your turn to cook. I'll follow discreetly."

Chapter Fourteen

A few days later, Ryan paused as he reached the top of the stairs, heading for his bed. It wasn't that late, only six o'clock, and Tuesdays weren't usually a bad day for him. They'd even had Monday off for Presidents' Day. But for some reason, he was totally beat.

He'd dragged himself home after the last class, planning to go into his own room and crash for an hour, but Mark's door was finally open. The kid had started his new school that morning, and gone to band practice too, but he clearly hadn't come home worn out. From inside Mark's room, the quick tones of noodling on the acoustic guitar carried down the hall. Together with the open door, it seemed like an invitation he shouldn't pass up.

Ryan stuck his head into the room. Mark looked up and nodded. "Hey."

"Back from practice? I didn't see your dad's truck."

"Dad had a thing to fix. He made me take the bus."

"Me too," Ryan sighed. "You can't get chauffeurs like you used to." He stepped into the room. "Can I sit?"

Mark waved toward the chair. "Sure."

Ryan sat and watched the boy's fingers dance across the strings. The tune became soft and plaintive. Ryan rubbed his thigh, digging his fingers in to loosen the tight muscles, and waited.

Mark looked up at him. "Does it hurt?"

"My leg?" Ryan shrugged. "Some. I lost a bunch of muscle, so I have to use what's left differently. It aches sometimes."

"Will it really not get any better?"

"Don't know. This is better, though. I had a brace for a while." *Six fucking months.* "Hated the hell out of that thing. Now I don't need it." The doctor had wanted him to keep using it, as protection. Fuck that.

Mark nodded.

177

Eventually, Ryan said, "School going to work out, you think?"

"Hard to say. First day. And I'm a freshman and a transfer. Lowest of the low."

"I remember." Ryan eyed him. "Can you do the class work? It would help your case for staying here with your dad, if you can bring your grades up."

Mark gave a short laugh. "No sweat. They looked at my grades from Loyola, and put me in basic everything. No honors, no AP. It should be easy."

"I guess that's good." Ryan leaned back in the chair and listened to the kid play.

After a while, without lifting his fingers from the strings, Mark asked, "Did you have, like, acne when you were a teenager?"

"Some. Not as bad as yours. If it's bugging you, maybe your dad could see about getting antibiotics for it. I hear there's more treatments now. Although I expect you'll grow out of it eventually."

"Not soon enough," Mark muttered. "I get so tired of being called zit-face."

"Already? First day?"

"I guess I was talking to this guy's girlfriend. But we were just talking. He told me to get lost. How was I to know she was taken?"

"No one gets taken," Ryan said, and then flashed on John, last night, underneath him. "In an ownership sense, anyway. He must be pretty damned insecure if he won't let her talk to a lowly freshman."

"I guess." Mark squinted at him. "I can handle him. It wasn't serious. This gay thing with you guys though. I don't need anything else getting the guys on my case at school. You're not going to, like, show up for teacher conferences with Dad or anything?"

"God, no. Why would I want to walk into a high school again if I don't have to? Don't worry. John put me down on your paperwork as an alternate local contact, because it makes sense. It doesn't make me an alternate parent. Most likely, no one at school will know your dad is gay, unless you tell them."

"Like that's gonna happen." Mark looked him over. "You're too young to be my parent anyway."

"Yeah," Ryan reflected. "I'd have had to be fourteen. I was probably a virgin then. No wait, maybe not." He grinned.

"Yuck! Jesus, TMI, dude."

"Hey, I'm talking girls here," Ryan told him. "Mary Jo Peterson. Red hair down to her butt, face like an angel, brain like cotton candy." He made a face. "Man, I had bad taste back then. But she was the hottest bod in the freshman class, and at fourteen I wasn't thinking much past that." He eyed Mark. "Did you leave a girl behind in California?"

"Nope." Mark picked out a dissonant chord. "Not enough money for the Loyola girls. They wanted guys with serious bank."

"Well, now you're in a band," Ryan pointed out. "Lead guitar is a hot ticket."

"I guess. Cal's the singer though. The guys won't even let me sing backup until my voice quits breaking."

Ryan laughed. "Won't be long. Is practice going to work out with your school schedule?"

"Yeah. I had plenty of time to get there today, even with staying late to get all the assignments written down. Band practice is good. Although Patrick broke up with his girlfriend. I guess she dumped him. He was pretty down." Mark shrugged. "On the plus side, he wrote this song called *Bitter* that's really cool. The melody needs a little work, but the lyrics are sharp."

"Nothing like suffering to improve one's art," Ryan quipped.

Downstairs, they heard the door open, and then John's voice drifted up the stairs. "Hey, where's my dinner?"

"In the Domino's Pizza oven where you left it," Ryan yelled back. "If you call for it and pay them, of course."

He heard John's footsteps on the stairs and then the man poked his head in the door. "Here you are." He smiled at each of them. "Hey, Mark, how was school?"

"Fine," Mark grunted.

Ryan stood slowly and then turned to John, an eye on Mark as he did so. "You go shower," he told John. "I'll call Domino's." He laid a palm on John's

179

cheek and kissed him, lightly and briefly. Mark didn't look up, but he didn't wince too badly. It was a start.

****

By Saturday, he was less certain. Mark was spending a lot of time locked in his room, appearing mainly for meals. Ryan wasn't sure if it was not wanting to see him and John together, or some other source of teenage angst. Direct questions got monosyllabic answers at best. School was okay. Practice was good. Homework was done. No, he didn't need anything. Ryan figured they had no choice but to let him stew.

John would have backed off on any contact with Ryan when the boy was in the room. Ryan, remembering past discussions, made a point of brief hugs and occasional dry kisses in front of Mark. Despite occasional exaggerated winces and mutters of "yuck" or "get a room", Ryan got the feeling that Mark was struggling as much or more with other issues. When the boy wasn't paying deliberate attention, their gestures of affection didn't even rate a glance. Mark's studied reactions seemed more a way to guilt trip his dad than genuine. Unfortunately the guilt thing was wearing on John.

Ryan was sitting at the breakfast table, struggling with the intricacies of adrenal gland hormones, two books and a chart open in front of him, when John came back in from taking out the trash and sat down across from him. Ryan looked up, and then slid his books to one side. "Problem?"

"No. I just… parenting is the most important job there is, and you have to fly by the seat of your pants."

I like the seat of your pants. Ryan kept the joke to himself, and searched for something supportive to say. "It's early days yet. And Mark doesn't seem actively unhappy. He showed me his math quiz. He got a B+."

"Really? He didn't tell me." John brightened but then frowned. "How come he talks to you more than to me?"

"I matter less?" Ryan speculated.

A clatter of teenage feet on the stairs heralded the wonder boy himself. Ryan and John watched as Mark went straight to the fridge, grabbed a coke, and then turned back to the stairs. But this time he hesitated, and came back toward them. He sat at the table, and cracked open the pop top.

"Coke. Breakfast of champions," Ryan quipped.

Mark winced instead of smiling. *Okay, then.*

"So, John," Ryan said, "do you want to do the grocery run or shall I?"

"Do you have the time? I thought you had an exam."

"Monday. It's Saturday. Not even a crack student like me can study for forty-eight hours straight. I have time."

"Thanks. I hate those freaking new carts," John said, faking ease. "I took out a display of Christmas window clings with the front end of the cart last time."

"Which tells me how long it's been since you did the shopping," Ryan said. "Mark, anything you want me to get?"

Mark shook his head, then stared down at his hands. "I have a question."

"Sure," Ryan offered.

"What should you do," Mark began slowly, "if you think someone you know is doing drugs?"

Ryan turned to John. *Definitely a real-parent question.* "That depends," John said. "It's different depending if it's pot or meth, and if it's a friend or just someone you know."

"Not pot, Dad, Jesus, I'm not that much of a ween. I'm not sure what drug it is, really. And his good friends don't seem to be worried."

"That's hard," John said. "If you like this guy and you can talk to him, maybe that's the first step. Find out what he's on, see if there's a chance he wants help. Or talk to his other friends, see why they aren't doing anything for him. But be careful. You don't want to get mixed up with that stuff. Is this someone I know?"

"Uh-uh. Just a guy at school. But I like him, and I don't want to see him go down."

"If it's meth, he needs help now. That stuff is nearly impossible to kick once you start. Otherwise… you have to decide if the teachers or his parents would be able to help."

"I can't tell anyone. He'd never speak to me again." Mark sighed. "I wish I knew what to do."

"Even adults have a hard time dealing with addiction issues. We get a whole semester class on it," Ryan offered. "Be there, talk to him, but don't get sucked in."

Mark nodded silently, but he didn't get up. He sat sipping his soda, gazing out the window. He seemed more at ease and Ryan felt his spirits rise.

"Hey, kid," he said. "Why don't you come along to the store? We can sneak in some more Oreos and Ho Ho's and stuff on your dad's dime."

John kicked him exaggeratedly, then hesitated as his phone rang. Ryan saw John's face go stiff, like a mask, as he glanced at the display and flipped it open, and guessed even before John said, "What is it, Cynthia?"

She'd taken to calling every day for a report on Mark, topped off with what seemed like a nasty and prolonged rant at John. Ryan wished John would just cut her off. But the man's innate courtesy or maybe lingering guilt apparently wouldn't let him do that.

"You are?" John's voice was wary. "Now?" He paused. "Okay. I guess I can't stop you. Yes, he's here." But he hung up the phone instead of passing it to Mark, as Ryan expected. John muttered something like a curse under his breath. "Your mother's at the airport," he told Mark. "She'll be here in an hour."

Mark leaped to his feet, his chair crashing to the floor. "I'm not going back with her. She can't make me. I'll just run away again."

John winced.

"Mark." Ryan nailed the kid with a look. "Pick up your chair and sit." He waited until Mark cautiously complied. "You're right," he told the boy firmly. "You're not going back with her if you don't want to. I promise. Neither your dad nor I will let that happen." He had to add, "Today," because a court order might change things. He turned to John and raised an eyebrow. *Your ball.*

"She's decided she wants to see you," John said. "She doesn't feel right making important choices about your future over the phone."

"She'll try to make me say I'll come home. I mean, back to LA. I don't want to see her."

"I'm sorry, son. She has a legal right. I can't just tell her to go away."

"Fuck that!"

John closed his hands on the edge of the table, the knuckles white, but spoke evenly. "If you really want to stay here, you need to be able to look your mother in the eye and say, 'I love you but I want to live with my father.' She needs to hear it from you and really know that it's your choice. Can you do that?"

Mark kicked at the cabinet with the toe of his sneaker. "Is *he* coming with her?"

"I didn't ask."

"I definitely don't want to see *him*."

"We'll be here with you," John said. "You don't have to do this alone. But if you're making adult choices, you're going to have to stand up to them."

Mark looked down at the floor, then nodded slowly.

"So," Ryan said, "we have an hour. Does anyone have an uncontrollable urge to clean the bathroom? Mark?"

"Do we have to?" Mark whined.

"Better cleaning than brooding. We'll get the Sunday cleanup done a day early. And I don't want Carlisle seeing this place in a mess if he shows up."

"I'll get the dishes and the kitchen," John volunteered.

"I guess I said the word bathroom." Ryan feigned dismay, but he actually wanted his hands too busy for brooding. "Mark, the vacuum is calling your name."

****

Ryan was scrubbing the sink when the doorbell rang. He scowled down at the porcelain, which didn't reflect his face because the enamel was forty freaking years old, and should have been replaced twenty of those years ago. The rust stains were *not* coming off.

He straightened and put his supplies away in the cabinet. Then he slowly made his way downstairs. John was at the front door. Mark appeared to be lurking in the kitchen. From the sound of the voices, Carlisle had come along with Cynthia. Then Ryan heard John say, "Torey! Hey, sweetheart, it's good to see you!"

Ryan sped up down the last steps, to see John sweep his daughter into a hug. Torey spotted Ryan as her father put her down, and ran up to him. "Ryan!" Her arms wrapped tightly around him too, and he hugged her back with a smile.

"Hey, princess, I like the hair."

"What about her hair?" John said.

Ryan grinned at her, "Highlights, right? He won't notice unless you dye it green."

A woman's voice said, "I don't think we've been introduced."

Ryan looked up to get his first glimpse of John's ex-wife. Of course, he'd seen the woman in photos around the house. But she looked more fragile, less self-assured, in person. Or maybe that was the effect of a long trip and the slight bulge of her stomach around the baby she carried.

"Ryan Ward," he said, not holding out his hand given the lack of space in the crowded entry hall. "You must be Cynthia. Come on in and sit down. Can I get you something? Water maybe, or hot tea?"

"Um." She eyed him.

"Yes," John said. "Everyone come in, this way, sit down." He led them into the living room and directed Cynthia toward the biggest chair. She eased down into it with what was probably an involuntary sigh.

The tall blond man whom Ryan was assuming was Carlisle sat on the arm of her chair. Possessive, or looking for the high ground? John perched uneasily on the edge of the couch. Ryan made his bid for status by sitting in the big recliner, low and at ease, knees apart. Position of confidence. The posturing would have been funny, if the kids weren't caught up in this.

Speaking of. "Hey, Mark," he called. "As long as you're in the kitchen, get your mother a bottled water, and then come on out here."

Mark appeared after a moment, water bottle in his hand and a mulish look on his face. Torey spotted him, and dropped quickly onto the open seat beside John. Mark perforce handed his mother the bottle and sat stiffly in the other wingback. There was a moment where they all just looked at each other.

Then Cynthia cleared her throat. "So, Marcus, how are you?"

"I'm fine."

"I...we, your father and I, wanted to talk to you." Her gesture indicated Carlisle, and Mark's brows drew in further.

"Stepfather."

"You need to listen to your mother," Carlisle snapped. "She's been very worried."

John shifted in his seat. "Um, guys, I think we all need to be calm about this. And I wonder if Torey shouldn't maybe go watch TV or something. This is really about Mark."

"No way," Torey said. "I want to come and live here with you too."

Ryan choked, but managed not to lose his calm posture.

Cynthia glared at John. "You see?" Her voice was shrill. "You took my son, and now you want to steal my daughter."

"No one's stealing anything. I didn't take Mark, you lost him. Anyway, getting mad isn't going to make things easier."

Carlisle turned to Torey. "You go upstairs, young lady. We'll talk to you later."

"No," John said. "If she's going to put herself in the middle of this, we might as well all be here together, let it all come out. But, Torey, we are going to talk about Mark first. Your turn will come later."

"Mark's always first," she muttered, but she subsided into the couch cushions, eyes wary.

"So," John said to Cynthia, "I assume you're here because you want to hear Mark's decision from him directly. So you can be sure that it's the right choice."

She shook her head hard. "It's not. He should be home, going to a good private school, living with his parents and his sister, not here at some dinky public school, living in a boarding house." She turned to glare at Ryan. "Speaking of which, why are you letting a stranger butt into our family business. You, tenant. Don't you have somewhere else to be?"

Ryan didn't shift position, but he raised an eyebrow at John. *Your call.*

John hesitated, then said, "He lives here. He's involved."

"I don't want him listening in," Cynthia said.

185

"He's no more a stranger than Brandon is."

"What are you talking about? Brandon's my husband."

John took a deep breath. Ryan kept his eyes on his man, trying to give him whatever he needed. *I can go, I can stay, you play it your way, babe.*

John said simply and clearly, "You brought Brandon into our family when you fell in love with him. I'm in love with Ryan."

"You what?"

"I love him. I live with him."

For once, Cynthia was silenced, her mouth opening and closing like a fish. Mark threw Ryan an odd smile. Ryan figured he was either enjoying seeing his mother flummoxed, or thinking this would take the heat off him and his decision. *Not likely. Think it through, boy.*

Sure enough, the first words out of Carlisle's mouth were, "Pack your stuff, Mark. You're leaving now!"

"No way!" Mark sat back solidly in his chair. "I like it here and I'm not going."

Cynthia found her voice. "You're not staying here with that... pervert." She pointed a trembling finger at Ryan.

"Now back off." John's voice became harder. "No name-calling. Ryan is my boyfriend, just like Brandon was yours."

"And did he know you had a teenage son?" Cynthia demanded. "Did he suggest bringing Mark out here? Having a young boy in this house with the two of you?"

"Watch it," John said. "Torey doesn't need to know how your mind works. Ryan and me getting together has nothing to do with Mark living here. Except that it's easier to care for a child in a household with two adults. Mark is my son. I would never do anything to hurt him."

"How do I know that?"

John's voice was rueful. "Come on. You've known me for twenty years, Cynthia. You didn't worry about Brandon with Torey, and you've only known him for four years."

"Six," Cynthia snapped with vicious satisfaction. Ryan could see the barb go home on John and did the math— a year and a half *before* the divorce.

Cynthia's hands suddenly gripped the arm of the chair and her husband's knee with white knuckles. Carlisle might've started rubbing her hand for comfort, but Ryan thought he was more likely trying to unclench her fingers from his flesh. "Oh God," she said in a painful gasp. "Oh God, you're gay! I was with you and you're gay! The baby... I have to get AIDS tested... if you... You could have brought home anything."

"Stop," John said harshly. "Listen to me, Cynthia. You're fine and the baby's fine, at least on my part. I was never with anyone but you, before Ryan. Not anyone."

"Like she should believe that," Carlisle sneered.

"She should. I've never lied to her. I wasn't with anyone else, didn't even think about anyone else, male or female, until after the divorce. Then I dated a few women, but didn't sleep with them. And then Ryan."

Cynthia was staring at John as if she wanted X-ray vision, but eventually she nodded. "Okay. Yeah, you always were the Boy Scout. But not telling me you were gay is still damned well lying."

"I wasn't gay, then. Or didn't know it." John glanced at Torey, who'd scrunched back into the couch beside him, her eyes wide. Ryan figured she was getting a little more adult conversation than she had bargained for, but maybe that was better than secrets. John turned to speak directly to Torey. "When I met your mother, first day of tenth grade, she was the prettiest thing I had ever seen. I fell in love, just like that. I spent the next two years chasing after her, until she let herself get caught. We had a wonderful senior year, and then after graduation we got married."

"Because I was pregnant," Cynthia said bitterly. She glanced at Torey and looked down, but went on in a low voice, "Would you have even looked at me after high school, if it wasn't for the baby?"

Still facing Torey, John said, "I planned to marry your mother all along. She's right, that I would have waited a while if it hadn't been for the baby, your older brother who died. We got married at eighteen, which is very young. But I didn't regret it. I still don't. I loved her. We had good years, and I wouldn't trade you and your brother for anything in this whole world. But your mother and I changed. What we had wasn't right anymore. Your mother met Brandon. And now I met Ryan."

"And he made you… gay?" Torey asked in a small voice.

"No, sweetheart," John said. "I kissed him first. I chased him and convinced him we should be together. Because we make each other happy."

"This is such bullshit," Carlisle said. "You're not fit to have Mark here. I know plenty of lawyers and judges. The law is on Cynthia's side."

Time to shift this back where it belongs. Ryan lifted his feet onto the coffee table with a resounding *thump, thump*, and let his gaze sweep around the room. "We need to take a step back from the gay issue here," he said firmly. Everyone stared at him. *Good.* "The important thing we're trying to decide is where Mark will be happy and safe, for the next few months anyway. He has a welcoming place here, he's started school and is doing well, he has a band he plays with."

"I grounded him from band until his grades improve," Carlisle snapped.

"Which shows you don't understand Mark very well. *However many* years you've known him," Ryan said. "Music isn't a luxury, like computer games, that you take away from him for punishment. Music is who Mark is."

"He's just a boy."

"He's a boy with a gift. He'll be doing some kind of music all his life, and he needs it. I've played guitar for fifteen years, and he's already better than I'll ever be." He nodded at Mark's grateful look. "The school here may not be up to the standards of the one he was in, but if he gets B's and A's, as he has this week, instead of D's, it's a better place for him. And if he's not being harassed here, it's a *much* better place for him."

"He'll never get into a good college from a school like York High."

"He won't get into a good college by flunking out of Loyola either," Ryan pointed out.

"In the end, it's up to Mark," John said. "He's fifteen. He's starting to make his own choices. Better living here with me than running away from you, Cynthia. Assuming this is still what he wants."

Mark blanched as everyone's eyes converged on him. He swallowed, but said clearly enough, "I want to live with Dad."

"And his *gay boyfriend?*" Carlisle demanded.

"And Ryan," Mark said steadily. "I like Ryan. He treats me like a real person. I want to stay."

"You'll get harassed worse for having fag parents than you ever did at Loyola," Carlisle said.

"Maybe, but I think I can handle it."

Carlisle's jaw tightened. "Well, I won't allow it. No kid of mine is living with perverts, like that's better than what I can give him. You're coming home and you'll damned well pass your classes and get into a college I can hold my head up to tell people about."

"This isn't about you," John growled.

"My home, my rules."

"Which is why Mark left. And why he's better off here."

Carlisle glanced at Cynthia. "Tell your son he's coming home with us."

Mark bounced up out of his seat. "No way. What are you going to do? Drag me through airport security by my hair? You only fucking want me back because this makes you look bad."

"Watch your language," Carlisle barked.

"Fuck you too."

"Mark." Ryan gave him a look. Escalation was not their friend right now.

"Mark isn't leaving with you unless he chooses to," John said. "He has a safe home here. His choice."

"She has legal custody. She can sue the hell out of you."

"To drag Mark back to a house he's run away from once? Who gains from that?"

Cynthia extended a hand toward Marcus. "Don't you want to come back with me, honey? I know we've had problems but it's your home."

"Not anymore."

"How can you say that?" she asked plaintively. "Don't you want to be with a real family?"

"This is a real family," Mark said stoutly. "Dad, Ryan and me. We do okay."

Good boy. Ryan gave the kid a firm nod, and saw him sit up a little straighter. "Why not let Mark stay with us through the school year," he suggested. "At the end of the year, see what his grades are like, how he's doing in the band, everything. See if he's found his place."

"I don't know," Cynthia reached behind herself, rubbing at her back. "I just… This is all so hard."

The woman is pregnant. And losing her son to her ex. Ryan softened his tone. "Cynthia, you look beat. Do you want to go lie down for a while? Nothing's going to change if you take an hour to rest. You need to think about the new baby, too."

She glanced at him, eyes narrowed as if she expected some kind of trick. But after a moment she nodded. "I think that might be good."

Ryan said, "Mark, why don't you take your mother upstairs to the spare room. I put fresh sheets on the bed. She can lie down for a bit." And if she snooped, there was nothing he was hiding anymore.

"What are you now?" Carlisle sneered. "John's wife?"

More like his husband. Ryan let it go. Who cared what the jerk thought of him?

"But," Torey said, as Mark got up to do as he was told. "What about me?"

Ouch. Ryan turned his attention to her. Trying to keep both Cynthia's kids was certain to have her turn this whole thing to scorched earth. *Please, let Tory be doing okay there.* "Did you get into that school play? The one you and Char were auditioning for?"

"Um, yeah."

"Good part?"

"Not bad. But Char got the lead, which is kind of unfair, 'cause she can't remember half her lines and I know both parts already."

"It's your first role," Ryan pointed out. "You need to ace it, knock their socks off. Then you'll be in a position to try for the lead again next time. There'll be a lot more plays before you graduate, if you're really interested in acting."

"I guess but... I want to live here."

"Walking out on your first part isn't the best way to make an impression," he said doubtfully. "I thought you were okay with school, getting A's and all. And it sounds like Char is a good friend?"

"She's okay."

"And think about this." Ryan took his feet off the table and leaned toward her, trying to lighten the mood. "You're going to be a teenager soon. Do you really want your dad and me to be your main source of information about clothes...boys...makeup...*tampons*?"

"Yuck. Ryan!" she protested.

"See? You don't even want me to say the word."

Ryan glanced at John, throwing him the ball. *Teamwork.* John cleared his throat and said, "Torey, you're welcome here any time. But we'd have to clear it with your mom—" Cynthia's indrawn breath was so clearly the beginning of a violent refusal that John rushed on. "And maybe your mom could use your help, with the baby coming and all, and you might enjoy that. And she can tell you a lot more about growing-up girl stuff than we can. Don't you want to be there when your baby brother or sister is born?"

"Maybe."

"Things will be, um, unsettled and kind of mixed up here, until Ryan and Mark and I get our lives figured out. If you can stand it, I'd like you to stay with your mom, at least till the end of the school year and the baby comes. Then we can do a giant review, see how everyone is doing, including you. Can you manage that?" Ryan wondered if Torey could hear the plea in John's tone. Ryan would bet John wanted nothing more than to scoop up both his kids and run off with them, but the law wouldn't be on his side.

"I guess," Torey said in a small voice. "But I miss you."

"I miss you too, baby girl. I promise, we'll make sure you get out here to visit more often. You can fly out for long weekends. The money isn't that big a deal."

Ryan teased, "If necessary, I'll sell blood to raise funds for your ticket."

"They won't take your blood, you know." Carlisle's voice was mocking. "You're gay."

"Well…" *Shit, out of the mouths of SOB's.* "Hey, John, we need to call off this relationship. It's going to cut into my secondary source of income."

Without hesitation, John winged a magazine at his head. Ryan ducked, grinning.

"We're getting silly here," John said with a mock glare at Ryan. "How about we give Cynthia time for that nap, and then talk again?"

"Right," Ryan seconded, with a wave at Mark to help his mother. "Come on, Torey. I'm in a mood for cookies, but the last time I baked, we ended up with chocolate-chip rocks. Maybe you can give me a hand." He stood up and headed toward the kitchen, trying not to limp with Carlisle watching. Torey followed him slowly.

As he dug out ingredients, his listened with one ear to the rise and fall of men's voices in the living room. John and Carlisle. He'd have to trust John's good sense to keep it civil.

"Did you really bake rocks?" Torey asked, pulling out the cookie trays from the cupboard.

"Not quite. They were a bit hard. You know, if you're going to be with your mom for a few more months, you should get her to teach you to really cook. Because we have three people in this house, and not one of us can do much more than boil water. Then if you decide you still want to move here later, you'll have a skill to bargain with." He inspected the recipe on the back of the chocolate-chip bag. Brown sugar. Did they even have brown sugar left? Could he substitute white? Was that what he did last time?

"I don't know what I want," Torey admitted softly. "It's so weird at home now. Mom gets sad and cries a lot. And Brandon doesn't think girls are good at anything."

"I'm sorry," Ryan said. "If it's any help, I think part of your Mom's crying is being pregnant, with the stress and hormones and all."

"Maybe."

"It's not… awful there, right?" He didn't want to hear it, but he had to ask. If worst came to worst, they'd take on the world for Torey, too. "Like, is anyone hurting you? You're not going to run off or… do anything drastic?"

"Like my butthead brother?" Torey sighed dramatically. "It just sucks."

"You feel safe, though?"

She gave him a guarded look. "Yeah. All Brandon does is yell a bit. Mostly at Mark."

"That should get better with Mark gone."

She shrugged, looking doubtful.

"You can call us, anytime. Me or your dad. Or Mark, although I'm guessing you don't want your brother's advice."

Torey shook her head.

"Honey, things may be hard right now. But you have lots of people who love you. You know that, right?"

She nodded, her eyes wet. Ryan pulled her into a hug. "Hey. It gets better. I heard that somewhere." Her arms tightened around him, and she sniffled into his shirt.

The front door banged. After a moment, John appeared in the kitchen doorway. "Brandon went for a walk to cool off."

"He's from California, isn't he?" Ryan said. "Cooling off won't take long in this weather." He freed an arm to reach out. "Come here, babe. Torey needs a hug." *And you look like you could use one too.* John's arms were big enough to gather them both in. Ryan rubbed the man's shoulder, and for a moment they all stood together, warm despite the cool kitchen.

****

John hunched his shoulders at the sound of Cynthia's footsteps on the stair, and glanced around the living room for escape. Funny how, even after four years, he recognized the determined rhythm that meant she was building up a head of steam. God, he hated fighting with her. It had always ended with icy-cold rejection, until she decided to forgive him. He remembered how hard he'd worked in the past for that forgiveness. He hadn't had a big fight with Ryan yet, but somehow he didn't think icy cold was going to be part of it when he did.

"John," Cynthia said to his back. "We need to talk."

"I know." He sighed and turned. "I sent Ryan out with the kids to a movie."

"You let him take Torey somewhere without asking me?"

193

John rubbed his face. "Yeah. I did. They were here a week at Christmas and he took them places then. I trust him with my kids. Hell, I trust him with my life."

"Well, I don't."

"And I don't trust Brandon," John pointed out. Even though he'd made damned sure Torey wasn't actually afraid of Brandon, that was miles from *trust*. "But we both have to live with it."

"Brandon wouldn't hurt the kids."

Neither would Ryan. John skipped the obvious and said, "Brandon pushed Mark and belittled him and made him feel like crap, until Mark was flunking school, and running away from home. There are a lot of ways to hurt a kid."

"You can't blame Mark's problems on Brandon."

"Maybe not but he didn't help any."

Cynthia frowned. "I didn't come in here to talk about Mark right now. That's not what this is about."

Unfortunately. Mark's future was the real important issue, but he knew she wasn't ready to go there yet. "What is this about then, Cynthia?" *Make her put it in words.*

"You and that… that… man."

"Ryan."

"How *could* you?" He couldn't tell if she was scolding him, or genuinely asking. "How could you want to be with him?"

"I love him." Plain, simple, and getting more certain every time he said it. Admitting the truth today might have made this whole mess more complicated, but it made his goals simpler. Himself, and Ryan, and Mark, and as much of Torey as he could get, and a life.

"You can't." Cynthia groped for the arm of the wingback and then sat heavily. "How can you be gay? We were together almost twenty years. I would have known."

"I didn't know myself. I never looked at anyone but you. And then you were gone, and I looked around, and there was Ryan, and we just fit. At first I thought we were only good friends, but then I realized it was more."

"And you… and he… sleep together?"

"Yes, we do."

She actually shuddered. "With Mark in the house? With *Torey*?"

"We're probably more discreet than you and Brandon are. You didn't get pregnant without sharing a bed with your lover."

"That's different!"

"Not by much."

"Of course it is. We're married. We're… normal."

Whereas we're not allowed to get married, at least not here in Wisconsin. "So you never slept with Brandon until you married him?"

She actually blushed. But then her spine straightened. "You can't compare us. And I don't want the kids staying in this house, if you're going to do disgusting things around them."

"Jesus, Cynthia. Grow up. The most I'm going to do in front of the kids is kiss the man. We don't—"

"You kiss him?"

"I love him. Of course I kiss him."

"I can't do this." Cynthia dropped her head in her hands. "I can't talk to you. I can't think about this. I can't imagine you and him."

"Well, don't, for Christ's sake. Do you think I like to imagine you and Brandon doing stuff?" He choked a laugh, as she looked up and glared at him, and shook his head helplessly. "We need to get back to talking about Mark, and what's right for him."

"He can't stay here. That's final."

"What are you going to do? Drag him back to California in handcuffs?"

"You have to tell him he can't stay."

"But I want him to stay!" John tried to lower his voice. This was hard for her, he understood that. "He's welcome here. He and Ryan get along well. He's aced his high school classes this first week."

Cynthia was just shaking her head over and over.

"Cyn, he's fifteen. He's starting to make his own decisions. And what I *really* don't want is him running off to busk on the street with his guitar somewhere, thinking he can make it on his own."

"That Ryan is encouraging him to play the guitar."

"He doesn't need encouragement. He's a musician. When was the last time you actually listened to him play? He's probably going to have a career in music. But if he stays with me, he just might finish school first, maybe even go to college. If Brandon tries to take his guitar away from him, we may never see him again."

Cynthia shrank into the chair. "Mark wouldn't do that. He's just a kid."

"He hitchhiked to get here."

"He what? You said he came on the train."

"And then hitchhiked. He's independent, he's angry, and he doesn't always make good decisions." John leaned toward her. "Cynthia, for his own good, you're going to have to let him stay here, at least for now."

"How long?" she demanded. "How long do you get to keep my son away from me?"

John bit his tongue hard to keep from saying, *maybe as long as you've kept my kids away from me.* "Until he's ready. Until he decides living with you is right again. Maybe until he's eighteen and goes to college. You'll get visits, I swear, even if I have to drag him out to LA myself. He'll come see his little brother or sister and visit you. But he'll live here, for as long as he wants to."

"To hell with that," Brandon said from the doorway. "That kid is not living here."

John looked up at the ceiling. *God give me strength.* He took hold of his temper by the skin of his teeth, and got ready to start the argument over again.

Chapter Fifteen

Ryan paused at the door of Mark's room Wednesday evening. The boy had been sullen and monosyllabic ever since his mother and stepfather's visit. Ryan had hoped that having Cynthia give in and head back to California without him would smooth things over, but Mark wasn't bouncing back.

Of course, Carlisle was still threatening to go to court to enforce the custody order. The man really hadn't thought it through, if he believed dragging a resentful teenager back to his house was going to make his life better. Ryan wasn't sure if Carlisle's refusal to let go was driven by homophobia, possessiveness, or a simple unwillingness to admit to a mistake. Whichever, the uncertainty was wearing on all of them.

He knocked, then pushed lightly on Mark's door. Mark was sitting on his bed with his guitar on his lap. He wasn't playing it, just staring off into space.

"Hey," Ryan said. "Your dad called to say they had a tree blow down in the quad. He has to get it cut up and hauled, so he'll be late. We could order pizza."

"Not hungry."

Ryan leaned in the doorway. "Anything I can do?"

"No." Mark looked up at him through brown hair getting rather long and shaggy. *Suggest a haircut? Sometime when he doesn't look like he wants to bite your nose off.* But Mark's expression was already shifting to uncertainty. "Ryan?"

"Yes?"

"Can I ask you something? I mean, if I ask you a question can we talk about it without you, like, telling Dad?"

"Probably," Ryan said cautiously. "Unless your safety is involved, in which case I can't promise."

"It's not that. It's…" He stopped, fingering the inlay on the guitar. His long finger traced the pale curves in the wood, round and round.

"Okay," Ryan said when the pause had stretched out long enough. "I promise." He went in and sat on the desk chair, and tapped the door shut with his foot. "Lay it on me."

Mark groaned. "No one says that anymore."

"Just being the father figure here."

Mark nodded instead of laughing. "It's one of the guys in the band. What I said before. About the... problem. Who to tell?"

Ryan rummaged around in his brain for the first part of this conversation, and then remembered a week earlier. "The guy doing the drugs?"

"Yeah."

"Mm. That's tough."

"I don't want to tell Dad who it is, because then he'll make me quit the band, and we're, like, awesome, most of the time."

Ryan wanted to say John wouldn't have a knee-jerk response to the news, but in the interests of keeping it real, he took a pass. John was definitely overprotective about Mark and the band. "So when you're not awesome? What do the other guys say?"

"See, that's the problem. They don't really see it. Because when we're playing, he's basically fine. A little spacey and absent-minded, but he plays okay. It's when it's just the two of us, writing songs, that he starts to... wander."

"So this is Patrick we're talking about?"

"I didn't say that!" Mark protested.

Ryan knew who wrote the songs for the band, but okay. "One of the guys. Have you talked to him about it?"

"Yeah," Mark said. "Like I said, 'hey, dude, that's some mellow weed you're on.' But he denies it. He says he's just tired lately."

"And you don't think that's true?"

"No way." Mark snorted. "He used to write these cool lyrics, you know. But more and more, they don't make sense. The words just ramble. And then in the middle of working, he'll wander off into some weird-ass conversation. Sometimes it's like he's not even talking to me. He's on something, and I don't think it's pot."

"He never offered anything to you?"

"Ryan, he won't even admit he's taking shit. So how would he be offering it to me?"

"Right. Sorry." Ryan gave it some thought. His mind wandered back to Alice, up a tree, wandering in mental space. "Does he seem... happy? Um, serene?"

"Kind of. Like, dissociated."

"Good word." Ryan nodded. "He said he knew that girl Alice, didn't he?"

"Girl? Oh. The one in the tree that you tried to save? The one who jumped from, like, forty feet, when you were about to grab her, and almost made you fall out?" Ryan had told Mark the short version. Obviously, someone had also given him the long version.

"The first time I met him, didn't Patrick say he worked with her?"

"Yeah, I think."

"I wonder," Ryan said slowly. "Patrick claimed Alice never did drugs. Now he says he's not doing drugs. Maybe there really is something in the lab, some contaminant or something. Maybe he's being drugged without knowing it."

"Like, on purpose?" Mark's eyes were wide.

"No." Ryan hesitated. "Well, maybe, but it's not likely. I'm thinking some kind of accidental exposure."

"So if it was accidental, then he could just stop going into the lab, and he'd be fine. Right?"

"I don't know." Ryan ran a hand through his hair. "This is all hypothetical. Maybe it's some recreational substance he and Alice use, and don't want to tell anyone about. But it's possible it's the lab. I wonder if we should tell Detective Carstairs to take another look."

"You can't!" Mark bounded to his feet, clutching the guitar. "You promised. You can't tell anyone. I don't want Patrick to get into trouble. He's not hurting anyone."

"Except maybe himself. Mark, you know Alice effectively killed herself on the drug, whether she took it on purpose or not. Don't you think for Patrick's own safety—?"

199

"No," Mark insisted. "I mean, yeah, I'll talk to him. I'll ask him if there might be something in the lab. I have to ask him first, before I tell anyone."

"I'm not sure we should wait."

"Two days," Mark said urgently. "No practice tomorrow. But Friday, I swear, I'll talk to him. It's been months since the girl fell. He's been fine so far. If I snitch, and Patrick gets busted for drugs, he'll never forgive me. The whole band will never forgive me. I might as well just shoot myself!"

"Stop. Enough. You'll have a life and a career, even if this band falls apart."

Mark shook his head wildly. "No way. You can't tell the cops. God, Ryan, please, you promised."

"All right," Ryan said reluctantly. "Till Friday. Then you talk to Patrick. Carefully and safely, while the other guys are around. Don't confront him with this while you're alone with him, okay? Promise me."

"What do you think he'll do? He's just... mellow."

"Doesn't matter. If you threaten to take away someone's drugs, it can get ugly. Promise you'll talk to him when the rest of the guys are there."

"Okay. Jeez. I promise."

"And then call me," Ryan added. "Call me either way. If he's doing drugs on purpose, we need to... at least talk about it. Maybe we can help him see it's messing up the band. And if it's not on purpose, then we need to tell someone in authority."

"Shit." Mark sat back on his bed and picked at the strings of the guitar, a few tentative notes. "I keep thinking I've got stuff under control, you know. But there's always something else."

"I know the feeling." Ryan stood stiffly. "For what it's worth, I think you're handling a whole series of tough problems pretty damned well."

Mark's eyes went bright, behind those shaggy bangs.

"And now," Ryan said, "Pepperoni pizza?"

"Sure," Mark ran through a rapid minor line, the notes clear and crisp. "I guess I could eat."

Ryan made the trek to his own room, stretched out on the bed with his phone, and called to order dinner. He could get in twenty minutes with his feet up before the food came.

"So," he said conversationally to the air, to the deity he wasn't sure he believed in, "when I said I wouldn't mind having kids, did I forget to mention I'd prefer they didn't show up ready-made as teenagers?" The silence was his answer. "Yeah, that's what I thought." He was coming to love Mark, and Torey was a great kid, but their teen problems made him envious of Drew's fatherhood, with his chocolate-pudding-on-the-carpet complaints. It would've been so much easier to start with toddlers.

****

John paused in his work at the end of Friday and stretched, thinking about the coming weekend. It could only be a vast improvement on the last one. He'd thought Cynthia and Brandon would never leave. They had talked Mark's choice to death, before bowing to the inevitable, and then started in on Cynthia's visitation demands. Mark didn't want to go back to California at all. In the end, they'd agreed to a month's cooling-off period first. Unless Brandon went through with his threats to take the whole mess to court instead.

It'd been hard to say goodbye to Torey. John really wanted to keep her with them too. That would be heaven, to have both his kids and Ryan, all together again. But it wasn't going to happen, and he hoped they'd done the right thing for Torey. A girl needed her mother. She'd left without too much fuss, gazing tearfully out the back of the rental car. God, parenting was the hardest job on earth. But temporarily getting settled with Cynthia was a weight off his mind. Now he, Mark, and Ryan had a chance to work out how to live together.

And in a few minutes, he'd be going home to Ryan. Just a little more paperwork to do. It wasn't a bad life.

John liked coming back to his office at the end of the day. Sure, it was a small space in a stuffy industrial basement, but he had a variety of campus maps on the walls, plant-care schedules, contractor numbers. On the biggest map, lines in green, yellow and red marked the walking trails he'd refurbished, the ones in need of care, and the ones he was planning for the future. A big photo of the lilac hedge in full bloom lent inspiration for the coming spring.

He was bending over his monthly budget report, when he heard a sound from the hallway, his door clicked, and then he was grabbed from behind. He smiled and turned in Ryan's arms. "Hey, you're here late today."

201

"Yep. I needed some library time, and I figured you could give me a ride home."

"You bought that new car, and it sits in the driveway."

"I like riding in with you in the mornings. And the car eats gas."

"So does my truck."

"Yeah, but *you* pay to fill up the truck."

John glanced at the closed door, and then kissed Ryan firmly. "I like having you around too."

"Funny how that works." Ryan returned the kiss, slowly and more thoroughly. "Does that door happen to lock?" He rubbed his pelvis against John.

"I'm not having sex in my office," John said firmly.

"No?" Ryan's mouth was warm and rough on his neck, teeth scraping over stubble.

"Um, no." *Okay, that didn't sound very convincing.*

"You're sure?"

He wriggled loose and stepped back. "I told Mark to call if his band practice ran late. He might come by."

Ryan smiled. "Okay. I can wait. Some."

John pulled out his cell phone to check for missed calls, and to help himself resist the temptation to wipe that smile off Ryan's face in the best way. *I wonder if this floor is too hard for him to kneel on.* There were no messages on his phone, but it rang as he was pocketing it.

"Speak of the devil," he said. "Hey, Mark."

"Dad." His son's voice was a harsh whisper. "I need help."

John glanced over at Ryan and toggled the phone to speaker. "What's wrong?"

Ryan stepped to his side to listen.

"He's out there, with a gun. And he's burning stuff!" Despite the words, Mark's voice was hushed.

"*What!* Who? Where are you?"

"Dr. Crosby's lab. I think it's him. Dad, I'm scared."

"Look," Ryan said clearly. "If someone has a gun, you need to call 911, now!"

"He might hear me." Mark barely breathed. "I think he shot Patrick."

Ryan snatched his own cell phone out, and was dialing 911 even as John said very softly, "What building are you in? Where's the lab?" He glanced at Ryan, and they hurried out of the office.

"I think it's Smythe," Mark whispered. "I'm on the sixth floor."

"That's probably right. Smythe has seven floors." John yanked open the stairwell door, with Ryan right behind him. "Mark, we're coming

"Oh, Jesus," Mark moaned. "He's lighting the walls on fire."

"You need to get out of the building, Mark," Ryan said urgently toward the phone in John's hand.

"I can't. He's right out there."

John flicked another look at Ryan. They were climbing the basement stairs, and he'd automatically slowed to Ryan's pace. Ryan put his own phone to his other ear, and said, "I want to report an emergency, fire." John ground his teeth. Smythe was two buildings over.

"Go," Ryan said to him. "I'll catch up. I'm on with 911."

John ran, taking three stairs at a time.

The back door to get outside from Croft Hall had been bolted for the night. He had to pause to wrestle it open, and left it swinging behind him for Ryan. The paths were ice-free, and he charged flat-out toward the looming bulk of Smythe Hall.

It was late enough that the sky was fully dark, and the streetlights were on. The windows up in Smythe were all dark, at least on this side. No one working late in a lab. No fire to be seen, either.

"Stay safe," John told Mark into the phone pressed to his ear. "Tell me what's happening."

"Patrick ran out, and Crosby went after him," Mark said on a soft breath. "I heard popping, like shots, and then he...Dr. Crosby came back. I'm behind the lab counter by the windows. He's out in the other room, between me and the door. He's got, like, a fireplace lighter or something. He's muttering to himself and setting things on fire."

It didn't make any sense. *Doesn't matter for now.* John focused on the essentials. "Is there another door you can use to get out?"

"No."

"The window?"

Mark's whisper was panicked, "I'm on the sixth floor. And I don't think they open."

"You can always break one."

"He'd hear me. It's too high!"

"I'm coming," John said. "I'm almost there. Where on the sixth floor? Where's the lab? What do you see out the window?"

"I'm hiding on the floor. I don't want to stand up. I don't see anything. I don't even know which side of the building this is."

"I'm at the front door." John reached out. He expected the door to be locked, but it opened to his pull. For an instant he hesitated, wondering if he should make a quick run around the building, to look for the lighted lab. *Fuck it, I'll find it from inside.* He stepped in. The lobby was dark, even for after hours. Only the emergency lighting was operating. The air felt heavy and still, as if the power was off.

The elevator was just to the left of the main entrance. John stabbed at the button, and then paused. *In case of fire, do not use the elevator.* In any case, the button stayed dark. He whirled and headed for the nearest stairs. The heavy metal door creaked as he pulled it open. The staircase was dim, lit by red exit lights, and as he pounded up the first flight, there was a faint scent of smoke. But there was also silence, no alarms, no sprinklers.

"Mark, talk to me," he said, swinging around the post and up the next flight. He had to press the phone to his ear, as suddenly the klaxons of a fire alarm began to go off.

"Dad." He could barely hear Mark. "The alarm started. I can't tell if he's still out there."

"Do you have sprinklers?"

"No. No water. Just noise."

"Can you peek out and see if he's still there, carefully?" He passed the third-floor landing and headed for the fourth.

"I think he's gone, but there's so much fire."

John was concentrating on his son's voice, and barely stopped in time to avoid tripping over a crumpled form on the landing between the third and fourth floors. "Damn!" He knelt beside the body to look closer. It was the kid from the band, Patrick. He lay face down, dark blood pooling on the floor under him.

John bent over the boy. The dim light made it hard to see, but Patrick lay still as death. His eyes were closed. John was reaching for a pulse when the kid groaned and moved an arm.

"I've found Patrick," he told Mark over the phone. "He's on the stairs."

"Is he dead?"

"No." *Not yet. Move him? Don't move him?* Patrick flailed his arm and slid a knee, arching as if trying to turn and get up. John caught him, easing the boy down onto his back. Blood soaked the front of his sweatshirt, and trailed down the legs of his jeans. John lifted the hem of the shirt gently. The skin of Patrick's abdomen was torn open in two ragged holes, steadily dripping blood. *Jesus.*

"He's been hurt, Mark. You stay safe."

Patrick's eyes opened. He looked up at John and muttered something.

"Don't talk," John told him. "You'll be okay." He shot an agonized glance up the stairs, but set down his phone and struggled out of his jacket and shirt. He wadded up the shirt and pressed it over the wounds on Patrick's body, trying to control the bleeding.

Patrick said, "Hurts," and then coughed, and his eyes rolled up, as his body went limp.

"I know." John found himself coughing too. He looked up again. The door to the fourth floor stood propped open, and dark wisps of smoke were drifting through. Most of it spiraled up the staircase in a nebulous cloud, but some was seeping down. From beyond the door, he thought he saw an ominous flicker of light.

That's the fourth floor. He held the makeshift dressing with one hand and grabbed his phone again. "Mark, you said sixth floor, right?"

"Yes, sixth."

"Damn. There's fire on the fourth floor too."

"Dad?" Mark's voice was high and thin over the speaker. "How do I get out?"

From behind John, Ryan's voice said loudly, "Stay by the window and stay low. The first responders will be here any time now." He turned to John. "We have to grab this kid here and get out. Seriously. Right now."

John turned to him in disbelief. "That's Mark up there. I'm not leaving."

"Shit." Ryan wiped his forehead with the back of his hand. "John, you know what we used to call guys who ran into a burning building without gear?"

"Stupid?" John bent to try to wrap the makeshift bandage more securely around Patrick.

"Dead," Ryan said in a harsh voice. "I *know* it's Mark. But it does him no good to have you dead in some hallway when the guys arrive to get him out through the window."

"Do you hear any sirens?" John clamped his phone between his shoulder and ear as he tied a knot in the shirt sleeves, already wet with the boy's blood. "I don't hear any. I'm not leaving Mark alone up there."

Ryan leaned in to speak into John's phone, their cheeks brushing. "Mark. Is there fire in the actual room you're in?"

"Nooo, but the next one."

"Close the door in between. You hear me?"

"He'll notice."

"If there's open flame, he's either long gone or too busy. Close the door and block the crack. Then go over to the window and wait. Don't open it or break the glass unless you can't breathe. Stay low."

"Okay." There was a pause. Then Mark's voice in John's ear said breathily, "I closed the door but I'm scared."

Ryan spoke over John's automatic reassurance. "You'll be fine. Stay on the phone with me and do as I say. You hear me, Mark?"

"Yeah."

John looked back and forth between the boy on the floor and the stairs that led to Mark. Still no sirens. Where was the damned fire department?

"Come on," Ryan said. "Let's get Patrick out of here. Now!"

John gritted his teeth. "You go. I'm going to get Mark."

"You fucking can't." Ryan's fingers bit into John's arm. "You can't help him that way. Trust me."

John just shook his head. If he turned around now, and something happened to Mark, it would kill him too. "I have to."

Ryan stared at John, his eyes wild. And then said, "Fuck. I'll get him."

John remembered the way Ryan climbed steps, hauling himself with a hand on the rail and his cane in the other. "You can't," John said. "Two and a half more flights. I need to…"

"This kid can't stand, but he's still alive." Ryan knelt stiffly and laid his fingers on Patrick's pulse, confirming it. "And this building's going bad fast. I can feel it. Listen, John." He looked intently into John's face. "I can't carry Patrick out. Not down stairs. If we're going to get him out alive, it has to be you. And if one of us is going deeper, after Mark, then it should be me. I've at least got a fucking hope in hell of knowing how to do it, and living to tell the tale."

"But…" John whipped around to look up at the streamers of smoke ascending the stairwell, then back down at Patrick. He felt nauseous. He wanted to say no, tell Ryan to get out with him now. He didn't want both of his guys at risk up there. *But Mark is up there.* "Please…" It came out as a whisper.

Ryan's hand landed hard on John's shoulder, as he levered himself upright again. "Get Patrick out and safe, fast," he said. "And then, John, for God's sake, *don't come back in.* That's a firefighter's worst nightmare— people who are out, going back in. Direct the rescue guys, tell them about me and Mark. Warn them about a guy with a gun. Have them get ladders and the net for a sixth-floor rescue. Then get clear and stay clear. Promise me. And trust me with your son."

If you die doing this then I've killed you. But he still heard no sirens, just the alarms. Only knowing Ryan was going for Mark would let John head back down himself, even with Patrick's life in the balance. "I can't let you go. Not if it's that risky. But I…"

207

"Hey, unlike you I'm a pro. I'll be fine." Ryan gave a short shake of his head. "We're five minutes out and still no fucking trucks. You're right. One of us needs to get Mark, and it has to be me."

That's my *son up there.* Every fiber of John wanted to head up those stairs, now. But this kid, Patrick, was whimpering and trembling again under his hands. If there was ever a moment to trust Ryan, this was it. "Yes," John said. *No choices.* "Go. But you damned well keep yourself safe too, you hear me?"

"Got it." Ryan switched phones with John. "I've got Mark. You've got 911. See you on the outside." He headed up the stairs again, before John could respond. John listened to his fast, uneven footsteps on the treads, even after he passed around the bend at the fourth floor, slammed the door there shut, and headed up out of sight.

For one more instant John hesitated. At his feet, Patrick whispered, "It was all for nothing. And then out of the dark, but the sign was there too." His voice wavered, and John didn't even bother to try to make sense of it.

He bent and hauled Patrick up in a fireman's carry. He was heavier than he looked, and long-legged. He made an awkward burden, his random motions complicating the job. John steadied himself against the rail, and then began a slow, careful descent. Patrick wailed and whimpered as he was jostled over John's shoulder. John gritted his teeth and headed down a step at a time. Above him, the clanging alarms began to compete with a crackling noise and a rush of air. *Was the stairwell getting brighter?*

Ryan and Mark were above that. God help them. There was nothing he could do except keep moving down.

At the front door, he staggered into the arms of a familiar campus cop. Caldwell caught their combined weight without falling, and helped him bring Patrick down the front steps. Sirens outside finally competed with the fire alarms beating against John's ears. There were two patrol cars parked nearby, and another approaching through the gloom. But he didn't still see the fire trucks.

"Ambulance?" he asked, coughing.

"On its way," Caldwell said. "Let's get the kid over here. What happened to him?"

"I think he was shot."

"Shot? Jesus!" The lights made the blood on Patrick a lurid red, staining his body from shoulder to knees.

John helped lay the boy down. "Yeah, you guys need to be careful! My son said there's a man with a gun around here somewhere."

"Your son?" Caldwell looked around them. "Where is he?"

John turned to stare up at Smythe Hall. The windows were not so dark now. On the fourth floor, the baleful glow of fire lit them. "Up there," he said. "On the sixth floor. With my boyfriend." *Most of my life is up there, in that inferno.*

****

Ryan hauled himself up the last flight to the sixth floor, cursing steadily under his breath. This was crazy; this was suicide. He shouldn't be in here without his gear. He'd be just one more victim for the guys to haul out when they finally arrived.

He'd lied about it being the right thing to do. But he'd seen the look in John's eyes. If he'd kept on insisting it was lethal, John would just have come up here himself. And gotten his damned, stubborn, fine, inexperienced ass burned to a crisp. At least Ryan had the training. He'd know exactly how he'd fucked it up when he died. *Better me than John.*

He stayed low, bent over as much as possible. Smoke rolled in a malevolent cloud up the ceiling above him. When he hit the sixth-floor, the fire door was still in place. He went through and shut it behind him. Then he dropped to a crawl below the haze, his stick in one fist, the phone in the other. The air in the hallway below the smoke was hot and harsh, but not nearly as bad as what he'd passed a couple of floors down. Still, Ryan knew how quickly things could change.

He paused, and put the phone to his ear. "Mark. It's Ryan, I'm on your floor. Is the guy with the gun still out there?"

"I don't think so," Mark said. "I haven't seen him since the alarms went off."

"Still no other way out?"

Mark's voice shook. "I don't see one."

"Can you yell for me, make noise so I can find you? Just keep the door shut and stay behind something, in case he hasn't gone."

"What if he comes back?"

"Show him the phone," Ryan said. "Tell him you're recording it all and cops are coming. He won't want to hurt you on candid camera. But odds he's gone." *Only a crazy person would stick around in this.* "Now where you?"

He heard Mark's yell of "Here" loudest over his phone and cursed. "Wait and try that again." A moment to silence the speaker, and then he listened. He thought he heard a faint voice from his left.

"Keep calling," he directed. "I'm coming."

As he crawled, Mark's voice got louder. So did the sounds of hungry flames somewhere below. Ryan knew those sounds, knew them intimately. He'd heard them from behind protective gear in a hundred other burning buildings. And once, he'd heard them as the fire burned over him, eating his flesh to the bone, ending that part of his life. *Don't think, don't remember.* He crawled toward the boy's voice.

A black plaque beside the door said "F. Crosby, MD". It was standing open and Ryan went in. The heat hit him like a blast furnace. He could almost feel his hair singeing. He dropped even lower, and looked.

The lab to his left was on fire. Ceiling panels dropped small embers onto the *thank God tile* floor. The Bunsen burners were all lit, their small domesticated flames witness to the fact that the gas was still on. Papers scattered across the counters in heaps that flamed and died. Flecks of ash drifted upward in the currents of hot air, edges still red and smoking. The wallboards at the far end were browning nicely. *Fucking old, substandard construction.* There was a pop and a whoosh as some flammable liquid in a bottle caught, flared and ran in lines of fire across a counter and onto the floor. A ceiling tile let go completely and fell, bright fragments scattering halfway to Ryan's feet.

"Mark!" he yelled. "You there? Make some noise."

All the way across the room to the right, he saw a door open and the boy's smaller form appeared. Mark stood in the doorway and looked at him, his shape wavering in the heated air. "Ryan!"

"Fuck. Close that door! Now!"

"But you…"

"Now!"

When the door had shut, Ryan pulled out his phone and turned the sound back on. "Listen up, Mark," Ryan said, as calmly as he could, leaning back out to look at the hallway. The ceiling out there was hard to see through fast-growing smoke. Could come down at any time. *Shit.* He crawled back into the lab. "What's going on in that room? Any fire?"

"Not yet." Mark's voice was raspy. "Smoke."

The smart thing would still be for Ryan to get out fast, while he might still reach the stairs, and tell Mark to wait for the pros. But the way the fire was creeping along the ceiling, it would be into that next room pretty soon, maybe before they arrived. The kid would probably panic. Maybe try to jump. Or stay and burn. *Shit, shit, shit.*

The sprinklers should have been going off, but there was no water. As Ryan surveyed the scene, he wondered in the back of his mind why the drop in pressure hadn't triggered the fire alarms earlier. Well, at least no water meant no steam burns.

Just real ones.

He rose to a crouch. The air was better down here than he'd have expected. Maybe because there was so little plastic or fabric in the ceramic and tile lab, and most of what was burning was above him. So far. Which still meant fucking awful air. He coughed, choking. *Go now or go home. Or get dead.*

You don't have to do this. His leg screamed with remembered pain. The odd whispering rush of hungry flames clawed its way from his ears into his brain, echoes of hell. *You should run now, get out. Tell the boy to wait by the window for rescue and get yourself out. Or make him try to come to you.* He crouched, frozen. There was a soft thump from the hallway behind him.

"Ryan? What do I do?" Mark's panicky voice asked. "It's getting smokier here."

"I'm coming in there," Ryan said over the pounding of his pulse. "Stand back. I'll be coming through the door fast. Get your jacket off and hold it ready. If any of me is smoking when I get there, beat on me with the jacket to put it out. Got that?"

"Don't, Ry," Mark begged. "It's too dangerous."

"I know what I'm doing. Trust me. Get ready." He stuck the phone in his pocket, and sucked in air.

The first step was like going off a cliff. Then he was moving fast past the flames, head down to protect his face. Brightness flickered in the periphery of his left view. *Ceiling. Fuck!* He felt something hot land on his left hand

and shook it off. A patter of blows across his shoulders, like being patted by small hands. He smelled scorching fabric. The air was so hot, it was like a solid force against his skin. A shower of sparks erupted off to one side and he dodged, cursing silently. Despite holding his breath, the heat seared him. Then he was past the bad bit. He hit the door to Mark, shoved the handle down, swung around it as it opened, and slammed it shut again on the flames behind him.

Mark ran to him. Ryan thought he was trying to hug him, and realized belatedly that Mark was trying to get at his back. The boy slapped at his shoulders with thick fabric. "Let me get this off." Ryan slid his arms out of his jacket sleeves, and yanked it off. Half the back was scorched, spots black and crumbled. Thank God for thick parkas. He felt no pain, but it had to have been close. Then Mark hugged him fiercely.

"God, Ryan, I was so scared."

Ryan gave him a quick squeeze and stepped back. "We're not out yet." He took a quick look around. No obvious other exit. He pulled out his phone to call John… *Oops, need to call yourself.*

John answered instantly. "Ryan?"

"I'm with Mark. We're in the lab, sixth floor." He looked out the window. "Overlooking the library. Where's the fucking ladder truck?"

"Not here yet," John's voice was hoarse. "On its way. Apparently there was a major fire half the fucking way across town."

"We're not going to get out the door," Ryan said. "And we won't be able to wait here much longer." He had an idea. "Can you head around underneath us, look at the fifth-floor windows, tell me how the room below us looks? You'll spot us by the broken window. Don't stand right underneath it, and get clear if something looks like it's gonna come down."

"Can do." From the sound of his breath, John was running.

"What broken window?" Mark asked.

Ryan considered the choices, and the fire. Breaking a window would cause air currents, which would feed the fire and could suck flame toward them. But he didn't see much choice. "This one," he said.

It was tougher than it looked. It took three full-strength blows with the handle of his cane before the glass shattered. He looked out and down. A police car, flashing lights, people staring up, and there, a running figure that was John. "Stay back till I finish with the glass," he said on the phone. He swiped the cane over the sill until all the jagged shards had cleared.

"I see you," John said.

"Fifth floor below me. What do you think?"

"Looks okay directly under you. At least from out here," John said. "Around front though, the fourth and fifth both look bad."

A loud sound from the lab behind the closed door decided Ryan. "We're going to have to move," he told John. "If the fucking ladder gets here, send them our way. But we can't wait. The lab is going fast. I'm going to try to rope down one floor."

"You have a rope?" John said.

"Not exactly."

Ryan put the phone away. He did a quick survey of the space. No exposed wires, no computer cables, just benches and glassware and a refrigerator. The fridge would have a cord, but not long enough to help. *Shit.* He went to the rack of lab coats hanging on the wall. They were sturdy cotton canvas, and the longer style. He yanked them down, and began knotting them together. Pain and tightness in his hands suggested he'd managed to scorch himself a little, but his fingers still worked. *Don't look, don't think.*

"Can I help?" Mark asked.

"No offense, kid, but I trust my own knots." There were six coats. With knots he was willing to trust, it made about eighteen feet of rope. He took it over to the window. Mark clung tight to his side, glancing back at the door. Then Mark suddenly flinched and gasped, a sound that was almost a squeak. Ryan looked back and saw a finger of brightness through the crack above the door. *Too fucking close.* "Time to blow this joint," Ryan said. There was an old-fashioned radiator beneath the window. Ryan knotted the improvised rope to it, and tossed it out.

"That won't reach the ground," Mark said anxiously.

"Nope. We're going down one floor and back in. Then we'll find some stairs."

"You think?"

"Confidence, kid." Ryan turned to him. "There's going to be two hard parts to this. First, you have to wait here while I go down and break out the next window so we can get back inside. You can't climb out until I tell you. Even if the fire is getting close, you have to wait."

"Okay." Mark's voice shook.

"I don't think this rope will support us both together. Stay right by the window. Breathe the outside air. Then when I call, you'll have to get out and down the rope by yourself. I'll show you how." He demonstrated where to hold, and how to get out the window. "The first bit over the sill is the hardest. Can you do that?"

Mark's eyes were huge in his face. "I suck at rope climbing in PE."

"Yeah. But this is down, not up." Suddenly there was an explosion from the lab behind them. Ryan whirled the boy in his arms against the wall, putting his own back to the fire. But whatever flammable substance had just caught, it was far enough away. The door held.

He let Mark go. The boy was shaking but he nodded, glancing over his shoulder. "Okay. I can do it."

"Promise? I don't want to have to climb back up and get you."

"I can."

Ryan gave him a swift hug. "Good man. Wait until I call you." He swung to a seat on the window ledge and took the cane in his mouth, lips stretched wide around it. *Like around John.* Stupid brain. Hands on the makeshift rope. If it didn't hold, odds were they'd both die. *God, if You exist, don't do that to John.* Ryan swung himself out.

Going down a rope mainly took arm strength. Ryan had put in the sweat and pain to get all the arm muscles he could. The makeshift rope held. One floor down, dangling over forty feet of nothing, he peered in the window. Dark. *In a fire, dark is good.* He took a life-or-death grip on the rope with one hand, and reached for the cane in his mouth with the other. Rope in one hand, feet braced on the wall, raise and swing.

It was a measure of his desperation that the first blow worked. Glass shattered inward. He dropped the cane, cursed as it fell out of sight, and grabbed for the rope with his second hand. *Don't fall, don't fucking fall.* The muscles in his arms screamed at the jolt of his body weight, but held. He got a foot onto the windowsill and the relief was amazing. With his bad leg, he kicked at the shards of glass still holding in the frame. They gave reluctantly. Finally he was able to swing himself into the room.

One glance showed it was better than the furnace upstairs. Ryan leaned out and looked up. Mark was looking down. "It's time, kid," Ryan called up cheerfully. "Piece of cake. I'll be reaching out around the rope. Come down slowly and I'll guide you in. Use your feet on the rope as well as your hands, just like I showed you."

For a long moment he thought the boy had frozen up. Then Mark's legs appeared over the sill. He slid out, chest on the sill, feet first, feeling for the rope with his sneakers. It swung, as Ryan tried to guide it from below. Mark kicked it, slipped and then found a grip. Slowly he moved one hand from the windowsill to the rope. Then the other.

"I don't know if I can hold on," he hissed. "Shit. Ow."

"You can do it," Ryan told him. "Just like in fucking gym class but this time you're gonna show them all how it's done. Just four feet or so to go, and I'll have your legs. Come on, nice and easy."

Mark inched downward in lurching fractions. Ryan held the rope, held his breath. The boy's feet were above him, and closer, and then he put a hand on one thin ankle. "Keep coming," he said. "Almost there." Two ankles, and now he'd catch any fall. He guided the boy's feet inward, and then Mark's grip was sliding. But he was in Ryan's hands and the slide brought him inside the sill and against Ryan's body.

"Oh Jesus." Mark was shaking. "Oh Jesus. I *never* want to do that again."

"Well, not without a real rope," Ryan said lightly, an arm around him. "And yeah, maybe a net. So, Spiderman, ready to find a way out?"

"No kidding."

"Let me go first." Ryan led the way through this new space. Off to the right, the ceiling was beginning to scorch. To the left, he spotted a door. It was locked, but the catch was in the door handle. He unlocked it, and laid a hand flat on the surface. Cool. He pulled it open quickly. "Come on."

They burst out into the hallway. Ahead and to the right, smoke hazed the air. The left looked marginally better. "This way." Fifty feet down the hall, he found a staircase. This door was cool too. He pulled it open. *Stuffy, smoky, but not too bad.*

"Looks okay," he said. "Move, kid, go fast and steady. And stay low. I'm right behind you."

"I'm not leaving you."

"Just go." They were on the stairs. Down was always harder on his knee than up. The last thing Ryan needed was to fall. "Mark, I need you to go down as quickly as is safe. Get out, find the firefighters, tell them exactly where I am then find your dad. Can you do that?" Ryan gimped down slowly, knuckles white on the rail. Mark was keeping pace with him.

"I want to stay with you."

Smoke drifted up the stairs, getting thicker. "Mark, the best thing you can do is send the guys with the gear up here after me. Okay?"

"Fuck! Okay. Just don't stop until you're out. Promise."

"Are you nuts? I hate fire." Ryan's breath was coming hard. "I'm hurrying, in my own way. Stay low and get gone."

Mark clattered ahead, feet swift on the stairs. Ryan sighed. Just himself now, and the leg, and the smoke, and four more fucking flights. Each step got harder. He must have wrenched his back or scorched it or something, because he could feel the pull up his arm and across his shoulders. He started coughing and couldn't stop. He had to pause for a moment, doubled over. Then he kept going. The firefighters met him on the last step.

One of them reached for him, but he shook them off. "I'm fine. I'm out now. Be careful up there, guys. You've got alcohol, oxygen tanks, gas lines, some bacterial biohazard, and no water."

"Fucking lovely," the lead man muttered through his mask. "Anyone else in here?"

"Don't know." For a bare instant Ryan remembered what it was like to be one of these guys, the adrenaline and the sense of purpose. But his throat was raw and his chest was tight, and all he wanted now was to get outside and find John.

He coughed, chest aching as he went past them, and out into the cold, clean, blessedly thin, breathable air. It turned out to be a side door, with a fine drift of snow dusted over the narrow steps. All around, the snow-covered grass was bright under the emergency lights. Just two steps down, two more steps and he'd be clear. Then he felt it happen. *Shit, not now!* But as his knee went out, he was caught in a familiar hold. Ryan looked up at John, and grinned manically. "We've got to stop meeting like this."

Chapter Sixteen

Ryan looked filthy, covered in soot, reeking of burned hair and smoke. John had never held anything so wonderful.

He pulled Ry in close and just shut his eyes for an instant. He would never forget seeing Ryan hanging by one arm over that five-story drop. And the moment when the cane fell from his hand. John saw the downward motion, and for one heart-stopping moment thought it was Ryan falling. And there was nothing he could do from below, even as he reached up to catch. Then the cane just missed his arm, and Ryan pulled himself up to the window.

In his arms, Ryan coughed, a wet, harsh sound. John guided him back, keeping an arm around his shoulders. "Come on. You need the paramedics."

"I'm fine," Ryan said, still coughing.

"Sure you are. But Mark's over there and he'll want to see you." John hurried his boyfriend toward the ambulance, parked under a streetlight. Ryan leaned on him heavily. His knee was obviously not good. John shifted his grip to give more support.

A paramedic hopped out of the back of the truck as they approached and strode toward them. "Where are you hurt?" he asked anxiously.

"He probably inhaled a bunch of smoke," John started.

"No, you. The blood."

"Oh." John looked down at himself. "It's not mine. It's from the boy who was shot."

"How is Patrick?" Ryan rasped.

"Still alive when the ambulance pulled out," John told him.

"What about that guy?" the paramedic interrupted, pointing at Ryan's foot.

John looked down. In the snow around Ryan's boot, red droplets were spreading.

"Shit! Ry?"

"I don't feel anything," he said. But he didn't protest as the paramedic took hold of him from the other side, and they helped him over to the back doors.

Mark was inside, sitting with an oxygen mask on his face. He yanked it off to say, "Ryan! Are you okay?"

The second paramedic firmly reseated the mask over Mark's nose and mouth, as Ryan was lifted up and onto the gurney. Ryan muttered, "Ouch. Damn it," and rolled on his side. John stood in the doorway as the two men bent over Ryan, attaching leads to his chest, a clip to his finger, who-the-hell-knew what kind of lines and monitors. Ryan managed to say, "Don't worry, Mark. I'm good," before he got his own oxygen mask.

John peered over one man's shoulder as the paramedic slit Ryan's jeans up the leg. From boot-top to just below the knee a deep bleeding gash marked Ryan's calf. The paramedic quickly moved to apply a pressure wrap. "That's going to need stitches," the other one said.

"How bad is it?" John asked anxiously.

"Not too. They might want to top him up a pint, but it should heal. We need to get both these guys in for chest films though."

"I want to come along," John said urgently.

"Sorry, no room," the man told him. "You'll have to follow us."

Ryan tugged off his mask to say, "John, get a cab. Don't drive."

John frowned. "What?"

Ryan coughed hard, and managed to say, "Look at your hands", before being masked again. John looked down. *Well, hell.* His hands were shaking. *Guess I haven't run out of adrenaline yet.* Or maybe it was just the cold. He shuddered, realizing for the first time that he was standing on the snow in his blood-soaked T-shirt. One paramedic caught the motion and tossed him a blanket.

"Wrap yourself up and get somewhere warm right now," he directed, "unless you want to end up in the bed next to them."

In bed next to Ryan sounded really good right now, but he couldn't afford to get sick. John stepped back, tugging the blanket around himself. The ambulance doors closed and it away pulled off the grass and out onto the road. For a moment John's mind went blank. They were both safe. He could stop praying and screaming in his head now. He should do... something else. *Phone. Cab.*

A hard grip on his arm turned him. "John Barrett. I should've known you'd be in the middle of this."

John sighed. "Detective Carstairs."

"I got a call," she said. "Arson, gunshots, buildings burning down on campus. And here you are."

"You have to excuse me," John said absently. "I need to get to the hospital and see my son and... Ryan."

Her face became a little less sardonic. "Are they hurt?"

"Smoke inhalation. Cuts. I don't know. I need to go find out."

"It was Ryan Ward who called 911, right?"

"Yes. Because Mark was inside the fire, but he called me instead."

Carstairs sighed. "Okay. Listen, wait five minutes and I'll drive you to the hospital. I need statements from all of you."

John caught her arm as she turned away. "Mark said it was Dr. Crosby, the guy who runs the lab, who was setting it on fire and shot Patrick."

"Someone saw him?"

"My son. Yes."

"Did he know why?"

"I... we didn't get that far. It was more important to get them out."

She nodded. "Okay. Five minutes. I'll brief my officers here, and then we'll go see what the real story is." She looked up at the flames emerging

219

from the upper floors of Smythe. "My car is over there, the blue Taurus. Go sit in it, stay outside the perimeter. Try not to get blood on my seats."

John half expected that with his luck the car would be locked, but when he tried the handle it opened. He slid in, keeping the blanket around himself. The interior was blessedly warm. He leaned his head against the door and watched as yet another fire truck arrived. The crews leaped out, immediately busy with hoses. At least the hydrant clearly had water. Police officers were stringing tape barriers, to keep onlookers back. In the quiet inside the car, the scurrying men and equipment seemed distant and unreal.

He jumped as the driver's door opened and Carstairs swung herself in. She started the car with a muffled curse.

"You haven't found Dr. Crosby?" John guessed.

"Not as far as I know," she said. "Although it would help if we even knew what he looks like. His staff page is down. Shit, what a mess. It makes no sense. I hope your boy has some good explanation for what's going on here."

John shrugged. Right now he didn't need an explanation. He just needed Mark and Ryan healthy, safe, home. Hell, he'd settle for safe and in the hospital for now. Safe and anything.

As she pulled off campus onto the main road, Carstairs turned to him, opened her mouth and then shut it again. She shook her head. "No."

"No, what?"

"No, I'm not going to take some kind of half-assed statement while I'm driving. I can wait fifteen minutes. It won't kill me."

John leaned his head back. "I don't know anything anyway." *Except how close I came to losing it all.*

"Well I hope to hell someone does," she muttered.

Twice on the drive she took brief phone calls, her end a series of okay's and get-back-to-me-with-that's. Once she called someone to get hold of Patrick's contact information from the student-records office. John closed his eyes and counted breaths. Yelling at her would not make this woman drive faster, and her attention was already divided.

The emergency room was busy, but not frantic. It took Carstairs a few moments to work her way up to the desk, but then her badge, and John's explanation that Mark was a minor, got them back into the treatment area. Mark and Ryan were in the same cubicle. Ryan lay face down on the bed. Mark was seated in a chair, but an oxygen mask still covered his face.

"Hey, guys," John said, as steadily as he could.

Mark's eyes brightened and he smiled through the plastic. Ryan's fingers waved in his direction. A doctor was bending over Ryan's shoulders. He straightened, and turned.

"Excuse me. Who are you?"

"I'm the boy's father," John said.

"I thought he was." He pointed to Ryan. "That's why we put them both in here."

"I'm the boy's other father," John said firmly. "How are they?"

The doctor glanced at Mark, who pulled down the mask. "He's my real dad," Mark said. "Ryan's like my stepdad."

"Ah." The doctor shrugged. "Your son is fine. No burns and his oxygen levels are good. The mask is a precaution. We'll send him down to radiology in a bit, to check his lungs on an X-ray, but I expect he'll be able to go home in a few hours."

"And Ryan?"

Ryan lifted his head. "I'll be able to go home in a few hours too."

"You shut up. I'm asking the doctor."

"Um, that's privileged information," the doctor said tentatively.

"I'm fine," Ryan said. "A few scorch marks, and the cut on my leg, which I don't really feel since it went through the old scars. I'll leave when Mark's ready." He coughed harshly.

"He should stay the night on oxygen and monitoring," the doctor said. "The cut needs sutures and I want to run IV fluids. He lost some blood."

"I freaking hate hospitals," Ryan muttered.

"Tough shit." John stepped over to him and looked down at Ryan's bare back. *Youch!* Patches of small red blisters dotted his shoulders. "You'll follow doctor's orders if I have to sit on you."

Ryan rolled an eye at him, and John could almost hear the comment Ry bit back. Something like, *"Sounds good to me."* It sounded good to him too. But once Ryan was healthy, not now.

"What can I do?" John asked.

"You can tell your son to talk to me," Carstairs interrupted.

"And who are you?" the doctor demanded.

She flipped her badge at him. "York PD. I have a man supposedly running around out there shooting people and setting fires. If this kid won't die without the mask, I need his statement."

The doctor hesitated, but then said, "He should be okay. But, Mark, if you feel out of breath or your chest is tight, you put that oxygen right back on."

Mark nodded. Slowly, he slid the elastic off his head and lowered the mask to his lap. John grabbed the last chair and sat at his son's side. The doctor returned to bandaging Ryan, although the tilt of his head said he couldn't resist listening. Carstairs glanced at him for a moment. "Can that wait?"

"I'm almost done. I do have other patients."

Carstairs heaved an exaggerated sigh, but asked nothing until the dressing was taped into place. The doctor paused at the doorway. "Someone will be coming to take both of these men down for X-rays," he said.

"I understand."

"These walls are fabric. I can't keep people away from here. This is a hospital, not a police station."

"I'll live," Carstairs said. "Just step outside."

He left and she drew the curtain across behind him. Then she turned to Mark, notebook in hand. "All right, kid. Let's hear the story."

"Um, where do you want me to start?"

"How about your name?"

"Marcus Barrett."

"John Barrett is your father?"

"Yes."

"John, I have your permission to speak with your son?"

"Yes," John said, "if he agrees."

"I want to," Mark said. "It's so weird. I don't understand what happened. Someone needs to do something."

"So," Carstairs said. "Start at the beginning. You're too young to be a college student. What were you doing on campus?"

"I play in a band," Mark said. "The other three guys are at Bonaventure, so we practice on campus."

"So you came for practice?"

"Yeah. Four o'clock, like usual. But there was a note on the board that Calvin couldn't make it. He's our bass and vocals and he kind of leads the band. So when Gordon showed— he's drums— he decided not to stick around. But Patrick got there, and we're writing a song together. So we decided since we were there anyway, we'd work for a while."

"You're referring to Patrick Remington, the boy who was shot?"

"Yeah. He plays flute and sax, and he writes the song lyrics. We do the music together."

"So you were in a practice room, writing a song. How did you end up in Smythe Hall? That's not the music building."

Mark hesitated and glanced at John.

"Go ahead and tell her," he said.

"I don't want to get anyone in trouble."

John shook his head. "Patrick has bigger problems tonight. If it might help figure out this mess and catch Crosby, you need to tell the truth."

Mark paused a moment longer and then nodded. He looked steadily back at the detective. "Patrick's been weird lately. Sometimes he's off the music, or he'll talk like he's spaced out. The other guys said it's just Patrick, he gets a little disconnected, but… it wasn't right. We worked for a while on the song, but it was one of his spacey days. He kept changing the lyrics, and they made less and less sense. Then he just put down his flute and started wandering around the room.

"I asked if he wanted to pack it in, and he started telling me about his girlfriend. How she dumped him. Then he said it was because he was ugly. Because his acne was coming back. Which, yeah, he had a few zits on his forehead, but I just had to laugh. I said, 'God, look at me before you complain.' And he said he knew the fix for that.

"He said the guy he worked for, Crosby, had a medication. It worked great. He said he used to look worse than me, but Crosby let him use this stuff he invented. It's not even on the market. He said him and this girl, Alice, that worked in the lab, they both got to try the stuff out. And it worked great. But then Crosby wouldn't give him any more."

Mark glanced at John. "He was all upset about it. Crosby wouldn't give him any more blue gel. He called it blue gel. He started saying how he needed it to get his girl back. I was like, 'Come on, man, she wouldn't dump you for three zits.' I mean, there had to be other reasons. But he swore he'd get her back. And then he said I should try it too. That it was like magic. And he could get some for both of us."

He frowned. "I guess I should've left or something. But he said the stuff was in the lab. And he had the keys. It wasn't like we were breaking in. He worked there. And he was going to go, no matter what I said. I was worried he might… I don't know. So we went over to Smythe."

"Was the building open?" Carstairs asked.

"No. Patrick had a key. He unlocked the door. We went in and then up to the sixth floor, to the lab."

"Was the power on then?"

"Yes. We took the elevator. It was kind of dark, 'cause by then it was probably six thirty and not many people were around, being Friday and all. But there were lights in the hallways and stuff. We went up to the lab, and Patrick had a key and we went in." He looked at Carstairs anxiously. "We didn't break in. Patrick had the key."

"I understand," she said. "Then what?"

"Patrick started looking for this blue-gel stuff. He was opening cabinets and just looking everywhere. It's a big lab. He was being dumb, looking in the same place four times, all random and shit. After a while, I went and sat by the windows and just watched him. Because he couldn't even tell me what the stuff looked like. I mean, blue gel, sure, but not if it would be in a bottle or a tub or anything. Then the lights went out."

"What did you do?"

"I wanted to get out of there," Mark said. "I was kind of freaked. But Patrick said it was just a power failure. The emergency lighting was on. And Patrick had one of those key-chain lights. So he kept on searching. And then Dr. Crosby came in."

"Did you recognize him?"

"No. Just, Patrick said, 'Hey, Dr. Crosby.' Like it was all normal for him to be there fucking around in the lab in the dark. And the man said, 'Patrick. What are you doing here?'—kind of angry. And Patrick said, 'I'm looking for my blue gel. I just want a little more. It's not fair to take it away.' And Crosby was all mad, and started cussing him out."

"Did he say why he was mad?"

"Just 'You shouldn't be here.' Stuff like that. And yeah, he said Patrick would wreck everything. And then he shot Patrick."

"Shot him? You're sure?"

"I saw the gun," Mark said. "I heard it. I don't know if he hit Patrick because Patrick, like, ran out the door. And Crosby ran after him, and there were more shots."

"Loud, soft, how many?"

"Shit, I don't know," Mark said. "A bunch? Four? Close by and then further away."

"And you didn't call 911 or try to get away."

"I was scared, okay?" Mark shook his head. "I couldn't believe it. Yeah, I was stupid. But he had a gun, and there was only the one door, and I was scared, and it happened so fast. And then he came back. Crosby."

"How long after he shot at Patrick?"

"It seemed like just a few seconds, a minute, I'm not sure!"

"You're doing fine," Carstairs said soothingly. "You had every right to be scared. Then what happened?"

"I ran and hid in the other part of the lab when I heard him come back, near the windows, behind the end of the counter. The guy was muttering about his work, it was all ruined, all for nothing. And then he lit the burner thingies and he started to set other stuff on fire. Like, he lit up all these piles of papers and stuff. Fire everywhere. Then it got noisier and I thought maybe he wouldn't hear me. So I called my dad."

John put in, "I was in my office on campus, not far away. Ryan was with me. We called 911. I ran the two blocks and got into the building, and found Patrick on the stair. Then the alarms finally went off. The fire was spreading."

Carstairs said, "The fire chief told me someone tampered with the alarm system. The water main to the building was shut off and so was the main power breaker, but not the gas."

"To make it burn better."

"Presumably. Mark, did you see Crosby clearly when he was setting the fire? Could you identify him if you saw him again?"

"I don't know. I was hiding, and just kind of peeking now and then, and the light was bad, all dim and flickery. I don't know."

"Okay. So Crosby was lighting fires. Then what?"

"Then the alarms went off, and I think he left."

"You don't know?"

"I was hunkered down in the other room. I was hiding, until Ryan came."

"You didn't leave the lab?"

"I couldn't. It was all on fire. I couldn't get across. I was trapped in back room by the windows."

"But you did get out."

"Ryan came. He helped me. We went out the window, and back in the next floor. And then down the stairs."

"But if you couldn't get out, how did Ryan get in?"

"I don't know." Mark looked over at Ryan. "It was all on fire. There was no way out, and I knew I was going to die. And then he just... walked through it."

"I ran like a fucking bat out of hell through it," Ryan said from his bed. "Stayed low and moved fast. I knew what I was doing. The kid didn't have the resources to get out, but I could get in. And then we were both trapped."

"So you found a rope and climbed out the window!" Carstairs sounded disbelieving.

"Made a rope out of Crosby's lab coats," Ryan said. "Saved by bad fashion sense. If he'd had the short jacket style, we'd have been screwed. There was just enough fabric to do the job."

John bit his lip hard. In the dark he hadn't made out what Ryan and Mark had used to climb out on. He'd assumed rope. *Knotted lab coats.* His stomach hurt.

"And you had nothing to do with setting the fires?" Carstairs said to Mark.

"No! God, no." He shuddered. "Why would I try to burn myself to death?"

"Maybe you miscalculated. Like painting yourself into a corner."

"Not possible," Ryan said firmly. "Even if Mark was the type, which he's not, the progression of the fire moved from the center of the room to the door. Mark was on the other side of the flames. He couldn't have done it. The arsonist worked toward the door and left that way."

"And I should accept your analysis because?"

"Eight years on SDFD duty. I know fires."

"And Mark wouldn't know where to shut off the building water supply, or e power," John added.

"You would." Carstairs sighed. "Okay, I'm just playing the game here. I believe you, kid. For what it's worth. Although I'll be happier if Patrick survives and corroborates your story."

"Do you know…?" John hesitated.

"He's in surgery," Carstairs said. "They'd have paged me if he died, but otherwise I don't know."

"That's something." Ryan coughed raggedly.

"Put that oxygen back on," John told him. When Ryan didn't immediately comply, John stood and bent over him.

Ryan looked up at him. "Did I tell you how good you looked at the bottom of those steps when I came out?"

"Better than you did at the top of them." John put the mask over his stubborn lover's nose and ran a finger across his cheek. He saw Ryan's eyes cut to Carstairs. But when he would have pulled back, Ryan reached up and pressed John's hand against his face with his own palm. His eyes smiled.

"So, Barrett, I need your statement," Carstairs said.

"Sure," John said, not looking away from those bloodshot green eyes. *He looks like hell, and he's still the hottest thing on the planet.* "Ask away. But I didn't do much."

"Except carry Patrick Remington out of the building, from what I hear."

"Yeah, that." *But Ryan walked through fire to save my kid.*

Chapter Seventeen

By the next afternoon, Ryan pretended to read while stretched out on the couch, but he was already heartily sick of being on crutches again. His leg didn't even hurt that much. It was tempting to just use it, but he was being good. The doctor had reluctantly released him, against medical advice, but warned him that abusing the leg might delay healing, and the last thing Ryan needed was to weaken that calf muscle any more. John would give him hell if he so much as put his foot to the ground. Ryan didn't plan to give him that kind of leverage.

The rest was just… annoying. A scattering of superficial burns across his shoulders and the back of one hand, making the crutches even more of a pain. It was almost familiar. He'd taken a handful of ibuprofen, for what that was worth. Mostly to please John. The cough came and went, but his chest no longer felt so tight. And Mark was doing really well. They'd been so damned lucky…

The doorbell rang, and Ryan got up, taking time first to peer out the sidelight by the door. Patrick's identity had hit the news, and cameras had caught his parents arriving at the hospital last night, as footage of the fire played over and over on TV. So far, either Mark's status as a minor, or simple luck, had kept the press from their own door. But Ryan figured it was only a matter of time.

The longer, the better, though. John had sent Cynthia a brief e-mail— *There was a fire on campus. Ryan and Mark were in the building but got out by the door with no injuries. Mark was checked by an MD, just to be sure, and he's fine. He'll call you in the morning.*

Then this morning, Mark had made the call to her, under protest and as uncommunicative as Ryan had ever heard him. John had chatted with Torey, keeping it casual. Hopefully, by the time other details got out, the story would have become old local news and Cynthia out in LA would never hear about how close their near miss had been. Luckily, the spectators with cell phones hadn't caught their rope descent, and only had dark and unidentifiable footage people running out of the building. If Cynthia ever found out the whole ...ath, she would probably try to drag Mark home to safety by his hair.

So Ryan was on watch for the approach of news vultures. The two people on the porch now weren't accompanied by lights and cameras, though. This was a different kind of annoying. John, coming from the workshop, was just behind him as he reached for the door.

"Quit getting up. I would have got that," John scolded.

"I needed to move around a bit." Ryan pulled the door open. "Detective Carstairs. Would you like to come in?"

"No, I planned to just stand here on your porch in the snow," she said sarcastically. She indicated the man behind her. "Detective Francis. He's working on the Crosby case with me. Hey, I brought you something." She held out Ryan's cane.

John reached around and took it for him. "That's pretty beat up," he said, examining the deep gashes in the wood where broken glass had scored it. "I was planning to make you another one anyway. You overpaid me the first time."

"No such thing as overpaid for that cane," Ryan said. "Don't you dare lose it."

John gave him a quirk of a smile, and stood it in the usual corner.

Carstairs was watching them. Ryan swung the door wide. "Come on in. Coffee?"

"I wouldn't say no." The detective's eyes looked bloodshot, and her clothes were creased. Ryan led the way to the kitchen, and balanced on one crutch to fill the kettle.

"Is Mark around?" Carstairs asked John.

"Upstairs." John nodded at the staircase. "That's him playing."

They were silent for a moment. The sounds of a guitar piece, fast and complex, drifted down.

"He's not bad," Carstairs said.

John's lip twitched. "I'll tell him you said so."

"Sounds like he doesn't need my applause," she said. "Anyway, I have a tin ear. Can you ask him to come down for a minute? It's important."

"Yes. I'll get him."

While John disappeared up the stairs, Ryan set the coffee dripping into the thermos. He kept his curiosity under control, and opened the fridge for milk, balancing awkwardly. Carstairs glanced at him. "How's your leg?"

"Mostly annoying," he said. "It'll heal."

"Good." She tilted her head. "Are your roommate and his kid doing okay too?"

Ryan smiled. "*My boyfriend* and his kid are fine, Detective."

John, coming back in with Mark, caught the remark. The brightness of his eyes was reward enough for that deliberate statement. John pulled out a chair at the table, and Ryan eased down off his crutches.

Carstairs turned to Mark. "Can you sit down too?" she asked. "We want to show you a set of photos, and see if you can pick out the man you saw in the lab."

He sat obediently but looked doubtful. "I can try."

"That's all we're asking."

"Is Patrick okay?"

Carstairs hesitated, then said, "He's off the critical list, which is all I can tell you. Here, have a look at these guys."

The other detective laid six photos out on the table in two rows of three. All showed pictures of middle-aged men with dark hair and glasses. Mark pored over them intently. After a minute he pulled out three. "Those are wrong. The two guys are too fat, and the other one has that big bald forehead. But I don't know about the other three. He might be one of those, or even someone else that's not in the pictures. I'm sorry."

Carstairs nodded, and at a flick of her fingers, her associate picked up the cards. "Pity," she said. "If we ever get him, we'll try a lineup. Maybe when you see him move, it'll ring a bell."

"*If* you get him?" John asked.

"Yeah." She shrugged. "Listen, I'm sorry for getting on your case so much over the deaths. You understand, it was nothing personal."

Ryan kicked John before he could be all polite and accept the apology. "You do know you caused nasty rumors all around campus about John. Murder. Drug dealing."

She had a great poker face. "He might've been guilty."

"But he wasn't."

"No. I'll make that clear in my reports."

"That's good. But I think you at least owe him an explanation."

"About what?"

"The case. What was going on with Crosby." *What the fuck was all that about?*

She rubbed her eyes. "You'll find out plenty on the news tonight. Half the details already got leaked to a sneaky reporter." She was clearly not happy with that.

John said urgently, "Mark's name?"

"I don't think so. Maybe? I hope not."

"Us too." Ryan said. "But then, even more, you owe *Mark* an explanation. It would be wrong for him to know less than the damned journalists."

Carstairs eyed him a long minute, then sighed. "Give me and Detective Francis a couple big cups of that great coffee, and I'll tell you what I can."

"Done." Ryan's curiosity was killing him. He'd refused to spend the night in the hospital, and John had finally consented to bring him home. For the first time since Mark's arrival, they had spent the night together in the big bed, just holding each other.

They hadn't talked much, a few short sentences about mundane things. Like, *we need to run by the grocery store tomorrow.* The important stuff was all said with touch, in the darkness. Mark had woken twice with screaming nightmares, and John went in to reassure him each time. Ryan hadn't slept deeply enough to dream. He'd been aware of his own new and better nightmares hovering. Now he was totally beat, and desperately curious.

John poured the coffee, doctoring Ryan's with milk to cushion the pain meds. Carstairs took a long swallow from her mug, and gave a sigh of satisfaction. "My candidate for sainthood? The guy who invented coffee," she said. "So. Dr. Crosby. We've been going through his computer, and talking to

232

his coworkers, and I think we have most of the story. I can give you a r̶̶
outline."

"Outline away," Ryan said.

She eyed him over the rim of her mug, making him wait, but then said "About seven years ago, Dr. Crosby was a little-known researcher in an obscure medical school. Then he found a new antibiotic inside ticks, if you can believe that."

Ryan shrugged, fatigue making him run his mouth. "Lots of weird places we've found them. I mean, bread mold, right? Sorry, go on."

"I guess. Anyway, this new antibiotic seemed to work on some disease-causing bacteria. Crosby did animal studies, and got a big drug firm interested, but only enough to fund him a nice grant. He probably had million-dollar signs flashing in his eyes."

I bet. The payoff could be huge. Ryan glanced at Mark, who sat with his arms crossed, hugging himself. *Did he almost die for that money?*

Carstairs said, "Things went wrong with the first human studies, which I gather was safety testing in healthy volunteers. If they'd panned out, he was all set to move into the private sector and really cash in. But it didn't work out that way.

"His test subjects got dizzy, or disoriented on his drug. Not at first, but by ten days out, they said it made them feel confused, and a couple were hallucinating. Crosby tried lowering the dose but he couldn't make it work without the side effects. The ethics board shut down the study. The drug company bowed out. All that money, down the drain."

The other detective said, "Nothing like losing huge bucks to make a guy crazy."

"And the fame," Ryan suggested. "No millions of people saved by the miracle of Crosbymed."

"Probably," Carstairs agreed. "But he didn't give up. Some subjects had told him that their acne cleared up on the drug. So he decided to reformulate it into a skin gel. Just smearing it on the skin surface didn't work, so he tried it mixed with a penetrating agent, something with a bunch of initials, to make the medication pass deeper through skin."

"DMSO?" Ryan guessed.

Yeah, probably. But he couldn't get permission for a human trial. The ...cs committee was playing it safe. So that son of a bitch Crosby decided to) ahead on his own."

John said sharply, "Drugging students?"

"Apparently. His notes show he hired four lab assistants with bad acne. One quit early. One turned out to be unreliable. The other two were Alice Tormel and Patrick Remington."

"Who both began acting strange," Ryan realized.

"Exactly. The stuff in the gel must have acted differently, more slowly. The kids' skin looked good, and Crosby's notes show he was really optimistic. But the effects didn't last. He tried long-term use, and the acne was controlled, but the kids began to act odd. Crosby tried adding a couple of other drugs to the mix, for the side effects."

"He was experimenting on those kids." Ryan felt new anger building. "Without telling them?"

"Probably, although until we ask Patrick, we can't be sure what they did or didn't know." Carstairs took another grateful swallow of her coffee. "Damn, this is the good stuff. Anyway, it didn't work out, whatever his reasoning. The kids got acne when they were off the med, and got high when they were on it. Then Alice did her swan dive out of the tree and died."

"She wasn't knowingly taking drugs. It was that gel," John said.

"Exactly. And Crosby got scared. It wasn't exactly murder, but at the least, he'd lose his license for unauthorized human research. At worst, he might face manslaughter charges. He began to think about winding the trial up, but he couldn't resist one more attempt with Patrick and a new formula. Meanwhile, Alice's roommate Kristin must've said something or suspected something. Crosby decided she was a threat."

Detective Francis put in, "It could have been as simple as Kristin going to Crosby and saying 'I'm worried about this stuff of yours that Alice was using.' Or she might have tried blackmail, or threatened to report him."

"He murdered her?" John asked.

"We're not sure. It might have been unintentional," Carstairs said. "She died of a skull fracture. He could have pushed her, or he could have whacked her over the head. In any case, she was dead. He buried her, cleared out her half-empty room, and left a note about her not being able to handle Alice's

death and going back home. The school didn't follow up, beyond some fc
letters. Which was lucky for him."

It must have taken some balls to go clean out a dead girl's dorm space.
Ryan asked. "You're sure it was Crosby?"

Francis said. "There's some physical evidence. Yeah, we're pretty sure."

"After no one noticed, Crosby probably thought he was safe," Carstairs
continued, "and he had his trial going with Patrick, and even put out an ad
for a new lab assistant. Then you, Barrett, found Kristin's body. And Patrick
started showing the symptoms of the drug again. Crosby's new formula
wasn't working and the risk was getting too high.

"He'd transferred money to an offshore account. When things went badly,
well, he was prepared to burn and run."

Francis said, "We don't know if it was just chance that Patrick went to the
lab the same night Crosby planned to get out. Or if something Crosby said
made the boy worried about access. Either way, last night Crosby destroyed
his home computer, packed his bags, and went to the lab. He shut off power
and water, cut the phone lines and disabled the alarms. Then he went upstairs
and started fires, beginning on the fourth floor, where his office was. Then he
went up to the lab on the sixth."

Carstairs turned to Mark. "There he ran into Patrick, looking for the very
thing he was trying to hide. Crosby has a registered handgun. Presumably that
was what he had with him, and used on Patrick."

"I don't know much about guns. It was small."

"Don't worry about it now. Crosby left Patrick for dead down at the third
floor landing, where Barrett later found him. Then the bastard went back up
to finish the arson in the lab."

Mark said, "Was he trying to burn me to death, you think?" It was clear he
was trying to sound calm, but there was a tremor in his voice.

Carstairs said, "You told us he didn't clearly see or speak to you? Shoot
at you?"

"No," Mark whispered. John reached over to rub his knuckles up and
down Mark's arm.

"Likely not, then."

"But why else would he come back up?"

"Still bent on destroying evidence, or making sure no one could cash in on s work later? He was pretty damned thorough about that. If he'd just meant o kill you, he had the gun."

Mark shivered hard, and John glared at her. She had the grace to look a little sheepish. "Which he didn't use, of course, so odds are, he never even knew you were there. Probably never will know." She glanced at John. "The boys were lucky you two were close by."

"And thank God for cell phones," Ryan muttered.

"Yep."

"So where is Crosby now, d'you think?" *Do we need to worry about him, if he does find out about Mark?*

"We've traced him directly from the lab to the airport. By the time we knew who we were after and put out a bulletin, he'd boarded a flight to Cancun. He used a false passport. We've contacted the Mexican authorities, but there's not much chance they'll lay hands on him. He got off the plane in Mexico, and vanished. He has a good bankroll somewhere out there to live on. He'd even taken out a second mortgage for extra cash."

"So you aren't even close to arresting him," John said.

"Not at this time," Carstairs agreed. "He's out of the country. Still, the police down there might get lucky."

"Do you think he'll ever come back up here on his own?" Mark asked.

"I doubt it," Francis said. "There's nothing here for him. Out there, he's free and has his money. Here, he's at risk of prison, and for what? He's not some psycho. This was about the cash and the fame, and there's nothing left."

"If you do eventually catch him," Ryan said, "will you be able to you convict him?"

"There's a lot of good evidence," Carstairs said. "But no smoking gun on some of the charges. Especially if Mark can't identify him from the lab."

Mark muttered, "Sorry."

She shook her head at him. "Better you tell the truth than make stuff up. But a lawyer could argue that Patrick's identification is inadmissible, since he was on a drug that causes hallucinations. I'm sure Crosby would go down for something, but it'd depend on the lawyers and the jury."

"You know what's ironic?" Francis told them. "We called the pharmaceutical company to get information, and apparently they were becoming interested in the idea of using the drug topically. They might take up Crosby's research themselves."

"Even though Alice and Kristin are dead?" John demanded.

"Hey," Carstairs said. "A real acne cure would be a million-seller. A few incidental deaths wouldn't deter a big pharma company from chasing that kind of profit."

"You don't think they were involved in the secret trials?" Ryan asked. "Maybe they're just going for deniability?"

Carstairs said, "Unlikely. I'd love to have someone to arrest, but sadly, I think Crosby was going it alone, and hoping to bring them back in for funding later."

"You've found out a lot very quickly," John mused.

Carstairs nodded. "I'm just that good. Also, it helps that Crosby was a better biologist than computer scientist. He tried to physically destroy his computers, not just erase them, and the stuff that burned in his lab and office in Smythe was a dead loss. But he took an axe to his home computer without knowing what he was doing, and the hard drive was still intact in the middle of the mess. Took our boys a couple of hours to get past his passwords and then we had it all."

"Helpful."

"Very."

"So now you finally have to stop looking at John as a suspect," Ryan said, only half joking. He realized he was still pissed about that.

"He was never that serious a candidate." Carstairs turned to John. "Everyone I talked to says you're a Boy Scout— helpful, honest, kind, and courteous. It'd be almost sickening, if you weren't such a nice guy." She actually smiled at him and Ryan.

"Thanks, I think," John said.

"Anyhow, that's where we stand." Carstairs drained the last of her coffee, and Francis followed suit. "This photo lineup was my last job for the day— meaning a very long yesterday. Now I hear a soft pillow calling my name. Tomorrow I'll be writing more reports till the cows come home. You all have a nice day."

John put a hand on Ryan's shoulder to keep him seated. "I'll show you out."

Ryan eyed Mark as the detectives made their way to the door. "Any plans for the rest of the day, Mark? You want to pick out something for dinner?"

"Actually." He turned to his father as John came back in the room. "Is there any chance I could go in to campus for a couple of hours?"

"To…?"

"The other guys in the band want to meet. We need to talk about what we're going to do while Patrick is recovering and stuff."

Ryan guessed that Mark also wanted to talk about the events of the day before with his friends. It might be good for him, to start to turn a nightmare into an adventure. "You gonna go look at Smythe Hall?" he asked. When Mark hesitated, Ryan added. "I'd be curious, if I were you. Hell, I am curious."

"Yeah, I figured I would."

"From now on, when the guys talk about scary stuff they've done, like hang gliding or whatever, you'll be able to say, 'That's nothing. I climbed out of the sixth floor of a burning building on a short makeshift rope. And then I went back inside.'"

Mark gave him a wry grin, then sobered. "Only because you told me it was safe. You said I could do it. When you came through that flaming lab for me… God."

"Adrenaline," Ryan said. "Once a fire junkie, always a fire junkie." He could see from Mark's skeptical stare that he wasn't buying it. "Okay, it was pretty scary for me too. But sometimes you just do what you have to. Especially for your kid."

"You're not my real dad," Mark said softly. "You didn't have to."

Ryan stared at him. "Yeah. I did."

Mark blinked and turned away. "So, Dad, can I go?"

"I guess so," John said.

"And I could hang out there for a while. Because then you and Ryan get a couple of hours to… snog or whatever."

"We what?"

Mark colored. "Look, I don't want to know about it, okay? But eve[...] can see that you and him, you just fit. Like, well for years now with you ar[...] Mom, there was always space between you. Even before the divorce."

"I'm sorry—" John began.

Mark waved him off. "With Ryan there's not. A space. So you should be together. It's stupid for you to have to be all distant when I'm around, and for Ryan to sleep in the guest room, and shit. I mean, I'm fifteen. I can handle it. I just... don't need any details, okay?"

John laughed softly. "Okay."

"So I'm gonna run up and get my guitar. Can you maybe drive me?"

"In exchange for two hours of privacy?" John laughed again and ruffled Mark's hair when he blushed. Mark ducked past him and John said, "Sure. I'll get my coat."

Ryan was still sitting in the kitchen when John returned. He heard the truck in the drive, and thought about going upstairs and getting naked into bed. But he didn't move.

John came into the kitchen and tossed his keys in the dish. His cheeks were flushed with cold, and his eyes sparkled.

"So," Ryan said, "what did it look like?"

"Um, I drove past," John told him. "The fourth through sixth floors look pretty gutted, but the structure didn't go down. It's a mess, though. Millions of dollars if it can be repaired at all." He hesitated then added, "The windows you used were both pretty burned out."

Ryan nodded. "I figured."

"God." John came over and just sat down on the kitchen floor, his head in Ryan's lap. Ryan ran his fingers through the curly auburn hair, rubbing gently.

"Hey," he said. "A gray hair."

"Sure. Kick a guy when he's down."

"You'll still be hot with completely gray hair," Ryan told him affectionately.

"If you ever fucking do something like that rope trick again, they'll all be white."

"Let's hope it's never necessary again."

239

John nodded, rubbing his cheek against Ryan's thigh. "Have I said how grateful I am that you did it, though?"

"About a million times."

For a long while they were silent, just the clock ticking, and Ryan's fingers winding through red, silky strands.

"Was it hard?" John asked. "To go in there? After your leg?"

"Oh yeah." Ryan was long past pretending he never got scared. "I stood there for a minute looking at the flames, and all I could think of was that beam coming down. And here was another burning ceiling. If it'd been anyone but Mark, or you, I don't know if I could have gone in."

John pressed a silent kiss onto the denim over Ryan's knee.

Ryan tugged his hair lightly. "In a way I'm glad it happened, though. Because I've been so twisted up in knots sometimes, sick to my stomach, wondering if I'd ever have the nerve to face a fire again. And now I know I can. And I know I really don't want to do that anymore."

"You don't miss it? The excitement?"

"Nope." Ryan shrugged. "When I joined the department, it was partly tribute to David and partly to do something to protect people. To be one of the good guys. But I think I also wanted the challenge, to face something that scared me. The adrenaline high. I don't need that anymore. And hey, being in a relationship, raising a teenager? Those are scary enough in their own way. Being a doctor, holding people's lives in my hands? I'll have enough challenges."

"Mark really likes you, trusts you," John said.

"I'm glad."

"He said you were the only guy who could tell him to rope-climb out a window and he'd do it."

Ryan laughed. "Given that he's around stupid-dare college boys, that's probably a good thing."

"Uh-huh." John rubbed his cheek on Ryan's leg again, a subtly different motion. "You smell good."

"Oh yeah?"

John's mouth trailed over denim, waking a new itch of need. "Clock'. ticking."

"He won't come home until you go get him. Which won't happen until we're done."

"We're doing something?" John's teeth worked their way over the increasingly hard ridge in Ryan's jeans. But Ryan suddenly wanted something else.

"Stand up."

"What?" John stood obediently.

"Here." Ryan steered John in close, standing between Ryan's spread legs. He put his hands up to John's belt buckle, opening it very slowly. John made a soft sound.

Ryan slid the metal tang free, pulled through the leather, out of his way. The stiff metal button yielded to his fingers and he tugged down the zipper tab, inch by slow inch. John's hands stroked his face, his neck. Pushing those jeans down let him get his fingers into tight, firm ass cheeks under thin boxers. He squeezed, and John moaned. "Let's go upstairs."

"Not yet. Blinds are closed. We're alone." Ryan leaned in, drawing his tongue over straining cotton. A dark spot appeared on the fabric and he licked at it, tasting salt. "Mm."

Ryan flexed his wrists, and John's dick slipped free of the descending shorts, slapping against the side of Ryan's face. Ryan turned to kiss it. He licked lightly, and then nuzzled against the red curls, breathing in John's scent.

"Don't you want to...?" The end of John's question was lost in a gasp, as Ryan deep-throated him with one swift motion.

Practice is a good thing. Ryan pulled back up, sucking hard. John's fingers caressed his hollowed cheeks, then went to his shoulders. Two months had taught Ryan some things about this man. He slid the fingers of his good hand deeper underneath, pressing over John's scrotum, and tasted the burst of slick precome across his tongue. John whimpered, bent his knees apart and jerked forward. *Oh yeah, so good.*

Ryan worked with his hand and mouth, sucking, sliding his tongue over and around, building John up. "Come on, Ry," John gasped. "Let's go up and sixty-nine."

Ryan pulled free for a moment to say, "Nope. You're mine." Then he resumed his assault. With a firm touch, he stroked John's soft sac, rubbing gently over his balls. He slipped one finger into his own full mouth, stroking the tip of John's dick as he did so. Then he slid that wet fingertip under, stroking the perineum, rubbing firmly, then pressing against John's ass. John groaned deep in his chest, and his hands went to Ryan's hair. Ryan pushed with his finger gently, insistently, gaining fingertip entrance, as John spread his legs as far as the jeans would allow.

Ryan found a rhythm of mouth and hands that had John vibrating between them, whimpering his name with indecipherable pleas. He bobbed his head, letting the spit drip wetly, keeping his teeth covered. Then he eased his mouth off John for a moment to look up. John's eyes were blazing, his gaze fixed on Ryan's lips, his face flushed and the cords of his neck drawn taut. "Come now," Ryan said. "Come hard."

He opened his mouth wide, and tried to relax his throat, as he gripped John's ass with his free hand and pulled him in deep. John's fingers clamped against the back of Ryan's head, with a roughness he only got when he'd pushed him to the brink. John thrust forward without finesse, and again, forward, faster, fucking into his mouth. Ryan tried to stroke the rim of John's opening with his finger, his hand cramped by the flex of John's strong thighs. He hummed, trying to breathe, trying to open his throat more, taken, possessed, filled with John. *Yes, yeah, give me all of it. Do me. Come for me.*

John groaned, and Ryan suddenly tasted the first gush of salty fluid. He swallowed fast, hiding his gag. He was still learning, and his throat was sore, but he wanted this, needed it. He pulled off very slowly, licking as he went, sucking on the rounded glans, trying to show how much this was for both of them. John's shaking hands dropped back to Ryan's shoulders, and he straightened his knees.

Ryan looked up. The fierce light in John's eyes had turned warm and soft. "God damn, Ry," he said. "You keep getting better."

One corner of Ryan's mouth tugged upward. "Good."

"Wow. Give me a minute and I'll see what I can do for you."

"No rush," Ryan told him. "I want you upstairs, on your back."

"That could be arranged."

Ryan reached down and helped John pull up his briefs and jeans. He batted away the thick, callused fingers, and carefully zipped, buttoned, buckled. John stood obediently under his hands, smiling.

"There." Ryan patted the fabric in the right spot to draw a sensitive breath from his lover. "All better."

"Not sure I could handle better."

Ryan stood carefully, ignoring the crutches he'd leaned against the spare chair. John's hand went to his elbow, a light touch of support. Ryan looked up into his face. *God, I love him.* And the landline on the counter rang.

"Leave it," John said.

Three more rings and the answering machine picked up. Ryan expected a telemarketer hang-up, but instead his father's voice came through. "Ryan? It's Dad. I just... We haven't heard from you in a while. I've called your cell but perhaps you didn't get my messages? I don't want to interfere with your life or anything but... maybe call me some time? Love you, son." Then he hung up.

John eyed Ryan gently. "Still hiding from your dad?"

I don't quite trust him to be okay with this. And then I feel guilty. "Not hiding. I just... he worries."

"So tell him you're fine. You don't need to give him any personal details, if you don't want him to know about us."

"I will. Soon."

"Look," John said. "You think he won't react well to me? Then he really doesn't have to know. I'm fine with that. You don't have to be out with your family. I can be just your landlord, for as long as you like. But he lost one son. I can imagine he likes to keep tabs on the rest of you. A brief, *'Hi, I'm good, how 'bout you'* call won't hurt you. Then we can go upstairs and play."

"I don't know." *I want to show you off. I don't want him to know. I'm an idiot.*

"Call him." John held out the cordless phone.

Ryan took it gingerly.

"Do you want me to go elsewhere?" John asked.

"God, no." Ryan took one of John's big arms and wrapped himself in it. The other arm came round him nicely. He took a deep breath and dialed.

"Hello?" His dad's voice was the same as ever.

"Dad? It's Ryan."

"Ryan! It's good to hear from you, boy. Is everything all right? Do you need anything?"

Ryan winced. Obviously his dad didn't expect casual conversation anymore. "No, I'm fine. Just wanted to talk."

"Oh?" He could still hear a hint of disbelief. "Well, that's good. That's great. How are you?"

"I'm… Everything's coming together, you know."

"Tell me."

"I know you've been worried about me," he said. "And I haven't called much."

"You've had a tough year. A really tough year," his dad said. "We understood."

"A lot of changes," Ryan told him. "But this, going to medical school, everything, it's right. I can feel it, it just fits."

"You always were trying to bandage up your brothers, from the time you could tie a knot."

Ryan laughed. "Yeah. Whether they were hurt or not. I feel like I'm doing what I was meant to do."

"That's good. That's important."

"And something good is happening in my personal life too." Ryan stopped.

"Really?" His father's interest sharpened. "You seeing someone special, Ryan?"

Ryan leaned back against John's chest. John's body pressed against his, solid and strong, moving with his slow, steady breaths. Ryan could lean, and not fall. "Someone really special," he told his father. "Dad, I've met this man…"

#######

About the Author

I get asked about my name a lot. It's not something exotic, though. "Kaje" is pronounced just like "cage" – it's an old nickname.

I was born in Montreal but I've lived for 30 years in Minnesota, where the two seasons are Snow-removal and Road-repair, where the mosquito is the state bird, and where winter can be breathtakingly beautiful. Minnesota's a kind, quiet (if sometimes chilly) place and it's home.

I've been writing far longer than I care to admit (*whispers – forty years*), mostly for my own entertainment, usually M/M romance (with added mystery, fantasy, historical, SciFi…) I also have a few Young Adult stories (some released under the pen name Kira Harp.)

In 2010, my husband finally convinced me that after all the years of writing for fun, I really should submit something, somewhere. To my surprise, they liked it. My first professionally published book, Life Lessons, came out from MLR Press in May 2011. I have a weakness for closeted cops with honest hearts, and teachers who speak their minds, and I had fun writing four novels and three freebie short stories in that series. I was delighted and encouraged by the immediate reception Mac and Tony received, and went on to release other stories.

I now have a good-sized backlist in ebooks and print, some free, some indie and professionally published, including Amazon bestseller *The Rebuilding Year* and Rainbow Award Best Mystery-Thriller *Tracefinder: Contact*.

I'm always pleased to have readers find me online at:

Website: https://kajeharper.wordpress.com/

Facebook: https://www.facebook.com/KajeHarper

Goodreads Author page: https://www.goodreads.com/author/show/4769304. Kaje_Harper

Other Books by Kaje Harper

Self-Published/Indie:

Tracefinder: Contact (Tracefinder #1)
Tracefinder: Changes (Tracefinder #2)

Second Act

Rejoice, Dammit

The Family We're Born With (Finding Family #1) - *free novella*
The Family We Make (Finding Family #2)

Unfair in Love and War (in the charity anthology *Another Place in Time*)

Not Your Grandfather's Magic (in the charity anthology *Wish Come True*)

Re-releasing in 2017:

The Rebuilding Year (Rebuilding Year #1)
Life, Some Assembly Required (Rebuilding Year #2)

Sole Support

Gift of the Goddess

Audiobook:

Into Deep Waters (Narrated by Kaleo Griffith)

From MLR Press:

Life Lessons (Life Lessons #1)
Breaking Cover (Life Lessons #2)
Home Work (Life Lessons #3)
Learning Curve (Life Lessons #4)

Unacceptable Risk (Hidden Wolves #1)
Unexpected Demands (Hidden Wolves #2)
Unjustified Claims (Hidden Wolves #3)
Unsafe Exposure (Hidden Wolves #4)

Storming Love: Nelson & Caleb

Full Circle

Where the Heart Is

Ghosts and Flames

Possibilities

Tumbling Dreams (in the anthology *Going For Gold*)

Free series stories:

And To All a Good Night (*Life Lessons #1.5*)
Getting It Right (*Life Lessons #1.8*)
Compensations (*Life Lessons #3.5*)

Unsettled Interlude (*Hidden Wolves #1.15*)
Unwanted Appeal (*Hidden Wolves #2.5*)

Can't Hurt to Believe (*Into Deep Waters #1.005*)

Stand-alone free novels:

Into Deep Waters

Nor Iron Bars a Cage

Chasing Death Metal Dreams

Lies and Consequences

Laser Visions

Changes Coming Down (in the free anthology *Hunting Under Covers*)

Stand-alone free short stories:

Like the Taste of Summer

Show Me Yours

Within Reach

A full list and links can be found at:
http://www.kajeharper.wordpress.com/books/

CPSIA information can be obtained
at www.ICGtesting.com
Printed in the USA
LVHW041158100219
607032LV00017B/826/P